ALSO BY DARCY COATES

CHAPTER 1

"EVERYTHING WILL BE OKAY." Clare leaned forward, hunched against the steering wheel as she fought to see through the snow pelting her windshield. "Don't worry about me."

The phone, nestled in the cup holder between the front seats, crackled. Thin scraps of Bethany's voice made it through the static, not enough for Clare to hear the words, but enough to let her know she wasn't alone.

"Beth? Can you hear me? It's all right."

The windshield wipers made a rhythmic thumping noise as they fought to keep her front window clear. They were on the fastest setting and still weren't helping much.

Clare had never seen such intense snow. It rushed around her, unrelenting. Wind forced it to a sharp angle. Even with snow tires and four-wheel drive, the car was struggling to get through the mounting drifts.

The weather forecast hadn't predicted the storm. Clare had been miles from home by the time the snow began. She couldn't stop. It was too dangerous to turn back. Her only choice was to press forward.

"Mar—alr—safe—"

"Beth, I can barely hear you."

"Marnie—safe—"

Even through the static, Clare could hear the panic in her sister's voice. She tightened her fingers on the steering wheel and forced a little more speed into the accelerator. "Yes. I'm on my way to get her. I'll be there soon."

That had been the plan: collect Marnie then drive to her sister's house. Beth's property had a bunker. They would be safe there, even as the world collapsed around them.

Clare had been asleep when the first confused, incoherent stories appeared on social media. She'd been in her kitchen, waiting for the coffeepot to finish brewing when the reports made it to an emergency news broadcast. She kept her TV off on Sundays. If not for Beth, Clare might have remained oblivious, curled up with a good book, and trying to pretend that Monday would never arrive.

But Beth watched the news. She'd seen the blurry, shaky footage taken just outside of London, and she had started rallying their small family. "We'll be safer together," she'd said. "We'll look after each other."

That included not just the sisters, but their aunt, Marnie. She lived on a farm an hour from Clare's house. Her only

2

transportation was a tractor. Clare and Beth made time to visit her regularly, checking that she was all right and bringing her extra supplies when she needed them. She was the closest family they had. Now that the world was crumbling, there was no way Clare could leave their aunt alone to fend for herself.

"Op—stop—stop!" The static faded, and Beth's voice became clear. She sounded like she was crying. "Stop! Please!"

"Beth?" Clare didn't move her eyes from the road. Soon, she would be at the forest. The trees would block out the worst of the snow and give her some respite. Until then, she just had to focus on moving forward and staying on the road.

"It's too danger—s—turn ba—"

"I'm picking up Aunt Marnie." Clare flicked her eyes away from the road just long enough to check the dashboard clock. "I'll be there before noon, as long as none of the roads are closed. We'll phone you and make a new plan then."

She'd thrown supplies into the back of her car before leaving: canned food, jugs of water, and spare clothes. Worst-case scenario, she could stay at Marnie's place for a few days until the snow cleared. Marnie might not have a bunker, but Clare wanted to believe they would be safe—in spite of what the news said.

The storm seemed to be growing worse. She could barely see ten feet ahead of her car. Massive snowdrifts were forming against ditches and hills, but the wind was vicious enough to keep the powder from growing too deep on the road. Even so, her car was struggling. Clare forced it to move a fraction quicker.

She couldn't see the forest but knew it wasn't far away. Once she was inside, she would be able to speed up.

A massive, dark shape appeared out of the shroud of white. It sat on the left side of the road, long and hulking, and Clare squinted as she tried to make it out. It was only when she was nearly beside it that she realized she was looking at two cars, parked almost end to end, with their doors open.

"Dangerous—" The static was growing worse again. "Don't—as—safe!"

Clare slowed to a crawl and leaned across the passenger's seat as she tried to see inside the cars' open doors. Snow had built up on the seats. The internal lights were on, creating a soft glow over the flecks of white. In the first car, children's toys were scattered around the rear seat. A cloth caterpillar hung above the window, its dangling feet tipped with snow.

Clare frowned. There was nothing but barren fields and patchy trees to either side of the road. The owners couldn't have gone far in the snow. She hoped a passing traveler had picked them up.

Or maybe they hadn't left willingly. A surreal, unpleasant sensation crawled through her stomach. The cars' doors hung open, and the keys were still in the ignition.

She pressed down on the accelerator to get back up to speed. The steady *thd thd thd* of the windshield wipers matched her heart rate.

The abandoned cars had absorbed her attention, and she hadn't realized the static had fallen quiet. She felt for the phone without taking her eyes off the road then held it ahead of herself so that she could watch both at the same time.

The call had dropped off. Clare tried redialing. The phone hung in suspense, refusing to even try to place the call.

"Come on," Clare whispered. She pushed her car to go a little faster, even though she knew she was testing the limits of safety. Reception was bad in that area, and the storm had to be making it worse, but Beth would panic if she couldn't reconnect.

Clare tried to place the call again. And again. And again. The phone wouldn't even ring. She muttered and dropped it back into the cup holder so that she could give the road her full attention. As long as she made it to Marnie's, everything else would be all right. They would find some way to contact Beth and put her mind at rest. And if it came to it, she and Marnie could hide in her rural farm until some kind of rescue arrived.

Something small and dark darted past her car. Reflexively, she jerked the steering wheel and only just managed to correct it before the car began to spin. Clare pressed one hand to her racing heart and clenched the wheel with the other.

What was that? A fox?

It had looked too large for a fox, closer to a wolf, really, and there were no wolves in the area. It had nearly stranded her, whatever it was. She needed to focus more and not let her mind wander, no matter how much it wanted to. The family had stuck together like glue her whole life. They would find a way to stick together now.

A bank of shadow grew out of the snowstorm ahead, and

Clare sucked in a tight breath as she recognized what it meant. The forest. Safety. Shelter. She resisted the urge to go full throttle and instead let her car coast in under the massive pines.

Banksy Forest was a local curiosity. Rumors said the growth had started out as a pine plantation. Even two centuries later, from the right angle, the neat rows were visible. But no one had come to cut the trees down once they reached maturity, so they had been allowed to grow and die as they wished, only to be replaced by more pines and any other plants that managed to have their seeds blown or dropped among them.

The forest held an air of mystery and neglect in almost equal parts. It covered nearly forty square kilometers, dividing the countryside. The oldest trees were massive. Lichen crusted the crevices in their bark. The weary branches seemed to droop with age, and organic litter had built up across the ground in banks almost as deep as the fallen snow.

Clare could still hear the storm raging. But entering the forest was like driving into an untouched world. Snow made it through the treetops, but with no wind to whip at it, the flakes fell gently. The temperature seemed a few degrees warmer, and the car's heater worked a little better. Instead of looking at a screen of white, Clare could see far along the path, as if she were staring into a tunnel. The forest was deeply shaded, and she kept her high beams on but turned the windshield wipers off. She breathed a sigh of relief as the rhythmic *thd thd thd* noise fell quiet.

The government maintained the road that ran through Banksy Forest. It was a simple two-lane highway that connected

Winthrop, near Clare's cottage, and West Aberdeen, where Bethany lived. The drive through the forest took twenty minutes, and shortly after it ended, a side road would lead Clare to Marnie's house.

I can do this. The path was clear, so she allowed the car some more speed. *As long as the storm lets up before the roads are too choked. As long as there are no accidents blocking the streets. I can do this.*

She reached for the phone to try Beth's number again, but before she could touch it, a strange noise made her look up.

CHAPTER 2

CLARE TRIED TO MOVE. She felt heavy and sluggish, like weights had been attached to all of her limbs. Her head throbbed. A slow, deep ache pulsed in her right arm.

She cracked her eyes open and flinched against the light. It wasn't bright. In fact, the room she was in was deeply shadowed, but even the soft glow sent spears of pain through her skull.

Where is this? Directly above her was a plain cream ceiling. It seemed a long way away, though—higher than her roof at home. She forced her neck to tilt so that she could see to the side.

To her right was a large, dark wooden door and strange wallpaper. Marnie had cheerful fruit-themed wallpaper in her kitchen, but she was the only person Clare knew who still decorated with it. The gray pattern was definitely not Marnie's warm white-and-yellow paper. It was decadent, with flourishes and floral shapes painted over a dark-blue background. The patterns were layered, weaving over and under each other and playing tricks on her eyes.

She spread her fingers to feel the surface she was on. It was soft. *A bed.* The crisp sheets were smoother than the ones on her bed at home.

Every movement was taxing, but she turned her head to the other side. She finally found the source of the light. Two candles were placed on a dark wood, ornately carved bedside table. Their glow was soft and warm compared to the harsh white light fighting its way through the gauzy curtains across the windows.

She blinked and squinted. Between the drapes, she was fairly sure she could see snow beating at latticed windows. The storm hadn't abated. She didn't know how long she'd been out of it, but she was nowhere near her car. Or anywhere else she recognized.

The last thing she remembered was driving. *Driving where? To Marnie's? It wasn't for a regular visit...was it?*

She remembered a feeling of stress. That wasn't normal. She loved Marnie. She remembered struggling to see through the snowstorm. That was also strange. She knew better than to leave her home when the weather was like that. The risk of becoming stranded was just too great. There had been something about a phone. *Did Marnie call me? Is that why I was racing to reach her?*

She tried to get a sense of where she was. Three tall, narrow windows were spaced along the wall. Curtains diffused the long strips of cold, white light growing across the carpeted floor and up the opposite wall, where an oversized fireplace crackled. The room was huge. Every piece of furniture was made from wood and held a sense of importance. Gilded cornices. Carvings. Intricate patterns.

Something moved, and Clare's heart rate kicked up a notch. Throbbing pain pounded through her head, and she had to squint against it. A man stood near the closest window. His dark clothes had let him blend in with the drapes. He faced away from her, staring through the glass as he watched the snow fall. She couldn't see much of him. He was tall, though, and wore a jacket. His hands were clasped behind his back.

Clare held perfectly still, breathing silently to avoid drawing attention. She didn't know the house, and she didn't know the man. The word *abduction* ran through her mind, and it was hard not to feel sick at the thought of it.

Quickly, Clare. Focus. Assess.

She wriggled her toes. Even that small effort was exhausting, but her toes worked at least. Without moving her head, she glanced down at her arms, which lay on top of the bed's quilt. The right arm, the one that hurt, was swaddled in bandages from the shoulder down to the fingers. She tried flexing her hand, and the pain intensified.

She could feel more bandages on her throat, her abdomen, and her leg, but none of them hurt like her arm did.

Bandages are a good sign. You didn't bandage people you intended to kill...unless you're a sadist and don't want your victim to die too quickly.

Her throat tightened, and Clare had to force her breaths back to a slow, even state to keep them quiet. Discreetly, and moving slowly, she wormed her left arm under the covers. She felt around the bandages on her midsection. They seemed to have been applied carefully. She was wearing underwear, but the rest of her clothes had been taken off.

The man swayed as he shifted his weight from one foot to the other. She couldn't get a read on him while he was facing away from her. But he was well over six feet, and broad shoulders suggested muscles hidden under his jacket.

Damn it. Clare looked back toward the door. It wasn't far away, but its size and age made her think it wouldn't open silently. *Maybe if I had a weapon…*

She looked for anything that might give her some kind of protection. The lamps fixed to the walls would make good batons, but only if she could break them free, and she didn't know if she was capable of that. The fireside chairs and small table would be too heavy to lift. But beside the fireplace, leaning against a stack of dry wood, was a set of metal utensils, including a poker. It was on the other side of the room, which was a long way to walk without being noticed. But it was the closest thing she could see that might offer her even a shred of defense.

Moving as slowly and quietly as she could, Clare squirmed toward the edge of the bed, silently cursing every time the sheets rustled. The wind beating against the house created a soft but persistent wail, and the stranger didn't seem to hear her. She got her legs over the edge of the bed and carefully, warily sat up. A wave of dizziness washed through her, and the headache intensified. She waited. The pain receded after a moment.

The stranger shifted again, tilting his head to look at something outside. Clare held still a moment to ensure he wasn't about to turn to her, then she fixed her attention on the fire poker. She could try to creep to it, but she had less risk of being intercepted if she ran. She pictured what she needed to do: a dash across the room, use her uninjured left arm to snatch up the poker, swivel to face the stranger, and be prepared to swing if he was coming after her.

Her mouth was dry. Her legs shook. She took a final second to steel herself then leaped forward.

She took one step before her knees buckled and dropped her to the ground. Clare gasped then bit down on a scream as pain tore through her arm and her midsection. Her vision flashed white as the migraine stabbed through her head. She couldn't move. She could barely breathe.

Something large appeared at her side. The man was speaking, but her ears felt as though they had been stuffed with cotton, and she couldn't make out any words. She clutched her good arm over the injured one, begging the pain to stop and trying not to throw up.

One arm wrapped around her shoulders, then the other slipped under her knees. Everything lurched as the man lifted her off the floor. The headache worsened, and Clare pressed her lips together to keep her pained gasps inside. Then she was placed back down on something soft—probably the bed—and the presence at her side disappeared.

Slowly, the pain began to recede like a swell washing back into the ocean. Clare cracked her eyes open. The cream ceiling swam. Her breaths still came in sharp, staccato gasps, but each one felt less strained than the last.

A cold, damp cloth pressed against her forehead. That felt good. She let her eyes close. The stranger spoke to her, but she still couldn't understand him. A moment later, she felt blankets being draped back across her body.

She tried to say, "Leave me alone," but the words came out slurred. A hand pressed onto her shoulder and squeezed very lightly, then it was gone again.

CHAPTER 3

WIND WHISTLED THROUGH GAPS somewhere deeper in the house. As Clare moved back toward consciousness, the sound, like out-of-tune flutes playing a song without any melody, taunted her.

She tried to roll over, and a hundred little aches and pains returned. She returned to her back and opened her eyes.

The room was the same. Cream ceiling. Dark wood doors. Tall, latticed windows with drapes pulled back and gauzy curtains muting the light. The man was no longer standing by the windows, though. He sat next to her bed.

Clare flinched back. He reclined in a chair, one leg folded over the other, and a mug clasped in his long fingers.

"Don't try to run again. You will only hurt yourself."

Finally, she could see his face. He was slightly older than she was—midtwenties, maybe. His thick black hair was a little longer than was fashionable. His eyes were dark and deep set, and his eyebrows rested low. He'd shed his jacket and wore a green knit top.

Clare pulled the sheets higher so that they were under her chin. A hundred questions wanted to be let out. *Who are you? What am I doing here?* She swallowed them all. She didn't know where she stood or how much danger she might be in. All she knew was that nothing about the situation was normal.

The man moved to place his mug on the bedside table and picked up a glass of water. "Drink. It will help."

Clare didn't want to remove her arm from the safety of the blanket, let alone move closer to the stranger, but she was desperately thirsty. The water sparkled in the glass. Her mouth and nose were dry enough to ache, and at that moment, the water looked like the most beautiful thing on the planet.

Cautiously, Clare extracted her hand from under the blankets and reached for the glass. She kept her attention focused on the stranger's expression. He looked impassive, as though there were nothing unusual about the day. He didn't try to move. She took the glass, pulling it toward herself quickly enough to spill a few drops. Clare brought the water to her lips, but before drinking, she tried to smell it. He noticed. His eyebrows pulled slightly closer together, but he made no comment.

She managed a very shaky smile and tried a sip. It didn't have any strange tastes, so she downed the whole glass. Her body silently rejoiced as she drank, and instantly, it begged for more.

The man held out his hand, and Clare carefully returned the glass to him. He placed it back onto the bedside table then picked up his own mug and settled back into the chair. He obviously didn't intend to start a conversation.

Clare couldn't stand the silence any longer. She licked her lips. "Who are you?"

"So you do speak." A very small smile flitted over his lips, but it was gone in an instant. "My name is Dorran."

She'd never heard of anyone with that name before. Mixed with the ostentatious decorations and abnormally large room, it left her with a sense of unreality, as though she'd tumbled through some portal into a fantasy world and couldn't find the way back out again. "Where am I?"

"My family's estate. Winterbourne Hall."

She frowned. "Where?"

"In the Banksy Forest."

She tried to edge a little farther away from him. "There aren't any properties in that forest."

"There is." He took a sip of his drink. "It is well concealed and not widely known."

Clare risked a glance behind her. Snow continued to swirl beyond the window. The room was warm, thanks to the fire, but outside looked bitterly cold. Even if she found her way out of the house, she didn't think she could run far.

"How…" She swallowed and tried to rephrase her question. "When…"

He tilted his head to one side, his voice soft. "Your car had crashed. I found you. You were bleeding out, so I brought you back here."

She closed her eyes. She remembered driving into the forest. *But what happened after that?* She strained, but even though scraps of memories teased the edges of her conscience, they stayed blurred.

Dorran was watching her closely. The scrutiny made her feel self-conscious. She pulled the blankets a half inch higher. "I don't remember crashing."

"Sometimes traumatic events can erase the memories immediately preceding them." His eyes flicked toward her arm. "You lost a lot of blood. But there are no broken bones. You were lucky in that regard."

She didn't feel lucky.

Dorran rose. He was moving slowly, but Clare still flinched as he walked around her bed. "I tried to call for an ambulance," he said as he opened a massive wardrobe. "But the storm has brought down the phone lines, and the roads are untenable. We must stay here until the storm clears."

Clare looked at the room's double doors. "Is there anyone else here?"

"Just us." He returned to her side and draped a dressing gown over the back of the chair he had been sitting in. "This is one of mine, but it is clean. Will you need help putting it on?"

"No," she said quickly.

"Then I will bring you some food. You were asleep for two days. You will be hungry, even if you don't feel it yet."

Clare watched him cross to the door and let himself out. All of his motions seemed careful and precise, as though he considered every movement before he made it. Once the door clicked shut, she held her breath and listened. Footsteps gradually faded. They seemed to go on a long way, though. *How big is this place?*

Still holding the blankets around her throat, Clare grabbed for the dressing gown. It was thick and too large for her. She struggled into it as quickly as she could, jarring her arm in the process. She squeezed her eyes closed and hissed as she waited for the pain to fade.

He says I crashed. Did I? I've driven down the Banksy Forest Road hundreds of times. I know it like the back of my hand.

She gingerly slipped her feet over the edge of the bed. The floor was carpeted, but it still felt cool, and her toes curled. *I've never seen any sign of a property inside the forest. Around it, yes. Farmhouses and barns. But inside? He's lying. Isn't he?*

She tried to stand. Her legs threatened to buckle again, and she clutched at the bed's headboard to stay upright. Her body seemed to have forgotten how to walk. She had to gradually coach her legs through the process of balancing and carrying weight, and even then, she staggered when she tried to step forward.

A table along the closest wall held a collection of odd items. As Clare passed it, she recognized her shirt. She grabbed it, but as it unfolded, she saw dark stains spread across the blue fabric. She touched them, but they were dry.

She flipped through the rest of the items gathered on the table, including her jeans, her shoes, and her bracelet. Everything was tinged with blood, even the jewelry.

Again, she tried to remember what had happened. She

pictured her home, the little rural house she'd bought for a bargain and fixed up. It had been a Sunday morning. She'd woken up early, brewed a cup of coffee, and prepared to curl up in her reading nook for a few hours, like she did every Sunday. She'd run errands and cleaned the house the day before. The following morning, she would be back to her job as an assistant at the nearest town's bookstore, unstacking new deliveries and returning mislaid books to their designated spots. Every day of the week had its fill of responsibilities, except for Sunday. Sunday was for relaxing.

But everything after brewing the coffee was a confusing fog. Scraps of memories and sensations taunted her. She'd been driving, but she couldn't remember why. She'd entered Banksy Forest. Beyond that was a blank slate.

Clare used the walls and furniture for balance as she made her way to the windows. She was laboriously slow. Every step was an effort, and when she finally reached the wall and rested her weight against the window ledge, she was breathless.

She pulled back the curtain. The window reached nearly to the ceiling but was only about as wide as her shoulders. Dark metal divided the panes. She looked for a latch to see if she could open it and climb through, but its supports only allowed it to open a few inches. She would need to find a way to break them if she wanted to use the windows as an escape.

Clare leaned closer to the window and shivered as cold air rolled off the glass. She looked down to check how far away the ground was and discovered she was much higher than she'd expected. The shrubs poking through the snowdrifts looked miles away. She had to be on the third floor, at least.

Steeling herself against the cold, Clare pressed her cheek to the glass to see along the building's length. One wing curved away in the distance. The house was immense—there had to be hundreds of rooms.

Everything about this is strange. I've never seen or even heard of a house this large. Where am I? Her eyes burned, and she rubbed her hands over them to quell the tears.

When she looked straight ahead, she could pick out small shapes among the endless white. One looked like a cottage. Others might have been greenery—trees or shrubs, she wasn't quite sure. And far in the distance, a massive dark shape, like a giant wall, ran across the horizon. It was barely visible, but as she watched it, she thought she could make out the tips of pine trees.

Is it…could it be possible…that it really is Banksy Forest?

The door clicked, and Clare shrank back into the curtains. Dorran paused in the doorway, a tray held in his hand, then he nodded at the chairs and table spaced around the fireplace. "Come and get warm."

Clare watched the door as her companion nudged it closed behind him. She tried to draw strength into her voice. "Can I have my phone, please?"

"I didn't find one with you." Dorran placed the tray on the coffee table. "Everything of yours is on that bench."

"Then…do you have a phone I could borrow?"

"I am afraid they won't work."

She looked for signs he might be lying, but she couldn't read him.

He lifted his shoulders into a shrug. "It is as I said earlier. I tried to call for an ambulance. I have continued to try since then. The lines are down."

She wasn't ready to believe him. If she could just get a phone, just try calling Beth—

Wait. I remember...

It was just a flash, but she thought she saw herself going through those motions in the car, dialing a number and growing frustrated when the call wouldn't connect.

Who was I calling? Marnie? No... Beth. I remember calling Beth. The snow was disturbing the signal and disconnected us. I tried to call her back because she would worry if I didn't.

Beth was worried. Worried because...

The memory danced away before Clare could grasp it. She had a vague sense of deep, crushing unease, as though they had heard very bad news. It felt like something out of a nightmare. Maybe it *was* a nightmare, a terrible dream she'd had while in the stranger's house, and she was conflating it with reality.

Dorran was watching her, standing beside the table, patient but expectant. The scrutiny felt too intense, and no matter how thick the dressing gown was, it didn't seem thick enough. Clare couldn't bring herself to meet his eyes. "Bathroom?"

Wordlessly, he motioned to the wall beside the fireplace. A door sat there, so shrouded in shadows that it had been nearly invisible.

Clare hobbled around the room. She tried to keep her back straight and her gait as steady as possible. It seemed like a bad idea to let him guess how weak she really felt. She made it to the door and slipped through, acutely aware of his eyes following her until she was inside.

The bathroom was relatively modern, at least. Every surface of the white tiles and expensive white porcelain shone. Another door in the opposite wall told her the bathroom served a second bedroom as well. Clare crept to the bathtub and sank down to sit on its edge. Her body ached. Her head ached. And emotionally, she felt broken.

Clare opened the dressing gown and checked the bandages on her abdomen. The white cloth was tinted pink. She clenched her teeth as she unwrapped it. Her nerves sparked with fresh pain as the fabric peeled off. Breathing heavily but trying to keep silent, Clare examined the injury. Three cuts, long and nearly parallel, ran across the left side of her abdomen. *What caused this? Glass, maybe?*

She visualized sitting in the driver's seat of the car as it crashed. The fractured windshield would hit her face, her shoulders, and her arms, not her stomach. That would be protected by the steering wheel and its airbag. She might have anticipated blunt trauma from an impact, but there was no sign of that. Only long, angry red gashes. Clare rewrapped the bandages with unsteady fingers.

I bet a knife could do this.

Nightmarish images of organ harvesting danced behind her

eyes, and panic sent tremors down her back. But she didn't think that was what had happened. The red scores were too shallow. She closed the dressing gown's flap and tied it securely.

Her view from the window had only shown one direction, but from what she'd seen, there were no other houses nearby except the cottage, and its windows were dark and empty.

She lifted her chin to stare at her reflection in the mirror opposite the bath. Her hair was tangled and oddly clumped. She felt around the matted area and found it was still tacky with dried blood, though not as much as she would have expected. Dorran must have tried to wash it out for her.

Clare would have given anything to speak with Beth, even for just a moment. She was more than a sister—she was the closest thing Clare had to a mother. Nearly a decade older than Clare, she'd taken on her care after their parents passed away. Bethany worried endlessly, but anytime Clare was faced with a bad situation or an impossible choice, Beth was always the voice of reason that guided her to the right solution.

She itched for her phone—or any phone. The stranger, Dorran, had said his didn't work.

Can I trust him?

The closed door separating her from the strange man felt too flimsy. If he wanted to keep her isolated or trapped, cutting off her contact with the outside world would be the first step. Clare tried to imagine where her phone might be. If the stranger had taken it, she would probably never see it again.

She fought to retrieve her last memory. She'd been driving as she talked to Beth. The phone had been in the cup holder. That was where she always put it.

If she had crashed, the impact probably would have jarred it free. Maybe Dorran really hadn't found it. Maybe it was in the back of the car or hidden under the seat.

She chewed on the corner of her thumb. Dorran said she had been in the room for two days. The phone's battery would be almost certainly dead, and she didn't have any cables in the car to recharge it.

But there might be another alternative. The phone wasn't the only item hidden in her car. She still had the little black box in her trunk. He couldn't have found that, surely.

She ran her hands over the bandages on her stomach. She was weak, but the forest had been visible through the snow, which meant it wasn't too far away. *I can make it. As long as I can get outside, I can make it.*

Clare's eyes drifted to the bathroom's second door.

CHAPTER 4

CLARE MOVED QUICKLY. SHE turned on the sink's tap. It gurgled and choked, then finally, a splatter of freezing water fell into the basin. Clare crossed the bathroom and opened the second door. Like she'd thought, it revealed another bedroom. Hers had been decorated with gray-and-blue wallpaper. The new room was painted all in red.

The running tap would buy her a few minutes, but if she was silent for too long, Dorran would check on her. She couldn't afford to waste time.

Her feet were bare, though. She could deal with the cold for a few minutes, even cope with being underdressed, but she didn't think she could wade across a field of snow then walk through the forest without shoes…at least not without slicing up her feet.

The new bedroom was almost a mirror of hers. A coat hanging on the back of the main door told her it was probably in use.

The lights were off, and she didn't want to risk wasting time or drawing attention by hunting for the switch. The bathroom's light was strong enough to work by. She wrenched open the wardrobe door. It was full of men's clothes, and, like she'd hoped, several pairs of shoes were lined up on the floor.

She assumed they were Dorran's. They would be miles too big for her, but she could deal with that.

She pulled out the thickest pair—boots that went up to her knees—and tied the laces as tightly as they would allow. Her mental clock was ticking down. She kept one eye on the bedroom door and the other on the bathroom door as she worked.

Her dressing gown was thick enough to keep her warm indoors, but it would be useless outside. She grabbed one of the jackets from the closet and pulled it on over the top. Then, trying not to let the new boots make too much noise, she moved to the main door and cracked it open.

Outside was quiet. Clare listened for a moment, waiting for any sign of movement, and when it remained still, she pushed the door fully open.

The hallway was just as opulent as the bedroom had been, with plush carpet, decorated walls, and light fixtures every few feet. None of the lights were on, though. The bathroom's bulb didn't reach far. She could see a glow coming from under a door a little farther down the hall—her own bedroom, most likely. She pulled the jacket tighter, rolled her feet to keep the boots from thudding too awkwardly, and set out into the shadows, guessing a direction.

As the gloom grew thicker and harder to parse, she became less and less oriented. Her legs were gradually remembering how to walk, but her energy was failing. She was breathless by the time she found the stairs at the end of the hall.

Clare looked over her shoulder a final time. No motion disturbed the gloom. She faced the stairs and tried to navigate them without breaking her neck.

She was almost blind except for a pale white glow spreading across the staircase's bottom steps. She used it to guide her path. One hand ran along a banister to hold her balance. The carpet was thick enough to muffle her steps, even when she increased her speed.

The ground floor was washed in light filtered through snow-crusted windows. It was simultaneously dim and harsh enough to hurt her eyes. Clare squinted as she examined the space.

Antique furniture, just as decadent and outdated as the set in her bedroom, filled the space. Doors led to different parts of the house. The tiled floor was polished into a shine.

There has to be a phone somewhere.

She hesitated a second, torn between hope and fear of what would happen if she wasted more time. But she was horribly tired. If there was a phone within reach, she couldn't afford to ignore it.

She crossed the foyer, turning in a slow circle as she hunted through the furniture. Cabinets and bookcases were recessed into the walls. Side tables held items she couldn't even name but were probably worth more than her car. Then a glimmer of bronze near the stairs caught her eye. Clare hurried to it. An old rotary phone sat on a small table, alongside a pen stand and stack of thick card paper.

She picked up the receiver and listened for a dial tone. There wasn't one. She tried entering Beth's number, dragging the dial around like she'd seen in movies, without any success. Then, acutely aware that her time was running out, she tried the emergency help line. There was no ringing and no answer. Dorran might have been telling the truth…or he might have deliberately disconnected the phone. She had no choice except to brave the snow.

The house's entrance stood at the opposite end of the foyer. Just like the one to her bedroom, the door was tall, dark, and seemed threatening. Clare had no time to waste on hesitation, though. She crossed the entryway in a dozen stumbling, unsteady steps, pulled the bolt free, and yanked on one of the oversized rings.

The door opened smoothly. Its hinges didn't creak, but the door's weight made it unwieldy. Almost as soon as its seal was broken, freezing air hit Clare. She sucked in a pained breath and squeezed her eyes closed.

It was horrendously, achingly cold, the kind of cold that slapped the breath out of her and made her double over. She didn't know how low the temperatures had dropped, but it was significantly worse than it had been when she'd left her home.

But she couldn't turn back. She stepped over the threshold and stumbled on a drift of snow. That side of the house faced away from the wind, and the snowbanks hadn't built up too high against the door. Even so, there was more than a foot of snow outside.

Clare pulled on her strength reserves and leaped onto the pile of white. She staggered forward, fighting against the chill spreading through her limbs. Walking was hard enough. Struggling through the snow was a thousand times worse.

Still, it was her best chance to reach safety. Hell, it was her only chance. She focused on the dark line visible through the driving snow: the forest's edge. She thought Dorran might have told the truth about that at least. She was looking at Banksy Forest, and it was no more than ten minutes away. She could make it that far, then find the road and her car. Her nightmare would be over.

As she left the shelter of the house, the wind buffeted her, slamming into her and worming through the jacket and dressing gown. She clenched her teeth until they ached. Even though the boots were up to her knees, snow still managed to sneak into them and freeze her legs.

The ground tended downward. She guessed that must be the front steps. When she stepped in the drifts, the soft snow gave way. Already worn down, Clare couldn't stay standing. She grunted as she hit the snow then tumbled, spreading her arms in an attempt to stop her descent. She came to rest on her back, gasping. Her face burned where the air cut at it, and her arm was on fire.

Get up. Get up, you idiot!

She rolled to her side, crawled forward, and managed to gain her footing. The snow was thicker there. Every inch was a battle. She kept her eyes focused on the forest ahead. Walking would be easier once she was inside. Just like while she was driving, the trees would protect her from the worst of the snow.

The memory came back. Driving. Entering the forest. Finally being able to see. There had been lights. Not straight ahead, like a car's beams, but coming from above her. And a noise. She couldn't remember what, though.

Her shoe jammed in something under the snow, and Clare had to wrench it free. She was walking between hedges. They were almost invisible, just gigantic white blocks on either side of her path, with sparse flecks of green peeking through. She had to be following the front path. That meant she would be clearly visible from all of the windows on that side of the house. She hoped her bedroom was on the building's other side.

Clare drew in whooping, wheezing breaths. Each inhale scorched her lungs and made her convulse. But she couldn't help it. She was starved for oxygen. No matter how deeply she breathed, it never seemed to be enough. Her body shook. Her mind was turning numb. One more step, then her knees buckled, and she landed in the snow.

Get up! Keep moving! She tried. She got as far as placing one foot on the snow, but she couldn't rise any farther.

You have to! For Beth and for Marnie. She tried again and got upright. She took half a step then tumbled. This time, she didn't even have the energy to get to her knees.

Banksy Forest was straight ahead, fading in and out of sight as the storm tried to hide it. She thought she could see dark shapes darting around the forest's edge. Clare guessed it was some kind of animal, probably frantic in the unseasonable snow.

The cold had gotten inside of her. It ran through her veins, turning her heart to lead. It froze inside her mouth and her throat. She coughed, but each new inhale only made it worse. Her eyes stung when she tried to keep them open, so she let them drift shut.

Don't do that. If you close your eyes, you'll never open them again.

But it was already too late. They were shut. Ice stung around the lids where tears escaped. She tried to reach forward, to drag herself closer to the forest, but her arm wouldn't move. She was so cold…so incredibly, horribly cold.

The falling snow was coating her. Soon, she would be invisible, lost to the world, buried in a garden of white, her body perfectly preserved until the snow melted. The thought terrified her. She didn't want to lie there all winter, unmoving and unchanging, forgotten. But she couldn't move. She couldn't even twitch a finger.

Through the muffling effects of the snow, she heard a deep, steady pounding. She thought it might be her heartbeat. But strangely, it was growing louder, nearer. A voice called to her. She tried to open her lips to answer, but she couldn't.

The crunching noise was right on top of her. Hands pushed on her shoulder, rolling her, then picking her up. She was going back into the house. And there was nothing she could do to stop it.

CHAPTER 5

CLARE FELT AS THOUGH she had been frozen solid, as if trying to move her arms would make them break off like icicles. The only things reassuring her that she wasn't dead were the steady thump of her heartbeat in her ears and the feeling of warmth across her skin. She was lying in front of a fire. She could hear the wood crackling, even see the light dancing on the backs of her eyelids.

Someone was carefully untying the boots and pulling them off. Her feet were somehow aching and numb at once. Clare gasped as a warm blanket was wrapped around them.

One hand went under her head and lifted. A pillow slipped underneath, then the hand laid her head back down. Clare cracked her eyes open. She was back in the bedroom.

Dorran knelt over her, his eyebrows pulled low, and his mouth tight. "Do you have a death wish?" He didn't sound angry. If anything, he sounded frightened.

Clare tried to answer, but it came out as a mumble.

Dorran rose and disappeared from her field of vision. Clare tilted her head toward the fire. She wished she could move closer to it, even though the nearest bits of skin were already turning pink. She felt like she might never be properly warm again.

"Here." Dorran knelt at her side then eased an arm under her back. He lifted her until she was sitting then let her rest against his shoulder. He was very close, closer than Clare would have liked. She could hear his breathing and even hear when he swallowed. His body heat spread across her back, cutting through the chill. He tossed a blanket over her lap, placed a bowl on it, and held a spoon out to her. "Eat. It is only canned soup, nothing special, but you will feel better for it."

She tried to take the spoon. Her fingers were too cold and stiff to bend right. Dorran dipped the spoon into the soup and lifted it to her lips.

Being fed by a stranger was one of the most surreal experiences of Clare's life. But Dorran was patient. He didn't complain about how long it took her to eat. When she dared glance up at his face, he looked almost serene.

Finally, when the bowl was empty, he laid her back down on the fireside rug and draped the blanket over her. Clare heard him moving through the room, carrying the bowl away and cleaning out the boots.

She no longer knew what to think. When she'd first woken up in Dorran's house, it had been all too easy to imagine he was some kind of monster. But if he were a cruel man, he'd had plenty of chances to hurt her. He hadn't taken advantage of any of them.

Bethany would have wanted her to keep her guard up. Beth had always been the cautious, nervous one out of them. She wouldn't let Clare go swimming unless a lifeguard was on duty. She never stayed out past ten at night. Every single one of Clare's childhood fevers and stomach bugs had sent them to the hospital waiting room.

Beth would want Clare to be careful, to be reserved about what she said around the man, to reject any friendliness, and to keep looking for a chance to escape. But that was Beth's way of thinking.

Clare tried to clear it from her mind and reassess the situation. She was frightened. That was probably unavoidable, considering where she'd woken up. She tried to ground herself, to find some kind of rational bearing. The man had been kind to her so far. Except for the cuts, which she still couldn't explain, there was no sign that she'd been abused.

And as long as she was trapped in the house, she was wholly reliant on the stranger. For food, for water, for everything. She had to take a chance and trust him. With the storm as bad as it was, she didn't have much of a choice.

The fire's heat gradually worked through her cold external layers and dried the dampness on her dressing gown. The soup warmed her from the inside. Her aches returned as the numbness faded, but Clare was almost grateful for them. They made her feel human.

She rolled over to warm her back and startled. Dorran sat in one of the two wingback chairs by the fire, within arm's reach, watching her. She hadn't expected him to be so close. Before she could moderate the words, they'd already left her. "Have you been staring at me this whole time?"

He looked taken aback. "I can face the other way if you prefer."

"No...sorry." She attempted to sit and groaned from the effort.

"Try not to move too much." He continued to watch her, but at least he was keeping his distance. "You lost enough blood to need a transfusion. You should rest until we can get you to a hospital."

He was talking about a hospital. That was a positive sign. Still, Clare didn't like lying on the floor. It made her feel vulnerable, as though she were something less than human. She eyed the second wingback chair. It was covered in an elegant green fabric, and the cushions looked soft. It was only a few feet away, and she would feel like more of an equal in it.

She lurched up, staggered, and would have fallen if Dorran hadn't caught her arm.

"What did I *just* say?" He sounded frustrated, and Clare flinched. Even so, he helped carry her weight as he eased her into the chair.

Clare collapsed back, breathing more heavily than the task warranted, and checked that the dressing gown was still wrapped tightly around her. It was. "You don't have to stay here," she said. "I don't need to be watched all the time."

"You walked into a blizzard." He slid back into his own chair, then sighed and used his thumbs to rub the bridge of his nose. "I am sorry. I do not mean to snap."

The apology surprised her. Clare wrapped her arms around herself, watching him carefully. He looked tired. His black hair was disheveled from the melted snow.

Is he a sadist who kidnapped you? Or a man who saved your life?

He'd told the truth about the phones being dead. He'd also told the truth about the house being inside Banksy Forest—as far as she could tell, at least. So maybe he'd told the truth about the crash. Her arm tightened over the bandages on her stomach. She swallowed and took a risk. "Thank you."

He blinked at her, and she broke eye contact. "For saving me. And helping me. Both times."

"You're…welcome." Dorran sounded surprised. He stood and crossed the room. When he returned, he carried a glass of water and two tablets. He placed them on the small round table between their chairs. "For the pain."

The tablets were unmarked. The cautious voice inside Clare's head—the voice that sounded like Bethany—told her not to touch them. But Clare was trying to make a conscious effort not to be so brittle. She tipped the tablets into her mouth and washed them down.

Dorran picked up his mug and returned his attention to the fireplace. Bright embers lay scattered around the wood being consumed. It must have been burning for hours. The heat rolling off it was delicious, and Clare found herself leaning forward in her chair. But she also couldn't stop herself from glancing at the man sitting opposite her. His face was full of strong angles, as though he had been carved out of stone. She still couldn't get a read on him.

It felt surreal. They were sitting together, enjoying the fire's heat as though it were something they did every night, as though they had known each other for years. It left her feeling unsteady. She couldn't stand the silence. "Do you own this house?"

"No. My family, the Morthornes, do." His eyebrows twitched down very slightly when he said the word *family*.

Clare kept her guard up for any kind of negative reaction. "It's a big place. Very…uh…"

"Pretentious?" He made a faint noise in the back of his throat, something that might have been a laugh. "Don't worry. I will not argue on that count."

Clare would have used more generous language, but Dorran was giving her a glimpse of his personality, and she followed it. "It must be an old building."

"Yes. Winterbourne has not changed much in the past century. My family…" He hesitated. "They are fond of tradition."

"But you aren't?"

"Some of it is just inconvenient, such as my name, Dorran, after a forebear. It is constantly misspelled."

Clare clutched at the common ground. "People keep trying to put an *i* into my name."

"What is it?"

She blinked, not comprehending.

He stared back. "Your name. You never told me."

"Oh! Uh, Clare."

"Clare without an *i*."

"That's it."

This time, when he smiled, it looked real, and it didn't immediately vanish.

Clare matched his grin and pulled her unhurt leg up to tuck under herself. "You were telling me about your family. How many are in it?"

He tilted his head back. "My mother, Madeline, two aunts and an uncle, six cousins, three second cousins, two nieces, and two nephews. We are not a small family."

"So many…" Clare's own clan was restricted to her sister and her aunt. She tried to imagine a family reunion with that many people attending. She didn't think she could physically fit them into her house without them standing on each other. "How do you remember all of their names?"

Dorran laughed. The noise was so unexpected that Clare jolted. It was deep and sharp, and even though it ended quickly, it left her feeling warmer.

"It is not *that* many," he said.

"All right. I guess not. Especially in this house. How large is it?"

"Inconveniently large." He shrugged. "It does not only house our family, but the servants as well."

Clare's eyebrows rose. "Servants?"

"Staff," he corrected quickly. Clare thought she saw a flicker of embarrassment, but it was hidden almost immediately. "My apologies. That is another part of tradition that is well outdated. My mother wishes for the staff to be referred to as servants."

"They must work hard to look after the house." The room was glamorous enough that Clare could easily imagine needing help to maintain it. It wasn't hard to picture the estate run like a Victorian-era mansion.

"Sixty of them," he confirmed. "Maids, a butler—not that we ever have guests—footmen, cooks, gardeners, and my mother's personal maids."

"You said she wanted to call them servants." Clare took a stab in the dark. "Is she the head of the family?"

He glanced aside, giving Clare the impression that he didn't like the question. "Yes. She inherited Winterbourne and has control over how it is run."

Clare sensed there was something more to it, something Dorran was avoiding. His posture had grown tense. She steered the conversation back to safer ground. "You said you were here alone, though, didn't you?"

"Yes. Every winter, my family travels south, to our estate in Gould. Once the snow sets in here, it is impossible to leave."

A second estate, like some kind of aristocracy. I counted myself lucky just to have a cottage. "Why didn't you leave with them?"

"I did, initially, but we changed plans early into the trip. I left them and came back, intending to spend the winter here alone. That was when I found you. The snow came in earlier than normal, and now, I'm afraid, we are trapped here until the storm clears and the roads are passable again."

Clare looked out the window. The sky beyond was still a map of white. "It's too early in the season for the snow to be very thick."

"I would think so too. But it has been snowing for two days now without respite." He sipped his drink and frowned. "This is unnatural weather. It came out of nowhere and refuses to stop."

Another memory hit Clare. Blowing past her like a cold wind, the thought was there and gone before she could do more than shiver at it. She'd been driving through a snowstorm, a bad one. There had been a car on the side of the road, abandoned.

"Now my priority is to get you back to civilization as quickly as possible." Dorran put his mug aside. "I cleaned and stitched your wounds, and we have antibiotics, but you will probably fare better in the hands of a proper doctor."

She cleared her throat. "And my sister will be worried. She might even be looking for me. I need to tell her I'm all right."

"I'm afraid we are cut off until the phones are restored."

She hesitated, a last thread of cautious doubt clinging to her and warning her not to share her secret. *Be careful*, Beth's voice said. *Trust*, her heart whispered. "I have a shortwave radio."

His eyebrows rose. "Where?"

"In my car. My sister bought it for me. She keeps another set tuned to the same frequency so that we can contact each other in emergencies." She shrugged and pulled the dressing gown a little tighter. "Because my house is rural, I'm usually the last to get services reconnected when something goes down. Once, I was snowed in for almost a week with no power to charge my phone.

I was fine, of course. I had food and water and everything. But Beth was frantic."

"And she will be listening for contact from you?"

"I'm sure she will. My call was disconnected shortly before…" She blinked and saw Banksy Forest's massive trunks passing either side of her car then saw herself glance toward the phone. "Before the crash, I guess. She'll be worried sick. She might even be looking for me."

"Your car should still be out there." He stood and crossed to the window, running one hand through his hair. "It was off the side of the road. I almost didn't see it. As long as no one has passed through and towed it, and I doubt they would in this snow, we should be able to retrieve the radio and signal for help."

"How bad was the crash? Do you think the car might still work?"

"I wouldn't expect so. The damage looked widespread. And even if it did run, the roads would be too heavily covered for you to get far." He turned back to her. "But the radio is within reach. We can aim for that if nothing else."

CHAPTER 6

"HOW QUICKLY CAN WE go?" Clare tried to rise out of her chair but had to sink back down as her legs shook.

"*You* will not be going anywhere for a while." Dorran passed behind her as he paced the room. "The weather is too vicious."

"I'm used to it." Clare knew she sounded defensive, but she couldn't help it. Moving to Winthrop had been an important moment for her. It was one of the first significant changes she'd made under her own power. Beth loved her, but she'd sheltered Clare, sometimes too much. Clare had handled every aspect of the move, though, from finding the house and hiring movers to having to pay for repairs on her car after spinning into a ditch on her first winter there. Three years later, she felt as though she'd made the region her own. She loved the winters. She was a competent driver once snow set in. She'd endured hours outside in sleet to set up protection for her garden. Dorran's questioning felt a little too close to Beth's endless fretting.

Dorran tilted his head. "I didn't mean to imply you couldn't. But you are injured, plus you will have less resilience to the cold with the blood loss. This type of weather isn't something to be taken lightly."

"I've seen snowstorms before."

"Yes. But the temperatures are abnormally low for this area. I have lived here my whole life, and I wouldn't risk the trip without precautions."

Clare chewed her lip. As much as she wanted to reach her car, she had to concede the point. She hadn't made it far when she'd tried leaving the house. "What kinds of precautions would you need?"

"Your car is perhaps an hour's walk away. I won't try until the storm lets up."

"And you don't know how long that will take?"

"I am sorry, no. But hopefully not long. I would have expected it to have subsided already."

Clare watched the blizzard beat at the window. "You don't have a snowmobile or something like it?"

His smile was grim. "My mother would never allow it. She believes that too much technology erodes our minds, makes us soft."

"Yikes," Clare whispered. "You must have had a fun childhood."

Dorran laughed. "Oh yes, I did."

Clare looked around, absorbing the room's details—the thick wallpaper and elaborate cornices. Every surface was polished until its dark wood shone. It felt stifling. She tried to visualize the family who lived there. *Are they all as odd as Dorran?* "So we can't do anything except wait?"

"I am afraid so. We are at the weather's mercy today." He stopped by her chair. "You will be tired. Let me help you to bed."

"I can get there myself," Clare retorted. She glanced at the four-poster bed on the opposite side of the room. She'd never in her life imagined that going to bed would be a hard task, but the ten paces separating her from it could have been a mile.

Dorran silently extended a hand. Clare sighed, swallowed her pride, and took it. His fingers dwarfed hers, but they were surprisingly gentle as he supported her.

The fire had done its job of warming her, and as Clare curled up in the bed, still wearing the dressing gown, she relished the extra-thick quilts.

Dorran stayed by the fireplace, reading an old cloth-bound novel and feeding new logs into the fire when it burned low. Clare was too exhausted to complain. And as she drifted under, she realized she was at least a little grateful for the company. The house, despite being caked in opulence, felt hostile, as though she were unworthy of staying in it. As if it barely tolerated her. The judgment seeped out of the walls and rose through the floorboards. It bled resentment.

Clare slept poorly. Her dreams were spotted with memories from her last day of normal life. But they were distorted, unnerving, and bordering on nightmarish. She thought there had been something on the TV that had worried Beth—something that a lot of people were upset about. That was the reason she had been driving to Marnie's.

When she startled awake, the light's angle told her it was early morning. She'd rolled onto her bad arm, and a line of fire erupted along its length. Clare groaned and pried it free.

"Here," a familiar voice said. Dorran stood at her side, wearing a beige knit top and offering a glass of water and painkillers. She gratefully swallowed the tablets and drained the water.

As she passed the glass back, she asked, "How's the weather?"

"Hmm." A grim smile was all the answer Clare needed, but she still turned toward the window. The panes rattled as a burst of wind buffeted them. Snow caked the metal.

She dragged a hand over her face. "Okay."

Dorran chuckled. "Do not give up hope. It might clear later today."

Clare nodded. All through the night, anytime she'd come close to waking, her thoughts had always turned to the little black radio hidden in the back of her car. Knowing it was so close but so unattainable was agonizing.

Enough complaining. You have shelter. There's a fire to keep you warm. And Dorran didn't murder you in the middle of the night. Things could be a lot worse, all things considered.

She reached her feet over the edge of the bed, but Dorran held out a hand to stop her. "You should rest. I can bring you food if you would like to stay in bed."

"Thanks, but I think I might go stir-crazy if I do nothing

today." She rubbed the back of her neck. Little bits of grime stuck to the skin. "And, um, I'd really love to clean up a bit."

"Of course. But don't push yourself." Dorran lifted a bundle off a nearby bench and held it out to her. "Your old clothes were unsalvageable, I'm afraid. But I found these in one of the maids' belongings. I'm sure she would not mind your having them."

Clare took the dress and underwear he offered. The dress was made of a thick fabric and had a gentle floral print, and like a lot of things in the house, it hinted at an older era. It was clean, though, and looked like it would fit her better than the too-large dressing gown.

"Thank you." Clare held the clothes close. "Do you have showers here by any chance?"

"Yes. We have showers. But I'm sorry—it would be best if you washed with a cloth today. We can't risk infection entering the cuts while they're still healing."

"Right."

He nodded toward the bathroom. "I'll fetch some warm water for you. Wash anything that isn't covered by a bandage. I'll help you with your hair."

As Dorran disappeared into the bathroom, Clare put the clothes aside and slipped out of bed. Her legs were working better. Everything was stiff, though. She had to put effort into straightening her back.

The hallway door was just barely ajar. Clare approached it. She'd seen outside her room the day before, but that had been part of a desperate ploy for freedom, and she'd barely paid any attention to her surroundings.

The hallway was colder than her room. Goose bumps rose over her exposed skin as she looked through the open door, and Clare hunched her shoulders defensively.

To her right, buried in the shadows that smothered the lightless hallway, a door creaked open. She frowned and leaned forward, trying to see through the gloom. The creaking sound dragged out then finally fell silent. Clare could have sworn she heard something that sounded like a sigh.

She stepped back inside her room, her heart beating furiously, and shut the door. Behind her, she could hear splashing noises coming from the bathroom. She crossed to it and stopped in the doorway.

Dorran knelt by the bathtub as he poured a bucket of water into a basin. He gave her a wry smile. "The water heater is broken. I suspect the system froze, ironically. I'll warm this over the fire."

"You don't need to do that. I don't mind cold water."

He chuckled as he lifted the basin and stepped past her. "It will only take a moment. And your morning will be so much better for it." He moved back into her bedroom, knelt in front of the fire, and scraped embers out of the dying flames.

Clare carefully lowered herself onto the rug beside him. "Dorran, are you sure we're alone here?"

"Hm? Yes. Everyone left." He placed the metal basin on the embers and sat back on his haunches. "Why do you ask?"

"I thought I heard a door open earlier."

"That will be the house. This abysmal thing creaks and complains constantly, and it's worse on windy days like today."

The high ceilings and ornate architraves seemed to have a way of always making their presence known, even when Clare wasn't looking at them. She shuffled closer to the flames. "How old is it?"

"Old." He rose and disappeared into the bathroom. When he returned, he carried a stack of towels and a bar of soap. "I will prepare some breakfast. Take as much time as you need here. I will knock before I re-enter."

"Thanks."

Tiny bubbles appeared in the base of the bowl as the coals heated the water. Clare dipped her fingers into the liquid and was surprised by how quickly it had warmed. Dorran gave her a brief smile then stepped into the hallway, closing the door neatly behind himself.

Clare waited a moment before undressing. Even though Dorran had left, she still didn't feel fully alone. The house had a presence that seemed to loom around her, watching her and judging her. She didn't belong among the antiques and heirlooms, and it didn't want her to forget that.

She dipped a washcloth into the water then began scrubbing her face. It was a relief to get rid of the grime. Days of sweat and dirt had built up, leaving her feeling tacky.

A floorboard creaked above her, and Clare lifted her head. The wind really seemed to be trying to tear the building down. It whistled and rattled, seeking out every tiny hole and every loose tile.

Clare moved the washcloth lower to clean her chest. Dots of

blood had stained her bra, and she carefully removed it. Now that she was paying attention to her body, she found a dozen little scrapes, mostly on her left side. They stung when the hot cloth touched them, but Clare was careful to clean them well. Courting an infection was a bad idea even under the best of circumstances, and Winterbourne was far from an optimal place to be sick. Dorran had said they had antibiotics, but she wasn't sure she fully believed him when the building seemed to be living in the seventeenth century.

The rattling on the roof grew louder. It took on a rhythmic tone, almost like a force was beating its fists on the tiles. Clare rose, a towel clutched over her chest, and crept toward the window.

The storm was heavier, if that were possible. She could no longer see the forest in the distance. Even the shrubs below her window had vanished under a blanket of white. She looked up. Lightning arced through the sky. Reflected across a million snowflakes, it was blindingly bright. Clare pressed her hand over her eyes and waited for the specks to fade. The rattling noise fell silent. After a moment, it resumed.

A chill rolled off the window. Clare shuddered as she moved back to the dying fire. She rushed through the rest of her washing, more eager to be dressed again than to be clean.

Beth, I hope you're not worried about me. I hope you stayed at home instead of coming to look for me. Because there's no way you could get through the roads like this.

The basin of water was discolored by the time she finished with it. Clare shook out the maid's dress and changed into the new clothes. The dress had obviously been designed for the milder autumns, even though it had full sleeves and a high neckline. Clare supposed it made sense that the family didn't own much cold-weather attire if they never stayed through winter. The outfit was a couple of sizes too large, but a cloth belt let her adjust the waist.

She folded the dirty towels into a stack then rubbed her chilled arms. A noise reverberated from the hallway. Clare tried to pinpoint its source. *Something sharp being scraped across stone?*

She crossed to the door. It barely made a noise as she opened it. Clare hesitated on the landing, staring into the gloom. Dorran hadn't turned on any of the lights when he'd left. All Clare could see was a warm candlelit glow coming from the staircase to her right and thin slivers of cold white light glinting out from underneath innumerable doors.

The sound repeated on her left from the path that led deeper into the house. Clare frowned. It sounded close, but she couldn't see anything.

The carpet muffled her steps. As she ventured farther from her room, the temperature plummeted. Clare hugged herself and breathed in staccato gasps. As her eyes adjusted to the gloom, she began to make out more of the hallway's features.

Everything had been built with a high level of skill. The moldings wove neatly around the support pillars that jutted out of the wall every ten feet or so. The wallpaper was flawless. Clare couldn't see any gaps or any sign of where one sheet ended and another began. The design on the ceiling swirled above her, creating a bizarre pattern that seemed to beckon her farther into the house.

The hallway split into three paths. As Clare reached the intersection, the scraping sound broke off in a clatter. Clare held her breath as she peered around the corner. The new halls were shorter—they only went on for twenty meters before terminating in cloth-shrouded windows.

"Dorran?" A puff of condensation escaped when Clare spoke. There was no sign of her companion.

Clare's toes were growing numb, and shivers were setting in. She couldn't tell if Dorran was right that she was more susceptible to the cold or if the temperature really was that much lower. She crept toward the window at the end of the hall.

The curtain was made of thick cloth that crumpled when she lifted it. The narrow window behind it was coated with frost. When Clare moved close to it, her breath clouded the glass. She rose up on her toes to see into the yard. The window faced the estate's front. She could barely see an outline of the hedges she'd run between the day before.

A floorboard groaned behind her, and Clare turned sharply. Her shoulder hit the wall, and the cloth crumpled back into place as she stared down the hallway. A shape leaned against the wallpaper a dozen paces away, blending into the gloom.

CHAPTER 7

"DORRAN?" SHE REACHED BEHIND herself for the curtain. The shadow didn't move as Clare grasped the fabric and began to pull it up. Stark-white light spread across the carpet as the window's edge was uncovered. She kept lifting, exposing more and more of the floor, and the light began to seep up the nearest walls. The shape was just beyond the light's edge. Her pulse jumped as she pulled the curtain higher.

A hellish scraping noise from above made her flinch. Something dropped past the window's exterior, and she swiveled toward it, but the object was so fast that Clare only caught a flash of motion in her peripheral vision. She whipped back to the hallway. The shadowed figure was missing.

Clare was breathing too quickly. She pressed one hand to her throat, which had grown tight. She could have sworn a figure was standing in the hallway. But she'd looked away for only a second.

There was nowhere it could have run to in that time. Even if it had slipped into one of the bedrooms, she should have seen the door closing.

I didn't imagine it. She swallowed as she reluctantly turned her back to the hall and faced the window. *I couldn't have.*

Outside, something small and dark marred the perfect white world. Clare had to bend close to the glass and crane her neck to see it. A rectangular shape, no bigger than her head, was embedded in the snow below the window. A fresh coat of white was already erasing it. Clare needed only a glimpse to guess what it was, though. *A roof tile.*

The wind continued to beat at the house, but its whistle pitch had risen a note as it burrowed into the hole it had created. Clare shuddered and stepped away from the window. She reluctantly let the cloth fall back into place.

She'd been unnerved by the wind earlier when she was in her room, but at least she had felt sheltered inside the mansion. The building was so big, solid, and hulking, she'd had trouble imagining that anything could so much as chip it.

But the house was crumbling. The wind had already eaten a gap in the roof and made a home for itself inside. How many more tiles would fall before winter was over?

She couldn't stop shaking as she followed the hallway back to her room. To reach it, she had to walk over the space where she thought she'd seen the figure. Clare eyed the smooth wallpaper as she passed it. There were no doors in that stretch of the hall, nowhere for the stranger to hide. She felt sick.

I didn't imagine it. Clare's footsteps grew faster as she became desperate to put the window and the hall behind her.

She stopped at the door to her room. The crackling fire was warm. Her bed, with tussled and unmade sheets, looked comfortable. But the space still didn't feel inviting. She imagined sitting in front of the fire, trying to get the flames to reheat the chill inside her chest, as she waited for Dorran to return. It would be just her. Alone with the house.

Clare ducked her head and passed the room, aiming toward the glow at the end of the stairs. It might not be as warm as her bedroom, but it offered something more—human company. The security of companionship would stop her mind from going wild at every little shadow and noise. She never would have expected to turn to the strange man for comfort, but at least Dorran stopped the house from feeling so empty.

The carpet-covered stairs creaked as she descended them. She could see the foyer, but it was empty. A single candle waited on a table at the base of the stairs, perched on an old-fashioned bronze candleholder, and Clare picked it up.

On the third floor, the wind made its presence known unrelentingly. It whistled, spat, and shook anything it could get a hold on. In the foyer, though, its spiteful effects were muted. Instead, echoes surrounded Clare. Every little step, every breath, was whispered back to her.

Condensation rose like smoke every time she exhaled. She eyed the front door but passed it, instead looking for paths that might lead to the kitchen. There was no light and no sign of Dorran.

She pressed on the largest door and found herself facing a dining hall that looked like something out of a period drama. The table was large enough to seat thirty, but its settings had been cleared. The serving tables were bare. Everything had been cleaned scrupulously. The mahogany wood shone, the tiles had been scrubbed until they glistened, and even the chandelier reflected her candlelight back at her.

The tiles were too cold to stand on, so Clare backed out of the room and shut the doors. They moved silently, their hinges so well oiled that they could almost fool her into thinking they were brand-new. They weren't, though. The wood was old—well maintained, but old. A thousand tiny scratches and scrapes had been buffed out through the years.

Clare tried the next door. The room was empty except for more doors, like some kind of transitional room. One of the doors had a line of light flowing out from under it. As she moved closer, Clare began to hear noises—scraping, scratching, snapping. Interspersed between them was a whistle, not too different from how the wind sounded, except this one had a tune. It was low and mournful. Haunting.

As Clare stood on the door's threshold, Beth's voice of caution returned, begging her to retreat and go back upstairs. Her room might be lonely, but at least it was familiar and safe.

The tune dropped in pitch, and the scraping noise grew louder. Clare had come too far to go back. She clutched the candle tightly as she turned the door handle.

Beyond the door was a kitchen. The space looked larger than

Clare's entire cottage. The line of counters running around the room's edge was broken by stove tops and a gigantic brick oven. Two thick tables with dried herbs suspended above them filled up the room's center. Pots and pans, blackened from use and sometimes dented, hung from the walls, between racks of knives, chopping boards, and kitchen utensils.

The room was dark, lit by only an oil lamp perched on the center table and two candles spaced over the nearest bench. Dorran stood there, knife in hand and eyes wild.

They stared at each other for a moment, both silent and unmoving. Then Dorran exhaled and dropped the knife back onto the chopping block. "Clare. You startled me. You looked like a ghost."

She glanced down. Her own candle lit her, but not well. She could only imagine what she must have looked like standing in the dark doorway. "Sorry."

"Is everything all right?"

"Yes. Fine." She stepped into the room, warily eyeing the knives on the wall and the bronze fixtures that flickered in the candlelight. "It's dark in here."

"I will fix that." The aisle was narrow, and Dorran's shoulder brushed Clare's as he passed her. He flicked an oversized switch on the back wall, and sudden, sharp light bathed the room.

Dorran blew out the candles and the lamp as he returned to the counter. He'd been chopping leeks. Not far away, a pot simmered on the stovetop. He pulled a chair out from under the nearest table and indicated for Clare to sit. Then he undid his coat and draped it around her shoulders before stepping around her and fetching something from a cupboard near the door. Clare gratefully hugged the fur coat around herself. The kitchen wasn't quite as cold as the rest of the house, but it was still biting enough to feel through the dress.

"Here." Dorran placed a pair of worn leather boots at her side. "These should stop you from freezing. I didn't expect you to come looking for me, or I would have left the lights on."

She wanted to laugh but didn't know if it would be rude. "Do you always work in the dark?"

"No. But the storm took the power out." He scooped the leeks into the pot and stirred it. "We have a generator—the house is so remote that we lose power at least three or four times a year—but our fuel supplies are limited. I am trying to conserve where I can just in case we are trapped for longer than a few weeks."

"Oh!" She frowned up at the large, high-intensity lights set into the ceiling as she slid her feet into the boots. "Sorry. I didn't realize. You can leave them off."

His glance was sharp. "We can afford to keep them on for a while, especially since you are not familiar with the house."

Dorran retrieved two bowls from under the sink, ladled the soup into them, then topped them with parsley. He placed one in front of Clare, and she saw that it was really more of a stew. Chunks of meat bobbed among the vegetables.

"This is nice. Thank you."

"It is still canned soup, I'm afraid, but I supplemented what I could." He sank into the chair beside her. "We have nonperishable food and frozen meat and vegetables, but almost nothing fresh."

"I suppose your family wouldn't want the food rotting while they were away."

"Exactly." He frowned. "The leek was a lucky find."

"A moment ago, you said you were conserving fuel in case we're trapped here for weeks. That's not likely, though, is it? Winter's only just begun. There's usually a few patches of warm weather before the cold really kicks in."

He didn't speak for a moment but stirred his stew slowly. "I am not sure what to think. This storm arrived unnaturally quickly."

Clare closed her eyes and once again tried to dredge up memories of that final day. She remembered brewing coffee that morning. It had been a fair day then. Sunlight—not warm, but bright enough—had been coming through her window.

That was her last reliable memory. Everything after that felt jumbled and was mixed in with what had to be dreams. Her recollections felt like someone had dumped two jigsaw puzzles into one box and told her to solve them.

She'd been driving to Marnie's. She was sure that was real. And she'd been on the phone with Bethany, though she couldn't remember what they had been talking about. But it had been snowing heavily. Beth had been worried about her. She thought her older sister might have been telling her to go back home, but it had been too late for that. She'd been closer to Marnie's house than to her own.

She thought she remembered something about a news station. *That* had to be a dream. She only watched TV in the evening and never followed the news because it just depressed her. And she had passed a car on the side of the road, but that had been so unreal that she wasn't sure whether it was an actual memory or not.

But she did remember the snow. "The storm came out of nowhere, didn't it? I wouldn't have gone driving if I'd known it would be that bad."

"The same for myself. We had barely even had frost the week before. Realistically, my family should have been able to stay here for at least two or three more weeks, but my mother likes to make our journey to Gould early, before there is any chance of snow. I asked to be let out not long after leaving the forest. The sky was clear then. An hour into the walk home, snow was falling between the trees, and I could hear the wind howling. It was not long after that when I found you."

"You walked home? From outside the forest?"

"It is less than four hours if you keep a good pace."

"You must have *really* not wanted to go to Gould."

He laughed. "I did not."

Clare sipped some of the soup. It was good, meaty, and rich. "I guess the storm caught both of us unaware."

"Yes. And I bring up the storm's suddenness to try to explain why I am being cautious." Dorran continued to stir his soup, scooping up bits of vegetables then letting them drop back in. "Weather in this region can be unpredictable. But the storm appeared in less than an hour and has lasted for three days now. *That* is not normal."

Clare lowered her spoon. "What are you saying?"

"I cannot be certain, but some part about this feels wrong. I intend to be cautious, to take precautions, to guard our resources. The storm may still clear, and the temperature may rise within a day or two. But we cannot rely on it. Lives are lost when people take good fortune for granted."

CHAPTER 8

NESTLED IN THE KITCHEN, in the heart of the house and with Dorran beside her, it was easy to forget how vicious the weather was. But Clare could still picture the outside world blanketed in snow so thick that the ground looked like it might never resurface. She was used to storms lasting a few hours, sometimes as long as half a day. Three days of unrelenting blizzards wasn't right, though. A sense of malaise crawled into her bones.

On the morning of the crash, Beth had been worried about something. She'd called Clare because of it. *Worried about the storm? No, if it had just been a storm, I would have stayed in my house and weathered it out.*

"If this *is* a worst-case scenario…" She spoke carefully, trying not to let her imagination run away from her. "How long could we live here?"

"I took inventory yesterday. We have an abundance of

firewood, so heat will not be an issue. Food is more limited. We have canned soup and rice, but only enough to keep us for a few weeks. We have three kilos of frozen meat and a small amount of frozen vegetables." He nodded toward the door. "We also have a garden."

Clare frowned. "That's got to be long gone, though, right? It would be buried under the snow by now."

"Not quite. I will show you later. It is not planted, but it may provide food once the nonperishable goods are gone."

"Right." Clare dropped her spoon into her bowl. She knew she had to eat, but her mouth had turned dust dry. For the first time, she imagined what might happen if the snow didn't let up. If deep winter had arrived early and the roads remained choked until spring, they would be trapped in Winterbourne. She couldn't picture spending four months there cut off from the rest of the world.

There's probably nothing to worry about. Like Dorran said, the weather around here is unpredictable. But it's not like it will hurt to be prepared in case of a worst-case scenario either.

Clare swallowed. "I can help. With the garden, or the cooking, or repairing the house. Whatever you need."

He blinked. "Thank you. But you should rest. At least for a while longer."

"I'm feeling a lot better today." That was the truth. The stiffness and the pains persisted, but she no longer felt as though she were about to collapse.

"I'm glad to hear it." He rose and carried his empty bowl to the sink. "I'll help you with your hair. Finish eating while I heat some water."

Clare had been used to Beth washing her hair when she was a young teen, on the occasions when she tried to do something fancy with it. And the hairdressers washed it before cutting it. But letting Dorran run his fingers over her scalp was a strange experience.

He had her lean back in one of the kitchen chairs and draped a towel around her neck while he balanced a washbowl behind her. Traces of dried blood had matted her hair, but unlike Beth and the hairdressers, he was incredibly careful as he untangled it. He worked through the knots slowly, alternately using shampoo and conditioner from glass bottles. His thick eyebrows were pulled together in concentration, but otherwise, he looked serene.

The experience was far too intimate for Clare. Desperate for a distraction, she started a conversation. "This really is inside the Banksy Forest, isn't it?"

"The estate? Yes."

"I can't believe I never knew it was here. It must be old."

"Very old."

"Older than the forest?"

"The same age. My family owns the forest."

"Oh!" Pieces were starting to fall into place. "Does that mean they planted it?"

"Correct. Several hundred years ago. This and many other forests." He scooped up a cupful of warm water and poured it over her hair, his other hand smoothing the suds out. Then the comb returned to a stubborn patch just above her temple.

Clare shuffled a little higher in her seat. She was still trying to get used to being touched by someone she barely knew. "Why did they plant them?"

"It was our business. We grew wood. It made our family wealthy."

She tried to glimpse his face again, but his head was down as he tried to ease grime out of the tangle without hurting her. "Why didn't they cut this one down?"

"Because the head of the family died unexpectedly. In her grief, his widow had a house built where no one could disturb her—inside one of the forests."

Clare eyed the kitchen. "She must have been very rich. I had no idea wood growing could be so profitable."

"It wasn't our only business, but it was our mainstay. Under good leadership, wealth tends to cascade. Unfortunately, since the house was built, good leadership has been rare in our family. The estates—and the businesses—were passed down through generations and gradually sold as expenses exceeded income. Now we have almost nothing left. This estate. The Gould estate. And this forest."

He sounded sad. Clare pulled the fur coat around herself a little more tightly. "Still, it's more than a lot of people have, right?"

"True." Dorran's inflection didn't change, but as the word hung between them, Clare sensed there was something more he was stopping himself from saying.

She lifted her eyebrows. "But?"

"I worry about the future." The words came out carefully, as though he didn't like to say them. "If we sold this building and lived modestly, we would have nothing to worry about. But my mother insists on holding this house and maintaining our traditions. Sixty full-time staff are not cheap. Repairing and maintaining a building this old and large is not cheap. We have money, but it flows out rapidly, and nothing comes in to replace it. By the time my mother is dead, I suspect we will be bankrupt."

Clare tried to imagine how that must feel—to come from a family of historical significance, to live a life of decadence, but to know you would inherit none of it. Winterbourne Hall was massive and clean, but she doubted it would be easy to sell. Banksy Forest wasn't a prime location. There were no beautiful views to attract luxury vacationers, and the snow made the place unlivable for nearly four months every year. The building, for all of the care that had gone into maintaining it, wasn't modern enough to attract a fair price.

Dorran's fingers caught on a snag, and Clare swallowed a gasp. He pulled back, sounding alarmed. "Forgive me."

"It's fine." She laughed. "You don't have to worry so much. You're doing a good job."

After a moment, his hands returned, moving more carefully.

"What about you?" Clare tried again to see his face. His dark eyes met hers then glanced away. "What will you do if your mother is spending all of her money?"

"Truthfully, I do not yet know. I would like to work. I would like to be responsible for something. But that is not an option as long as I live here."

"Why don't you leave?"

He closed his eyes. The muscles in his jaw twitched. Before she could identify the emotions he was trying to conceal, he opened his eyes and his features returned to neutral. He dipped the comb into the water before answering. "I cannot."

His tone made it clear he didn't want to continue that line of conversation, but Clare was too curious to stop. "Why not?"

"The world is not particularly welcoming to someone like me."

"Someone like you?"

He poured fresh water over her hair, holding one hand across her forehead to keep it from running into her eyes. "Strange."

"What? You're not strange."

"You are being kind. I know what I am."

Clare bit her lip. She wanted to argue, but he *was* odd. She hadn't been able to get a read on him at first, and it had terrified her. She had preferred to chance the snow than spend the night in his house. But that had been before she'd talked to him.

She thought she was starting to understand Dorran. He wasn't strange in a bad way. He was just stilted and uncertain. He buried his discomfort under formality. And he was sad. That was what bothered her the most. He tried to hide it, but it slipped out occasionally, hidden in his expressions and movements. The tilt of his eyes. The way his smiles never seemed truly uninhibited. How methodical he made every motion. It seemed as though all of the life had been crushed out of him somehow.

He gently nudged her to sit upright and used the towel to squeeze the moisture out of her hair. Clare wanted to say something else, to find a way to tell him that he wasn't too strange for the world and that he didn't need to spend the rest of his life hiding in his secluded mansion. But she couldn't find the right words.

"I think I fixed it well enough." The towel dabbed across her forehead, catching the last drips. "No hair dryers, I'm afraid, but we can sit you beside the fire to dry it."

"Thanks." She touched her hair, relieved to finally feel clean again.

Dorran tipped the dirty water down the sink and left the towels in the empty basin. "Before you return to your room, would you mind taking a detour? I would like to show you something."

"Sure."

He lit two candles in the stovetop, fixed them into candleholders, and gave Clare one. Then he led her to the door, switching off the kitchen's lights as he passed them.

Clare pulled the coat tighter as they crossed the empty room and approached one of the doors in the back. Since he'd given her his coat, he only wore a shirt. "Aren't you cold?"

"A little. But I don't mind it. Careful here."

He led her down five steps and into a stone room. A large bolted bronze door opposite them caught in their candlelight. Unlike the main parts of the house, the area hadn't been well maintained. The bronze was tarnished, and dirt had accumulated between the stones lining the floor. Bare bulbs hung from the ceiling to light the walls.

"Is this part of the house for the staff?" Clare guessed.

He gave her a quick smile. "Correct."

A tall stone archway to Clare's left drew her attention. She could see a step down, but no farther. Shadows clustered inside the entryway, and she thought she could hear a very faint dripping noise coming from the space.

Dorran was focused on the door ahead, though. The small window in it was too fogged for Clare to see through. Dorran put the candle on the ground while he unbolted the door and pulled it open. Then he motioned Clare into the room.

As she stepped through the doorway, lights flickered to life, starting right above her and reappearing every four feet down the long, rectangular room. The space was warmer than the rest of the house, enough that the cold no longer bit at Clare's face. Shelves lining the walls were full of metal and wood implements. At least twenty raised garden beds were spaced evenly throughout the area, and organic smells filled her nose. After spending so long in the house's stuffy hallways and rooms, being surrounded by something natural was like a breath of fresh air.

"Is this…"

"Our garden." He stepped in behind her and closed the door. The lights were warmer than the kitchen's, and they highlighted Dorran's dark eyes and the line of his jaw. "It is expensive to have food delivered to the property, so most of what we eat is grown on-site. The gardens were dug up shortly before the family left. Sadly, the chickens and goats are gone too."

She leaned over one of the garden beds. The soil looked rich and dark.

"If we have nothing but canned vegetables and rice to eat, we will soon start craving fresh food. I thought it would be wise to restart the garden. It will use up our fuel faster but will help extend our food stores."

Clare thought it was probably a smart move. She brushed her hand over the dirt. "It's still warm."

"It was heated until a few days ago. The insulation has protected it from the worst of the cold." He pointed to the lights above them. "They're full-spectrum bulbs, which imitate sunlight. They will need fuel to run. But we can save gasoline by heating it through the furnace. That is my main motive for being cautious with the lights. If we budget carefully, we should have enough fuel to keep the garden lit and warm for a while."

"It's heated by a furnace? Like a real, wood-burning furnace?"

"Yes. In the basement, below our feet." He paced along the garden beds, examining the freshly turned soil. "We have plenty of seeds. I thought we could start with plants with a short harvest time. Lettuce. Beans. Some of the seeds can be eaten as sprouts too. I will come back later and begin work."

"Why don't we start now?" Clare tilted her head. "I had a garden at my cottage. I can help."

"I would appreciate it. But your arm is still healing, and you must be tired. Perhaps another day."

She laughed. "You don't have to worry about me so much. And I want to help. I think I'd go crazy if I had to stay in bed all day."

69

"Hm. As long as you're not too tired." His eyes warmed. "I'll see to reviving the furnace. You could begin planting. Gloves are on that shelf. Seeds are on the bench. I will be back within twenty minutes."

"Sounds like a plan."

Clare pulled on a pair of thick gloves as she watched Dorran leave through the tarnished door. He seemed familiar with the staff's areas of the house. Something told her that he was used to working in the garden. If she'd been stuck in the mansion with no freedom and no real job, she probably would have started looking for chores to do too.

The seeds were arranged in large labeled glass jars on a bench running across the back wall. The quantity surprised her. She was used to buying packets with a hundred or two hundred seeds for her own garden. Winterbourne had tens of thousands.

I guess the garden has been running for a long while. Feeding a large family and sixty staff three times a day would be no small feat.

The shelf also held an array of miniature stakes and pens. Clare used them to mark out the area she was planting. Her own garden was more of a hobby than a necessity, and she grew as many flowers as vegetables. Winterbourne's garden was a different matter. She tried to guess how many plants would provide full meals for two people without planting so much that it became a waste. More challenging was the fact that the jars only listed the plant variety, with no instructions on how deep or far apart the seeds needed to be buried.

Clare set several rows of tomatoes and lettuce, which she had practice with, but hesitated on everything else. She liked to be useful, but Dorran had left the garden completely in her hands, and that was more pressure than she was comfortable with. *Even if I get out of the house within a few days, Dorran will probably need the garden to get through the rest of the winter. I can't mess it up for him.*

She bit her lip as she stared at a jar of capsicum seeds. She couldn't remember how it liked to be planted. She put it on the edge of the garden bed and went in search of Dorran. He'd said he would be in the basement, which she guessed was accessed by the archway they had passed on the way to the garden. Clare picked up her candle as she left, being careful to close the door behind her to keep the heat inside.

She approached the archway but stopped on the top step. No light came from the basement. Cool air rolled out of it, prickling her skin. She tucked her chin into the coat's collar. The stairway made her uneasy, as though it exuded a toxic odor that her conscious mind couldn't detect but her subconscious shuddered at. She stared into the black abyss, and all she wanted to do was turn and run.

Don't let this house sweep you up in its aura. It's just a basement. Nothing more. She took in a deep breath, held it, then stepped into the void.

CHAPTER 9

THE CHANGE IN ATMOSPHERE was palpable. It covered Clare like water, sinking into the crevices in her clothes and saturating her. Her hair, still damp, chilled her. She held the candle ahead of herself so that the light could cover the walls, but the flame guttered as it fought against the frigid air.

"Dorran?" She tried to call for him, but the word came out as a gasp. Her only answer was a slow, steady dripping noise.

With each step she descended, she felt less connected to the real world. When she looked back, she could no longer see the archway, the garden, or any trace of light. It was just her and the darkness, wrapped around each other, tangled so badly that she began to worry they would never be separated again.

Her feet finally touched even ground. Clare's breathing was shallow, but even so, the cold air invaded her body and robbed her warmth. She licked dry lips as she tried to see into the room. The candlelight caught on a handful of dulled shapes—something metal, something glass. She couldn't identify any of them. She couldn't see Dorran. But she could hear a scratching noise. It came from above her and below her all at once, like fingernails on stone or dying breaths dragged through rotting lungs.

"Dorran, answer me."

A thud disturbed the stillness. She swung in its direction. Her candle flickered. She had never been bothered by the dark before, but at that moment, Clare felt as though she would rather die than be lost in the shadows in the basement. She held her hand around the flame to protect it and only began breathing again when the flame stabilized.

Soft, thudding footsteps echoed out of the darkness. Clare lowered her hand and squinted through the gloom. If Dorran was responsible for the sounds, he was working without a light. She took a step closer, then another. Someone drew in a deep, rasping breath. She passed a tall wooden shelf. On it, dusty glass objects glittered. *Wine bottles, maybe?*

The scraping noise became louder. It hurt Clare's ears and made her teeth ache. She silently begged it to stop. Motion became visible through the shadows ahead. Someone or something was bent low near a stone wall. Clare's thin light was just enough to let her see shoulders rising and falling.

"Dorran?"

The figure turned toward her. Eyes glinted—horrible, inhuman eyes peering out from behind long, greasy hair. Then the figure darted away, escaping from her circle of light, disappearing into a narrow doorway in the stone wall.

A sharp, broken scream cut through the cold air. Clare didn't realize it had come from her until she felt the ache in her throat. She stumbled backward, and her shoulders hit one of the shelves. Muffled clinking noises surrounded her as the bottles rocked.

She couldn't stop shaking. The thudding footsteps echoed around her, beating fast, like her own heart. The scraping noise joined it, louder this time. It surrounded her and overwhelmed her.

"Clare?" The voice was faint.

She turned toward it. In the distance, golden light glinted through the shadows. It promised safety. She ran for it. Her shin hit one of the shelves. She fell, gasping as cold stone scraped her hands and jarred her bandaged arm. A wave of pain rushed through the limb. The candle skittered over the floor and died in a splutter of wax.

"Clare!"

Footsteps drew nearer. She tried to stand, but trapped in the darkness and choking on the pain, she was too disoriented. She stumbled again and bent over, trying not to be sick. Then arms were around her, pulling her up. She was surrounded by warmth. When she opened her eyes, a lamp, larger and stronger than her own candle, was sitting beside her feet. It cut through the shadows to create a little oasis of light.

Dorran held her up so that she rested against his shoulder. He kept her steady, one hand on her back, the other holding her hand. His voice was tense. "What happened? Are you hurt?"

She sucked in ragged, uneven breaths. Her tongue felt heavy. She couldn't form the words, and they fell out in an incoherent slurry. "I saw someone."

"Clare?"

She shook her head, her mind a jumble. "I...I was looking for you."

"Ah." He exhaled. "Forgive me. This is the wine cellar. It is my fault—I should have shown you where to find the door to the basement."

His hands were unexpectedly warm. The numbness was fading, but the panic was not. Clare glanced behind them, at the wall. "There—there's someone down here."

"What?"

Clare raised a hand toward where she'd seen the hunched shape. "I saw someone. I...I think it was a woman. She came out of the door in the far wall."

Dorran stared into the darkness, confusion clear on his face, then he looked back at her. "Clare, there are no doors in the cellar. Just stairs leading to the main floor."

"But..." She paused for a second, trying to clear the panicked fog from her head and the tightness from her voice. "There was a woman. She was digging at something. Digging at the stones, I think. When I got closer, she ran into the tunnel. It's *right there*." She pointed again. The lamplight, although stronger than the candle, still couldn't reach the walls.

Dorran was silent. Then he took a deep breath and said, "Show me."

He helped her to her feet. She stumbled, and he put his arm around her back to hold her steady then picked up the lamp with his spare hand. Moving cautiously, Clare led him past the shelves. Shadows danced around them with every step, slinking across the stone walls and darting over the ceiling. A thousand dust-caked bottles glittered out of the gloom.

Clare came to a halt facing the stretch of wall where she'd seen the woman. She was sure it was the right place. She recognized the erratic stone tiles lining the floor. But the doorway was gone.

"I..." Her throat tightened. She stepped out of Dorran's support and approached the wall. The spot where there had been a gaping opening was nothing but rough, interlocked stones. She pressed her hands against them, feeling around the cracks, as she tried to make sense of it. "It was...I..."

"Clare."

"It was right here!"

"Clare." Dorran came up behind her and gently pulled her back from the wall.

Tears stung her cold face. She stared along the wall's length, scanning both directions, but the surface was unbroken. *There was a woman crouched on the ground. Crouched and scrabbling at the stone. When she saw me, she ran through the doorway that was right here. Right here...*

She felt like she was unraveling. Her mind was fracturing, the pieces floating away, and as fast as she tried to grasp them and pull them back in, more were lost.

But she and Dorran were alone in the basement. There were no noises and no rasping breaths. They were the only ones there, encased in their little globe of light. And he was watching her, concern thick around his eyes, waiting for her to speak.

"I'm not crazy," she whispered.

"No. Of course you're not." He pulled her closer, one hand brushing across her shaking back. "This is my fault. I shouldn't have left you alone."

"I didn't imagine it." Her voice cracked. She didn't know if he'd heard her.

"The light must have been creating tricks for your eyes. This house—it plays with your mind, especially if you are not familiar with it. It is a damned waking nightmare." He was trying to give her an escape, an excuse.

And with the empty wall stretching endlessly behind them, she had no choice but to take it. "Yes."

"Let's get you back upstairs, where it's warmer. And I'll find you something to drink. You will feel better once you're out of this maze of a wine cellar."

She nodded. Her mind was at war, killing itself as it tried to hold on to reality. Dorran kept his hand on her back as he turned her toward the stairway. Clare stopped at its base and stared up, suddenly exhausted. The stairs seemed to go on forever.

"Here." Dorran pulled her against his chest, scooped one arm under her legs, and lifted her as though she weighed nothing.

Clare clutched at his shirt but didn't try to argue. He held her carefully, her head tucked in at his neck, as he carried her up the stairs and back into the main parts of the house. He was warm. Slowly, she relaxed her grip.

"Bed or fireplace?" he asked as he climbed to the third floor.

"Fire." That was an easy question to answer. She was starved for warmth.

Dorran used his shoulder to bump the bedroom door open, then he placed her on the fireside rug. The embers were near dead, and the heat was leaking out of the room. Dorran knelt and fed wood into the fire until it was crackling again. Then he draped a quilt over Clare's shoulders. "Will you be all right on your own for a moment?"

"Yes."

She didn't see him leave, but she heard the quiet click of the door as it shut behind him. She exhaled then pushed the blanket off and stood.

I'm not crazy. She stared at her hands, frustrated that they continued to shake. *But there was no door. But I'm not crazy. But I know what I saw. But I'm not crazy…*

She left the fire to approach the windows. The day was nearly gone. A golden sunset glittered through the falling snow. The forest was clearly visible, a ragged band of black stretching across the horizon. It continued to snow, but the storm was over.

Thank mercy. She wrapped her arms around herself as she choked on tears. The radio was within reach. It would be reckless to try for it that night, while the temperatures were brutal and with dusk setting in, but daylight was less than twelve hours away. She would speak to Beth. She would find a way to leave Winterbourne before it sent her truly insane.

The door creaked as it opened, and Clare flinched.

Dorran stood in the entrance, holding a tray with two bowls of soup. He smiled. "Come and sit by the fire with me, where it's warm."

CHAPTER 10

THAT NIGHT WAS THE most peaceful Clare had spent in Winterbourne. She and Dorran sat side by side on the rug by the fire, blankets wrapped around their shoulders as they ate the soup and talked. Dorran didn't mention the scene in the cellar, and Clare was grateful for it. She still didn't know what to think had happened. Or what to think of herself. Instead, she focused on what was important—making contact with the outside world. *Leaving.*

She wouldn't have any regrets if she never saw Winterbourne again. But she was surprised to realize she would miss Dorran.

They talked about the garden—a safe, neutral topic—and about what plants they wanted to grow and how many. As she'd suspected, Dorran had spent a lot of time there while his family occupied the house. His mother refused to visit what she called "the servants' quarters." And while she disapproved of Dorran's hobby, she didn't disturb him when he worked there.

"In late spring and summer, it is warm enough to grow some hardy plants outside," he said. "I enjoy that. Being out of the house. Merri would join me on most days, though she complained when the frost set in."

"Is Merri one of your nieces?"

He laughed. "No. My dog. She is gone, sadly, spending the winter in Gould with my family. If I'd been able to bring her back with me, our incarceration would be a lot more entertaining." His smile faded, the way it did when he talked about his family.

Clare watched him curiously. "Your mother wouldn't let you take Merri with you?"

"No."

He placed his empty bowl to one side and stretched his legs toward the fire. All humor had left his face. Clare could tell he wanted to say more. But he was hesitating, standing on the edge of a cliff, unsure of whether it was safe to jump.

She leaned closer and lowered her voice. "What is it? You can tell me."

"This is not a healthy family," he said at last, the words halting and hesitant. The wood in the fire popped and fizzed. He stared at it, his face tense and his thick eyebrows pulled tight. "Everything we do is to maintain a pretense. The pretense that we are still the wealthiest estate in the area. The pretense that we are revered, adored, above reproach. The pretense that time never moved past our glory days."

Dorran had been guarded about what he said, but Clare had read between the lines enough to guess who was responsible.

"That's what your mother wants, isn't it? To stay locked in that bubble of time?"

"Yes. And she is fanatical about it. Any staff who question her values are dismissed harshly. Those who remain have absorbed her obsession. They became swept up in it—almost like a cult. They treat her word like law, and she will not accept anything less. Time away from the house is heavily restricted." He pressed his eyes closed. "Disobedience is punished, sometimes harshly. Withholding food for minor infractions. Caning for more serious lapses."

Clare's throat was tight. "But that's illegal."

"It is. But no one will report her. Some are too loyal. Others are afraid of the consequences. Our family's influence is diminished compared to what it once was, but not gone. And my mother does not forget grudges."

Anyone who kept her staff on such a tight leash could not have been an easy mother to live under. Clare spoke carefully. "Does she control what you do too?"

His smile was tense. "She does. I cannot leave the estate."

"Never?"

"I see the world twice a year, through the windows of our car, as we travel between Winterbourne and Gould."

Anger, cold and sharp, bloomed in Clare's stomach. *What sort of mother would lock her own child up like that?* It was quickly followed by a different question. *Why does he put up with it?*

Dorran adjusted his posture, folding one leg under the other. "It is not so bad. I had a good education through tutors. And the house is large, which makes it easy to avoid my family and easy to keep busy. I spend much of my time with the staff. Many of them are good company."

Clare shook her head. "Even so, don't you want to leave?"

He chuckled and glanced aside. "I do. But that is not why I am telling you this. I want to explain, and to apologize."

"Apologize for what?"

"Sometimes it is hard to know what is right, what is normal. When you spend your whole life trapped inside a family with an unhealthy view of the world, what is bizarre becomes your every day. What should be abhorrent becomes your reality."

Dorran ran his fingers through his hair, brushing it back from his forehead. His eyes moved, darting over the flames as he tried to piece together his thoughts. Clare waited, knowing he would need a minute.

"I am not used to speaking with people outside my family," he said at last. "I know I have not been the best of company. I did not know how to talk to you, especially at first. I made you uncomfortable, and I am sorry for it."

"You don't have to apologize for that."

He met her eyes. It only lasted a second, but the sincerity in his gaze was arresting. "I hope you will pardon me for any lapses in manners. They are not intentional. And..." He paused again as he chose his words. "I know trust is not something I can expect to come easily. But you should not be afraid to ask for anything you want or need while you stay here. I want you to be comfortable."

"Thank you." Clare wanted to say more, to tell him she was sorry for the family he'd been trapped with, to say how much she appreciated what he'd done for her. The words were crowding onto her tongue, too jumbled to come out, but she didn't want to let the silence hang. She rested her hand on his forearm.

He glanced at it, and his smile grew warmer, almost fond. It held more real joy than Clare had seen in him before. His other hand came up to cover hers, the fingers heavy and careful. He only held it there for a second before he stood, moving away from her touch.

"Your cuts need redressing. I should not have left them this long. I will return soon."

Clare waited until his footsteps had faded, then she released a held breath. Something was still bothering him. She wished she could look inside his mind, even just for a moment.

When Dorran returned, he looked serene again. He carried a pot of water, which he set on the coals to heat, and an old metal kit full of bandages, equipment, and surprisingly modern-looking plastic bottles. He took one, checked the label, then tipped out two pills, which he handed to Clare. She swallowed them.

"Because our family was so large, and because contact with the outside world was so unreliable, we had a doctor on staff. He worked in the kitchen when his medical skills weren't needed. In his spare time, he taught me a little."

Dorran placed surgical scissors and a needle driver into the pot of water, their handles poking above the steam, to boil. He then laid out a towel and indicated for Clare to give him her arm.

Using gloves, he fished the scissors out of the pot, waited for them to cool, then began cutting away the bandages.

It was the first time she'd seen her arm since the crash. Nausea rushed through her, and she turned away as she tried not to panic. Her arm was red and covered in mottled bruising. Gashes ran along it like lightning marks. Dorran had stitched them. Black thread wound through the red flesh like a nightmarish tapestry.

"It is all right." Dorran spoke softly. "It looks worse than it is. The cuts are shallow, near the surface. No broken bones. Even the muscles are mostly intact."

Clare took a deep, gulping breath. She still didn't trust herself to speak.

"I was as careful as I could be. Scarring should not be significant. It will only take a moment to clean this, and then we will bandage it again."

"Okay," she managed.

Dorran bent close as he worked on dabbing away caked blood. He was gentle, but even with the pain tablets, Clare had to bite the inside of her cheek to keep silent.

Several of the stitches had torn—probably during one of her falls—and he had to cut them free and restitch them. Clare tried not to look. She'd never been very good with blood. It wasn't a full-blown phobia, but it left her feeling queasy. Trying to distract herself, she grabbed on to the topic that had been on her mind all evening. "The storm's over."

"Yes. It looks much clearer."

"I want to try to go to my car tomorrow and get the radio."

"Hm." He kept his head low as he focused on stitching one of the cuts. "The snow is deep, and the air is still frigid. It will be risky to go tomorrow, especially if there is a chance that the storm will return."

She hissed as the needle punctured her skin, then she closed her eyes to clear her thoughts. "I don't want to wait any longer. Beth will be frantic. And maybe, if we can contact her, we can find a way out of here. A helicopter, maybe."

"All right. I can't promise I will be able to reach the car, but I will try."

She cracked her eyes open. Dorran had finished stitching, and he set the needle aside before pouring clear liquid from a bottle onto a cotton ball.

"I'll be going with you," Clare said.

"This will sting."

She kicked her foot out and swallowed a cry as the antiseptic touched the cuts.

Dorran looked apologetic. "It will be over in a moment. Hold on."

Clare was sweating and shaking by the time he'd finished. He pulled fresh bandages out of the kit and began wrapping them around her arm. He didn't speak until he was nearly done. "I don't think it would be a good idea for you to accompany me. It is a long walk, and in harsh conditions. Better if I go alone."

"Safety in numbers," she countered.

He gave her a quick look.

She lifted her chin. "I can do it. I know I can."

"You probably could." Dorran finished tying off the bandages. "But remember what I said earlier about minimizing risk. About not relying on the best-possible scenario, no matter how likely it seems. You could probably make the trip to the car and back. But while you live in this house, I am responsible for your well-being. And I will not risk it when I can do the job myself."

Clare wanted to argue. Whenever she thought about the radio, she pictured getting it herself. Sending someone else in her place felt wrong. But Dorran was already making a concession by traveling there before he thought it was safe.

Leave it for tonight. You can ask again tomorrow. The weather might have improved by then.

"Leg next," Dorran said, and Clare tried not to cringe. The arm had been such a challenge that she'd forgotten about the other patches of bandages scattered about her body. Reluctantly, she extended her leg and braced herself.

The other cuts turned out to be minor compared to the damage to her arm. She'd lost a strip of skin on her leg—it had probably scraped against the road—but the injury wasn't severe enough to need stitches. It still stung like a nightmare when Dorran cleaned it, though. She had a nick in her neck and three cuts across her abdomen. Like her arm, they had needed stitches, but Dorran said the cuts hadn't gone deep enough to be a serious risk.

Clare lay on her back, holding a blanket over her chest for modesty, while Dorran cleaned the stitches on her stomach. She was surprised by how comfortable she was with it. She'd always been shy about showing too much skin—something Beth's caution had reinforced—and if she'd imagined the experience before arriving at Winterbourne Hall, she would have thought it would be embarrassing at best, horrible at worst. But she didn't feel any of that with Dorran. She felt safe.

"There, finished." He pressed along the edges of the gauze to ensure it stuck to her then rocked back on his heels. "You've done well."

A sharp gust of wind rattled the windows, and Clare startled. A door farther down the hallway banged open.

"Just the wind," Dorran said. He packed away the kit and shut the lid. "I'll make sure it's closed. But don't let it alarm you. This house likes to complain."

He left, walking smoothly. He was confident, unafraid of what was lurking in the hallway. As Clare pulled her coat around her shoulders, she wished she could feel as secure as he did.

CHAPTER 11

THEY ENDED UP SLEEPING on the rug, bundled in blankets and pillows, taking advantage of the fire's warmth. Clare was secretly glad. She didn't want to be left alone in the house. The wind beat at the windows, and the floorboards in the attic groaned, but human company made it easier to tune them out.

The wind grew worse during the night, and as Clare drifted in and out of sleep, she began to imagine the sound of fingers scrabbling at the tiles above them, so much like the noise from the wine cellar. In the early hours of the morning, she thought she heard a scream. She shot upright, breathing too quickly, her heart galloping. The noise had already faded, though, until she couldn't tell if it had been the wind or part of a dream. Clare brushed loose hair behind her ear and pulled her knees up close to her chest.

Dorran lay near her on the rug, one arm under his head as

he slept. The fire's glow softened his face. She'd never noticed before, but he had long eyelashes. They brushed his cheeks and twitched as he dreamed.

The fire was growing low, so Clare crawled to it and fed it a fresh log. It crackled as the wood crushed the embers.

She felt cold despite the room's warmth. When she lay back down, she moved a little closer to Dorran's side. His forearm had slipped out from under the blanket. She tugged the quilt back over it then pulled her own blanket up around her throat and tried to relax.

She'd nearly fallen asleep when a heavy thud broke through the daze. Clare opened her eyes. Dorran still slept, his features relaxed and his breathing deep and slow. Clare twisted to see the window. It was hard to be sure with the curtains blocking the view, but she thought pale, ghastly daylight was starting to replace the moonlight.

Something's wrong. A sense of dread passed over Clare. It started in her shoulders, tightening the muscles, then wormed its way down her back. *Something's wrong. Something's wrong.*

She held still, wrapped in blankets, as the dread filled her stomach and turned her cold. Light from the fire and light from the windows mixed uneasily, cold and hot, neither strong enough to remove the gloom. The wallpaper's twisting pattern felt more insane than ever. The cornices and edging hoarded shadows jealously.

Something's wrong. But what?

An exhale came from near the door. It floated out of the

shadows, weary and rasping, and Clare's heart skipped a beat. She slowly turned her head.

Dark furniture blended into the gloom, becoming nothing but a jagged row of menacing shapes. One shadow stood out from the others. It was moving.

The woman swayed by the open door. A dirty white nightdress clung to her emaciated body. Greasy brown hair brushed gaunt cheeks. The eyes bulged, glassy and too intense. One arm was crossed over her torso, and her bony fingers clutched at a hole in her dress. A hole in her *skin*. White bone poked out of dark-red flesh. The woman twitched as she swayed, unsteady on her feet, and every breath made the bones rise and fall in their sockets.

Clare opened her mouth to scream, but only a whine escaped. She felt frozen. The woman peeled back her lips, revealing cracked teeth and bleeding gums. She took a rocking step toward Clare. The trance broke.

"Dorran. Dorran! Dorran! *Dorran!*"

He jolted as he woke. Clare clutched at him, shaking him as she screamed. The woman flinched at the noise. The smile widened, becoming an insane grimace, as she stepped back through the open door and disappeared into the hallway.

"What?" Dorran, half-asleep, gripped Clare's hand too tightly. "What is it? What's wrong?"

"The woman! She's *real*. She was there. *Right there!*"

Slow and ponderous, the bedroom door drifted shut. Dorran stared at it then looked at Clare. His face hardened. "Stay here."

He rose out of their makeshift bed and grabbed the poker from beside the fire.

Clare scrambled to her feet and stayed close to him, afraid to be left alone. "I'm coming."

Dorran narrowed his eyes at her but didn't argue. He held the poker ahead as he leaned through the doorway, looking first left, then right. Clare rested one hand on his arm to keep herself grounded. They held that position for a moment, and all Clare could hear was their breathing and heartbeats.

"Did you see which way she went?" Dorran asked.

The moment had been so frantic that Clare wasn't sure. "I think...I think left."

Dorran turned in that direction. He moved smoothly, keeping his center of gravity low. His eyes were constantly roving. He reminded Clare of a stalking cat. She followed and watched their backs. The hallway seemed empty. When Dorran reached each door, he slowly, silently twisted the handle then shoved it open with his shoulder. A quick scan was all he needed to check that they were empty. They passed bedroom after bedroom, all neatly made and vacant. Then he checked a sitting room and a nursery.

At last, Dorran stopped at the end of the hallway, beside the window Clare had looked out of the day before. He lowered the poker, but the intensity didn't leave his face. He looked at her, asking a silent question.

"I'm sure I saw her," was all Clare could say.

"Go back to the bedroom. Lock the door. I will search the rest of the house."

"You shouldn't go alone."

"Do not argue." His voice was quiet, but his dark eyes held a warning.

She hadn't seen him look so focused and dangerous before. She let him lead her back to her room.

Dorran kept his eyes on the hallway. "I will be back soon, and I will call before opening the door. If anything else tries to come in, scream. I will hear you."

"Okay."

He shut the door. A moment later, she heard a click as he locked it.

Clare crossed to the fireplace and sank onto the layers of blankets and pillows. She was shaking. When she closed her eyes, she could see the woman again. The blotchy, discolored skin. Broken teeth and bleeding gums. Long hair that had thinned into straggly clumps. The hole in her side...

Clare bent over and pulled her knees up under her chin. The hairs on her arms all stood up. She'd never seen an injury like that before. She had no idea what might have caused it...or how the woman had still been standing.

I shouldn't have left Dorran alone. I should have insisted on going with him in case he needs help, in case he doesn't see her coming.

A hundred scenarios, all sickening, played out in Clare's mind. She tried to listen to the house to see if she could hear what was happening, but no noises reached her room. Clare squeezed her hands together until the knuckles ached. The wind was relentless, wearing down her patience. She stood and began pacing. She went to the window and stared across the unblemished blanket of snow that coated the landscape. The storm had cleared, and the sun was rising, but her surroundings were no easier to discern. Everything was the same shade of blurred, glaring white. Even the forest in the distance was barely distinguishable except for the ribbon of dark-brown trunks visible underneath their snowy caps.

Please, Dorran. Be careful.

She crossed to the door and tried the handle. It was locked. She went through the bathroom to the conjoined bedroom and tried its door, but Dorran had locked that as well.

A new nightmarish scenario played through her mind. *What will happen if Dorran never returns?* The doors were massive, and their locks were heavy metal. She didn't think she was strong enough to beat them down. Jumping from the third-floor window would probably kill her, no matter how fluffy the snow looked. If something happened to Dorran, she would be trapped there until she starved.

Clare returned to her own bedroom. She paced from the fire to the bed and back. Dorran had left his coat hanging on a hook by the door. He would be cold without it. She chewed at the corner of her thumb. Then a soft knock at the door made her catch her breath.

"It's just me," Dorran called. "Everything is fine."

Thank goodness was her first thought, followed closely by *Did he find the woman?*

The key scraped against metal as he unlocked the door. When

he stepped through, he looked tired. He gave Clare a small, brief smile before crossing to the fireplace and returning the poker to its holder. He didn't meet her eyes. "There is no one."

"But…" She felt choked as she moved from the closed door to Dorran. "Did you look everywhere?"

"I did. Every single room."

"What about the wine cellar?"

"Yes, there as well." He turned to face her, held out a hand, then let it drop back to his side. "Sometimes intense dreams can seem like reality—"

"No." She shook her head furiously and crossed her arms. "I didn't dream it. I was awake. And this is the third time I've seen her. There's someone else in this house."

"Clare." He closed the distance between them and grasped her forearms. His voice was very gentle. "When my family leaves for Gould, we have a count to ensure all parties are present. Every single man, woman, and child was packed and embarked on either the bus or one of the cars. *Everyone.*"

"Maybe…maybe…"

"When I left the group, I left alone. I walked back along the road alone. The blizzard set in before I found you. No one could have followed me. And even if they had, the doors and windows have all remained closed."

Angry, confused tears stung her eyes, but she blinked them back furiously. She tried to step out of Dorran's hands, but even though he never held her hard enough to hurt, he didn't let her go.

"I don't know what's happening, Clare. But I promise this house only holds two people—you and myself."

"There's got to be…" Her voice was strangled. "I'm not crazy. I'm not imagining it. Are… Do…" Again, the lump in her throat caught her words. "Does this house have any…any stories about ghosts? A maid, maybe, who died? With…with an injury in her side?"

His reply was a whisper. "Ghosts? No. Not in this house."

"I'm not crazy."

He looked incredibly, intensely sad. His head dropped, and he spoke so softly that she wasn't sure she was supposed to hear. "How can I make this better? How can I help you?"

She knew the answer to that question. "Let me go to my car for the radio."

He took a slow, ragged breath. Clare couldn't stand it any longer and leaned forward to rest against Dorran. Slowly at first, hesitantly, his arms wrapped around her back. The embrace was gentle, and Clare hid her face in his chest as she finally let the tears escape.

"All right," he said, and his voice was just as tight as hers was. "All right. We will both go."

CHAPTER 12

THEY DIDN'T TRY TO debate the figure Clare had seen. There was nothing else they could say without arguing in circles. But in an unspoken agreement, she and Dorran stayed close together through that morning's routine.

She could feel him watching her when he thought she wasn't looking. She wished she could say something to make things normal again. If she said it had all been a dream, that she'd been trapped in a fog of sleep when she'd seen the woman, she knew he would accept that, and the tension would be over. But she couldn't bring herself to lie.

And she still couldn't explain what she'd seen. The gash in the woman's side had been large and old. The flesh had begun to dry and turn dark as though it had been exposed to the air for too long. She'd looked demented. But she'd moved toward Clare with a purpose, like she wanted something. And she had only fled when Clare screamed.

I'm not imagining it. But already, doubt was starting to seep in. Not trusting her own eyes was a horrible thing, but her conviction crumbled with every passing minute.

She knew Dorran thought the house was affecting her, that the high walls and grim furniture were making her paranoid. He turned on every light they passed as they made their way through the building. When he spoke to her, his tone was warm and encouraging. He was trying to help, but in some ways, his kindness made it worse. She didn't want to be coddled. She just wanted to know she wasn't crazy.

One thing held her together. They were going to get the radio. For the first time in four days, she would have some contact with a world other than Winterbourne, and she felt like that by itself would make everything right.

Dorran was being cautious about the trip. He went through the house, collecting layer upon layer of clothes for Clare. Two sets of socks—one to keep her feet warm, the other to keep them dry. Jackets and layers of pants that needed their cuffs rolled up to fit her, followed by gloves that were a little too big, but secured with twine tied around the wrists. Finally, a knit hat and a thick wool scarf to wrap across her face.

"These are some of the lowest temperatures the area has seen," he said when he caught Clare frowning at the outfit. "And it's a long walk."

She was sure he was overreacting. She lived not far away. The winters could get bitingly cold and had never been bad enough to require more than a good thermal coat. But she also knew Dorran didn't want her coming at all. So she swallowed her objections.

She felt a little better when he went through the same process for himself, wrapping on layers of clothes. And she had to admit it was effective. Even though the house was like a fridge, she felt pleasantly warm.

Finally, Dorran boiled water and filled two insulated flasks. He tied one to Clare's belt and one to his then added a small toolbox.

"Ready?" he asked. She nodded. "Good. We're going to the shed along the side of the house first. It has snowshoes and shovels, which we will need to reach your car. Follow in my wake. Call out if you become stuck."

"Roger that," she said, trying to inject some lightness into the situation, but even though Dorran's eyes scrunched up in a smile, he didn't laugh.

They approached the front doors. Dorran looked her over a final time, seeming to run through some kind of internal checklist, then, satisfied, he wrenched open one of the double doors.

Clare's heart sank. The snow had built up against the door nearly to her chin. It created a solid wall of white. More flakes drifted in through the narrow opening to melt on the tile floor.

"Do you think you can manage this?" Dorran asked.

She hardened her expression. "Yep."

"All right. Come here. I'll help you up."

He gripped her around her waist and lifted. Clare scrambled on top of the snowbank, feeling it slip and compact under her, then finally got enough momentum to tumble down the other side. She rolled, skidding on the snow, and finally came to a halt in the valley. A moment later, Dorran followed her. He was a little more graceful and stayed on his knees as he slid down the slope. When he reached Clare, he offered his hand and pulled her up.

She stood, felt her balance wobble, then regained it. She adjusted the scarf over her face and gave Dorran a thumbs-up. He nodded then beckoned for her to follow.

The snow was cold, but the wind was infinitely worse. Even bundled up, Clare could feel it snatching at her warmth and trying to worm in through the layers of clothing. It whistled around them, beating flurries of snow against their bodies and screaming in Clare's ears. Dorran kept up a fast pace, but every few steps, he looked over his shoulder to check on Clare. She felt faintly pleased that she was able to keep up with him.

Their path led them alongside of the manor. The stones had been caked in ice, giving it a hostile, spiky texture. Clare sank to her waist in the snow, making every step an effort. Sometimes she stumbled and had to use her hands to clamber back to her feet. Dorran had a better footing, but he seemed to be struggling too.

They fought their way around the building. A mound in the snow appeared up ahead, and when Clare squinted, she realized she could make out the top part of a hut. Dorran quickened his pace as they neared it, then he dropped to his knees and began digging to clear a way into the building.

Clare knelt beside him, and together, they scraped armfuls of snow away from the door. When the handle was finally revealed, Dorran took a key out of his back pocket and crouched to see the lock. He struggled for a minute to unlock the frozen metal. The door swung into the hut, and he motioned for Clare to slide in.

She took a quick breath to brace herself, turned around to point her legs at the opening, and dropped in. Her boots thudded as they hit the floor, and she stepped back to let Dorran follow.

As soon as he was inside, he slammed the door and pulled the scarf away from his face. "Are you holding up all right?"

"Great," she said, trying to make her expression match her voice. The hike had worn her down more than she had expected. The blistering cold and exercise had combined into a surreal sensation—her core was hot, but her limbs were chilled. Despite the layers, she was shaking. She promised herself she would never doubt Dorran's judgment about clothes again.

The cabin they'd entered was small and crowded. Dozens of shelves were stacked full of gardening equipment, most of it rusty and cobwebbed. Clare guessed this was another part of the house that its owner never visited.

Dorran pulled off his hat and ruffled stray flecks of snow out of his hair. "It is a longer walk to the forest. If you are tired, you could return to the house. I can reach the car alone."

"I'm good to keep going."

"I promise I won't think badly of you if—"

She elbowed his side and grinned. "Stop trying to talk me out of it. I'm coming."

He sighed, but it was parsed through a smile. "Very well. Let's get you some snowshoes. That will make the hike a little easier, at least."

A row of the shoes had been stacked against the back wall. Dorran picked out a set and fit them under Clare's boots. He checked and double-checked the fasteners, then he had Clare walk up and down the cramped cabin to make sure they weren't likely to fall off. Once he was satisfied, he fitted his own and retrieved a shovel and pickaxe from one of the shelves. Then he opened the door and again lifted Clare so that she could scramble over the bank of snow, slipping and kicking awkwardly. He threw the shovel and pickaxe after her then hauled himself out and closed the cabin's door behind them.

The snowshoes were unwieldy, and Clare had to struggle to get standing. When she did, she held out a hand to carry one of the implements, but Dorran just chuckled and shook his head. He tugged his scarf back into place, put the tools over his shoulder, and set out toward the forest.

The snowshoes made a world of difference for crossing the open yard. It still took effort, but she no longer felt like she was about to topple with every step.

As they passed the house's front again, Dorran nodded to the left. "If you ever leave Winterbourne alone, be careful not to stray too far in that direction. There is a pond, and it is most likely liquid right now."

Clare stared at him. "*Liquid?*"

"I am not joking." He laughed. "The furnace in the basement directs heat toward the garden. But it has an automatic valve to redirect the flow of air outside if it ever starts to rise above a certain temperature. That release valve channels heat out near the lake. It won't be enough to make it *warm*, but it won't be solid ice, even in this weather."

Dorran must have been able to recognize the courtyard's layout under the snow because he led them along the easiest path, weaving around obstacles and keeping them on level ground. Before long, the snow flattened out. Clare guessed they had left the courtyard and were in what must have been a field separating the house grounds from the forest. The wind was louder and harsher without the hedges to buffer it.

She kept her gaze fixed on the line of trees ahead. The forest encircled the estate, winding around them. The day had low visibility, but seeing the trees was still easier than it had been during the snowstorm.

Dorran yelled to be heard through the wind. "The road is straight ahead. A path leads from our property's driveway to it, though it will be submerged in snow by now. We have a better chance striking through the forest, where the trees will have sheltered the ground at least a little."

She had no breath to reply, so she nodded instead. Dorran adjusted the tools over his shoulder and put his head down as he forged on.

A harsh flash made them both freeze. Clare's first thought

was that someone had taken a photo of them, but that was impossible—they were alone on the icy terrain. Dorran turned to face her, and his eyes, the only part of his face visible, reflected Clare's own confusion.

Then a deep rumble followed the flash, and her breath caught. *Lightning.*

Dorran stared into the distance, squinting, and Clare followed his gaze. The sky had turned a sickly green color near the horizon.

"What is it?" Even though she yelled, the wind snatched away her words.

Dorran shook his head. "It...it may be hail."

"Is it safe to keep going?"

He looked from the skyline to the forest, then at the house, and finally at Clare. He stomped one shoe to clear the snow from it as he looked back at the sky.

"Dorran?"

"We will press on a little farther. But be prepared to turn back if the storm nears."

She nodded, and Dorran began walking again. He'd increased his pace, and Clare had to breathe in gasps as she struggled to keep up with him. Every few paces, he looked over his shoulder to check on her. The rest of the time, he alternated his attention between the green-gray haze in the sky and the forest's edge.

They were getting closer to the trees. They passed a mound of snow to the left. *The groundskeeper's cottage.* She'd seen it from the window the day before. Its roof had been coated, but the walls and windows were still visible. Now only traces of gray wood peeked out between the snow banked over it.

Another heavy rumble shook Clare. It reverberated through her, vibrating every atom of her body. Another lightning flash followed immediately, along with a second, closer, crack of thunder.

Dorran stopped. He dropped the tools and stared at the storm. While only one corner of the sky had been tinged green before, now half the heavens were dark. He shook his head and began backing up. "It is moving too quickly."

"The forest is close." Clare could distinguish the individual trunks, frosted with snow, their boughs weighed down until they sagged. "We'll be sheltered in there."

"No." He kept shaking his head as he grabbed Clare's arm and tugged her back. "We have to go. We have to go now."

CHAPTER 13

CLARE WANTED TO ARGUE, but the alarm in Dorran's voice was sharp. She knew better than to ignore his caution. She turned, and together, they ran for Winterbourne.

More thunder rumbled behind them, but this time it didn't fade. It grew louder.

Not thunder. Hail, Clare realized. *Hail beating on the trees.*

She chanced a look behind them. The horizon had become a haze, almost like dense fog had fallen over the forest. The trees trembled where they were touched by hail.

The sour taste of fear flooded her mouth. The storm was moving fast, faster than anything she'd seen before. They would take at least ten minutes to reach the house, even running. The hail would be on them in seconds.

Dorran yanked her arm. "The cottage," he yelled, his words almost drowned out by the thunder of a million spits of ice whipping into each other. Clare looked to her right and saw the snow-coated mound. It was close. She followed Dorran as they sprinted for it.

A new noise joined the thunderous roar. Subtle thumps sounded as hail impacted the soft snow. The noises blended together, becoming almost painfully loud. Clare didn't spare the time to look behind them. The cottage was close, no more than twenty meters.

An icy stone impacted the snow ahead of her. She didn't see the hail itself, but she saw the hole it had created. Then another landed, above and to the right. Hail the size of her fist drove into the snow like meteors.

Dorran gasped and staggered. Clare reached out to him, and he yanked her against his chest, shielding her.

"Go," he yelled.

She lurched toward the shelter. Dorran followed, leaning over her.

A hailstone clipped her shoulder, and she hissed. Dorran's hand pressed over her head to protect it. She felt him flinch as another stone hit his back. They closed the distance between them and the cottage. Clare dropped to her knees. Her head rested against the frost-painted wood as she began digging snow away from the door. Dorran leaned over her. A hailstone hit her thigh, and hot pain bloomed out from the spot. She dug deeper. The stones created a thunderous tempo as they pummeled the shack's roof, the snow, and the two stranded humans.

She saw a glint of bronze. *The handle.* Dorran bent close,

gasping as he fit the key into the hole and turned it. He slammed a fist into the door. It swung open, and he shoved her in.

Clare grunted as she hit the floor then rolled out of the way. Dorran tumbled in after her. He kicked the door, slamming it closed, and the drumming was finally muffled.

They lay on the wood floor for a moment, panting. Then Clare unstrapped her snowshoes with numb hands and kicked them off. She crawled to Dorran. "Are you okay?"

"Yes." He was breathing heavily. She couldn't see much of his face under the scarf, but his eyes were scrunched closed.

She reached out to touch him but hesitated. "Is there anything I can do?"

"No."

She pulled off her scarf, and her lips smarted in the cold air. She looked about. The wooden cottage wasn't large, but it felt homey. A small kitchenette ran along one wall. A single bed took up the other, opposite a small brick fireplace in the back wall. A thin layer of dust coated the surfaces. "I'm going to start a fire… take some of the chill out of this place."

Dorran gave a brief nod.

Clare got to her feet. Her legs were shaking, and her lungs ached. She felt numb—not just physically, but emotionally. The storm had come on so quickly that it still didn't feel quite real. She knew Dorran was hurt. How badly, she couldn't tell, and he didn't seem to want to say. She couldn't do much for the pain, but she could make sure he was warm.

The fireplace was smaller than Winterbourne's, but the bracket beside it still held a small pile of logs. Kindling had been stacked in a bucket, and she found matches on the mantelpiece. Clare had to pull her gloves off to arrange the kindling and get it lit, and within seconds, her fingers began to cramp from the cold.

She heard movement behind her and turned to see that Dorran had unfastened his snowshoes and clambered to his feet. He approached the kitchenette, swayed, then bent over to spit a mouthful of blood into the sink.

"I'm sorry." Even though the hailstones thundered across the tin roof, she still whispered. "This is my fault. I shouldn't have asked to go to the car."

He crossed to her and dropped to his knees on the stones in front of the fireplace. It took him a moment to speak. "Not your fault. I would have been caught, with or without you. I've never seen a storm move so fast."

"Is it bad?"

"The storm?"

"No." She reached up to touch his arm. "You're hurt."

"Bruises. Nothing worse."

Now that he'd removed his scarf, she could see swelling developing on his cheek. He was complaining a lot less than she would have if she'd taken the same beating.

Clare swallowed and turned back to the fire. It was starting to catch. She fed it as quickly as it could handle, eager to have something to cut through the chill. Dorran sat still, but his eyes were unfocussed. He was probably in shock. She remembered the flask tied to her belt, pulled it off, and undid the cap.

"Drink," she coached, holding it up to his lips. He stirred back to wakefulness and let her tip his head back. She poured too quickly, and he choked on it. "Sorry, sorry!" She grabbed one of her gloves and used it to wipe water off the corner of his mouth.

He chuckled. "It's fine."

She tried again, more carefully, and helped him drink the rest of the flask. Once he was finished, his head bowed.

"Hang on a moment." Clare stood. Her own bruises were starting to form, making her shoulder and leg stiff, but she knew she'd gotten off lightly. She owed Dorran a lot.

The bed in the corner of the room was made, but it wasn't close enough to the fire to gather any warmth. Clare yanked the sheets free, lifted the mattress, and dragged it off the bed frame. A moment later, Dorran joined her and helped her push the mattress in front of the fireplace. Then they collapsed onto the bed and pressed close to the fire and each other, sharing the blankets as they draped them around their shoulders.

Color was returning to Dorran's face. He grimaced and rubbed a hand over the bridge of his nose. "I do not understand."

"What do you mean?"

"That hailstorm. The blizzard before it. This area has never seen weather like it, especially not so early in the season." He took a deep breath. "And then…you keep seeing a woman. The fact that you crashed in the first place. All of this, every single thing, is so strange. I cannot piece it together."

She swallowed thickly. "I don't understand either. Since I woke up in your house, everything has felt surreal. I thought it was just Winterbourne. But...I think it's more than that. I can't remember why I was on the road on the day I crashed. I mean, I know I was going to my aunt's, and I know I was talking to my sister, but I don't remember *why*. It was a Sunday. And I always stayed at home on Sundays."

He shuffled nearer until they were almost pressed together. The closeness and the warmth felt good, like food for her soul. She closed the distance and leaned her head against his chest, where she didn't think the hail had hit him. After a moment, he moved his arm and wrapped it around her. He felt so solid, so safe. She closed her eyes and breathed deeply.

Unrelenting hail continued to beat the roof above them. But the fire was growing to combat the cold. As her body temperature rose and her adrenaline faded, exhaustion began to overrun Clare. She struggled to keep her eyes open. "What will we do if the storm traps us in here?"

"We will find a way out. You are strong. So am I. We will figure it out."

She nodded and finally let her eyelids close.

CHAPTER 14

CLARE WOKE FEELING COLD. She squinted her eyes open. An orange glow lit the bricks in the fireplace, but it came from the last remaining coals. She turned toward the wood basket. It was empty. Dorran must have gotten up during the night to feed more fuel into the fire.

They'd fallen asleep on the mattress, under the blankets, still wearing their layers of clothes. The bed had been designed for a single person, so they'd had to lie almost on top of each other to fit. But the cold had made it necessary, and the thick clothes meant it felt less intimate than it could have. At least, it had when Clare had fallen asleep. Waking up, she found Dorran was nestled against her back, his arm draped over her waist.

"Hey." She patted his gloved hand gently. "Let me up."

He mumbled something, and his arm tightened around her.

She hadn't expected that and laughed. "Wake up, Dorran."

He finally stirred. She felt him tense as he realized where they were, then the arm lifted away from her. "Please excuse me."

"Ha. It's fine. You don't have to worry so much." Clare rolled out of bed. In spite of the fire's best efforts, the cabin had grown frosty during the night. She shivered as she crossed to the window.

Outside, the field sparkled. Thousands of hailstones had been preserved where they'd fallen, creating a glass-like blanket in the morning sun. To her surprise, the hail had beaten the snow down. Instead of being waist-deep, barely a foot of it remained.

The house rose out of the frozen ground like a jagged cliff wall to her right. Opposite it, the forest stretched away, its black line gradually fading into the mist. Clare caught sight of motion around the tree trunks. It looked like some kind of animal scurrying along the frozen ground. She moved closer to the glass, trying to see through the icy fragments clinging to it, but the animal was already gone.

Dorran sat up, rubbed his face, then rolled to his feet. He was moving stiffly, but his expression was passive as he joined Clare at the window. "There must have been sleet accompanying the hail last night. It was enough to melt some of the snow. That will make our return easier."

Clare was still watching the forest, and Dorran noticed. His expression tightened. "I don't think it would be wise."

"Right. Of course not." He was hurt. They were both tired and hungry, not to mention cold. "We should go back to the house."

"I know how important it is to you." Dorran rested his hand on her shoulder then turned toward the door. "We can try again another day. With luck, the hailstorm will be the worst of the weather."

She could guess what he was thinking, though. The storm had come out of nowhere. If they had spent even a few minutes longer in it, they would be facing injuries worse than bruises. It was hard to justify a two-hour walk to the car and back when a wrong move could mean death. But it smarted to be so close to the car and to leave it.

"I would like to move quickly, while the sky is clear," Dorran said. "Do you feel well enough to go now?"

"Yes. Definitely." She grabbed her snowshoes and tied them on while Dorran fit his own. His face twitched when he bent over, but he didn't make a noise. When he straightened, he looked pale but still smiled at her.

Despite her scarf and hat, the wind bit at Clare's skin as she stepped outside. Walking on ice was more of a challenge than crossing the snow had been. They moved side by side, holding each other for stability.

Progress was agonizingly slow, but the forest began to recede, and the mansion grew nearer. It was Clare's first time seeing the outside of it clearly. It surprised her. She'd imagined the building would be symmetrical and stately, but in reality, it was a Frankensteinesque creation.

"It has a special kind of look, doesn't it?" Clare asked.

"During our prime, my ancestors added to the house every few years, depending on how the family and the profits grew." Dorran spoke loudly to be heard over the crunch of their shoes and the wind. "Each new wing, new extension, and new addition can be traced to a marriage or a birth. It became a point of pride. The construction only stopped when profits dried up."

Clare recognized an effort to keep the style consistent. The trim and the windows all matched. The stone colors and sizes varied with each new addition, however, and some seemed to have been added with wild abandon. The manor had a presence about it. The same kind of presence she'd felt inside its rooms— quietly judgmental.

"The hail wasn't kind to the roof," Clare said. Black holes pocked the dark tiles. Some were small, while others were large enough for her to sit in them.

Dorran sighed. "That will mean leaks and a harder time heating the place." He must have seen Clare's expression because he added, "Don't worry. We will manage."

"What happens if the weather never improves?" Clare cleared her throat. "Sorry. I know that sounds paranoid—"

"Paranoia is not always foolish. And these are extraordinary circumstances." He tilted his head back to stare up at the building. "But try not to worry, if that is possible. I will be taking precautions to keep you safe."

Clare's shoe slid on a slippery patch of ground, and she felt color rising in her face as Dorran caught her and righted her. She managed an awkward laugh. "I feel a bit useless. You've done nothing except look after me since I arrived."

"You are helpful."

"No. I'm pretty sure I'm not."

The corners of his eyes crinkled as he smiled under the scarf. "I likely would have gone insane by now if I was alone in this house."

"Really? I thought you wanted to spend the winter away from your family. Isn't that why you left the group?"

"Hm." They had neared the steps leading to the front door, and Dorran slowed as they tried to navigate the slope. "I softened the details of that story. I did not leave. I was expelled. I spoke out of turn, and my mother thought a winter in what amounts to solitary confinement would be a suitable punishment. And it would have been, except for the unexpected surprise of your company."

Clare tilted her head. "Couldn't you have gone to town instead and stayed in a hotel?"

"I have no money of my own."

"You could have sold some of the things in the house. Some of the trinkets look like they might be gold. I know it's borderline stealing, but under the circumstances…"

"Ah, Clare. You see the world so cleanly." He was laughing again, but the chuckles held a strained undercurrent. The sadness was back. "Come. Let's get you somewhere warm."

They were at the front door. Dorran opened it and helped Clare through the gap. Once the door was closed again, they removed their snowshoes and stripped off their scarves and hats. Dorran motioned for them to leave the equipment in the room's corner.

"We may need it again. We'll keep it close. Do you remember the way to your room?"

She nodded.

"Go there. Make yourself comfortable. I will heat some food and bring it up."

"Can I help?"

"Thank you, but I'll take care of it." He shucked off his jacket and hung it on a hook beside the door. "I need some time to collect my thoughts."

They split up. Dorran headed toward the kitchen, and Clare climbed the stairs. As she approached the second floor, she couldn't help but wonder what the house felt like when it was full of people. There would be lights shining out of every room, as well as chatter and laughter coming from every corner of the house. The kitchen would be full of energy and noise. She might have trouble climbing the stairs without bumping into someone coming the other way.

She let her chin drop as tired legs carried her up. The house might have felt alive with enough people in it, but with just her and Dorran, it felt unnaturally, horribly hollow. Noise traveled too far—the creak of a tired floorboard, the snap of a closing door. Sounds bounced around her, making it hard to guess their origin and playing with her mind.

With no one to tend to it, the fire in her bedroom had gone out. Clare turned on the lights and stood on the threshold for a moment. Daylight came through the windows but didn't reach far enough to touch the back wall. She'd been gone less than a day, and already the space had started to feel neglected.

She went to the bathroom first and cleaned up. The water

coming out of the tap felt like pure ice. She'd tasted enough cold for a lifetime, but weariness outweighed a need for warmth, and she scrubbed her face and body with the cold water as quickly as she could.

Her cheeks looked pale in the mirror, but she decided to blame it on the poor lighting. She changed back into the dress Dorran had given her and topped it with one of the thick coats. Her hair was tangled from the hat and the wind. There wasn't much she could do for it, but she tried to make herself look as respectable as she was able to.

Dorran hadn't returned. She knew he didn't want her worrying about him, but ignoring the impulse was impossible.

She stepped back into the hallway, where the air felt still and stale. Dust particles floated around her, suspended like sediment in a soup. The house might have felt lively, even comforting, when it was full—but at that moment, it reminded her of an old animal lying in the snow as it gasped its last breaths. Wind and hail had torn its tiles off. The window frames would go next, rotted by water and age. The stones would be the last to crumble. But time was unforgiving. It would never stop eating away at the house, chipping it down, year by year, century by century, until it had erased it from existence.

An unseen door groaned as it moved in the wind. Clare pulled her jacket's collar a little higher and hurried toward the stairs. If Dorran could withstand the bleakness that seeped out of the building's walls, he was a more resilient person than she was.

She thought she remembered the way to the kitchen, but

she became lost somehow and found herself in a parlor. Even swallowed by gloom, the room was dripping in opulence. Chairs, little tables, and brushed rugs had been arranged so perfectly that to disturb them felt borderline sacrilegious. Clare backed out of the room and tried again. A sliver of yellow light under a door gave her a clue, and she followed it through the empty hallway to the kitchen.

Dorran wasn't there, but he'd lit the fire and put a pot on the stove. Another bunch of dried herbs had been taken down from the hook above the kitchen bench and left, half-chopped, on a board. A moist red sheet of paper told Clare he'd added frozen meat to the soup.

He'd used a candle to light the room, and shadows clung to the space. Clare moved slowly as she approached the pot. The stove had been left on a low heat, but the soup had already boiled and was splattering against its lid, so she turned it off. As the bubbling noise faded, she began to hear ragged breathing coming from the back of the room.

Clare moved toward the noise, slowly and cautiously. The breathing was interrupted by a quiet hiss, like air being sucked through clenched teeth. It came from behind a small wooden door set into the back wall, not far from the fireplace. The door had been left ajar. Clare swallowed then reached for it, her fingertips nudging the wood to slide it open.

CHAPTER 15

THE ROOM WAS SMALL and stacked with shelves, most of them empty. Dorran sat on a chair below the single lightbulb. His jackets and shirt were draped over the nearest shelf. He held a damp cloth, which was tinged with red. He shot Clare a tense glance then looked away.

Clare pressed a hand to her mouth. His back was a mottle of bruises. Angry reds mixed with dark purples, as though an artist had thrown fistfuls of paint across the canvas. Blood trickled from one of the marks below his shoulder blade, where the impact had broken the skin. She knew he'd taken the brunt of the hailstones, but she hadn't expected the damage to be so bad.

Clare lowered her hand. Dorran wouldn't meet her eyes. Bizarrely, she had the sense that he was ashamed.

"You should have said something," she whispered.

"It's fine." He picked a dry towel off the shelf and slung it over his shoulders to hide the marks. "It is not as bad as it looks."

"I don't believe that." The bowl of hot water beside him was stained pink. "Dorran, I'm so sorry."

"It's fine," he repeated. "I've had worse."

Those words sent a chill running through Clare. She wrapped her arms around her chest and tried to swallow through the lump in her throat. "From your mother?"

His face twitched. He still wouldn't look at her. "When I was a child. Not recently."

She didn't know what to say. His posture was tense, as though he were trying to shrink away from her. He didn't want to be pitied. He didn't want to be seen when he was vulnerable. But she couldn't leave him.

"Here." She stepped forward and carefully touched his fingers to ease the wet cloth out of them. "I'll help with the ones on your back where you can't reach."

"You don't need to worry. I can look after myself."

"I know. But you've done so much for me. Trust has to go both ways, doesn't it?"

He finally met her eyes. It only lasted for a second before he turned away again, but the look was full of crushing loneliness and stifled longing. He stopped arguing. Clare's heart ached for him as she rested against the nearest shelf and pulled the towel away from his back. She hated how angry the bruises looked. They had to hurt every time he moved. She dipped the cloth in the hot water and pressed it against one of the marks. He sucked in a sharp breath, and she pulled back. "Sorry!"

"It's fine." The tension was dissipating, and he actually laughed. "Don't worry about hurting me. I just need to get them cleaned."

She returned the cloth, moving more carefully this time. With a tentative dab followed by a soft press, Clare cleaned up the flecks of dried blood and grime from around the cuts.

While she worked, she glanced across the back of Dorran's head. His dark hair was tousled, and clumps stuck together. She couldn't tell if it was from melting snow or blood. "Did any hit your head?"

"No."

She tried running her fingers across the back of his skull, but he flinched away. Clare bit her lip. "If you have a concussion—"

"I don't. I promise you. The worst I have is bruising."

She didn't know if she could trust him to tell her the truth. He rested his arm on the shelf and tilted his head down while she worked lower on his back.

He's not used to being looked after. His whole life has been spent trying to appear stronger than he actually is.

"Dorran…" She swallowed and flipped the cloth to a clean patch. "After this is over—after the snow melts, and we can get in touch with the outside world—I'd like you to come with me."

His head lifted.

"I don't have a large house. Nothing like this. But it's big enough for two people to share. We've done all right here, just the two of us, haven't we? So if you want to—if you wouldn't mind—I hope you'll come and stay with me."

Her left hand rested on his shoulder, and she felt a shiver travel through him. He took a breath as though he were about to reply, but he didn't speak. Clare waited. She wished she could see his face, but he resolutely—almost deliberately—faced away from her.

When he spoke, his voice was tight. "I am sorry. I cannot accept your offer."

"Oh." Embarrassed heat rushed over her face. "Right. Sorry. That was really presumptuous of me—"

He took a breath. "No. It's not that. You…" He tilted his head back to stare at the wood ceiling, and after a moment, he continued in a steadier, calmer voice. "There is more at stake here than my wishes."

Clare carefully moved to a new patch of raw skin. Her pulse felt like something alive, jumping through her veins. "What do you mean?"

"Every choice has consequences. Mine especially."

She frowned. "Are you worried about your family looking for you? My house is rural. We can stay quiet. They can't find you if they don't know where to look."

He turned and wrapped her hands in his. Drips of water ran from the cloth and trickled between their fingers. Even though his eyes looked sad, Dorran was smiling. "You care too much. I am grateful. But once the snow clears, you will leave, and I will stay. That is just the way it has to be."

123

"I…" She looked down at his hands.

He squeezed hers lightly then took the cloth back. "You have been a great help. If you will excuse me, I must check on the gardens. The temperature will be dropping now that the furnace is out, and our seeds will need water. Please eat some of the soup. The pain tablets are on the shelf above the stove. Take two then have a sleep. I will be back to check on you shortly."

He scooped his shirt and jacket off the shelf then left. She could hear him moving through the kitchen, but he only stayed for a moment before the door clicked closed.

Clare let her head drop. She didn't understand him. He hated his family—she could guess that much—but he refused to leave them. She didn't know what he needed from her, or from himself, before he could feel free.

She blinked back angry tears as she carried the dish of water to the sink and tipped it out. The pot on the stove had stopped bubbling but was still warm when she touched the lid. She found a bowl, ladled out a portion, then sat at the table, but she couldn't do much except stir her food. Clare knew she should feel hungry. She hadn't eaten since the previous day's lunch, but her stomach was in knots.

A fresh wind picked up outside the house. She hoped it wouldn't start snowing again. Despite how vast the property was, it stifled her. It was strange to simultaneously feel claustrophobic and lonely.

She made herself eat the soup. Dorran wasn't a bad cook. Even with limited ingredients, he seemed to have a knack for making their meals taste good. But she was starting to crave fresh food, especially something green. She hoped the garden would grow quickly.

Her legs ached from the hike, and the cuts on her arm refused to stop stinging. The bottle of painkillers waited on the shelf, like Dorran had said they would. She tried to read the label, but it had been handwritten in a script so faded, she couldn't make it out. Dorran normally gave her two, but Beth's cautious voice in the back of her head said it wasn't wise to take drugs she didn't know, especially if there was any chance they might be addictive. She compromised by tipping one tablet into her palm and washing it down with a mouthful of freezing water from the tap.

Dorran wanted her to rest, but despite how tired she felt, she didn't think she could sleep. She stood in the kitchen, shoulders hunched, as she stared at her surroundings. She didn't want to go back to her room. But she didn't want to walk the halls aimlessly either. The wind was growing louder. She thought she could make out soft pattering noises through the brick walls. *Snow? Sleet? Not more hail, I hope.*

She shivered then glanced back at the pot of soup. Dorran hadn't eaten any. She could take a bowl to him. If what she'd said had upset him, the food might work as a peace offering. And even if it didn't, it would at least save him a trip back to the kitchen.

Clare checked that the liquid was still hot then poured out a large bowl, making sure to give him plenty of the meat. She dipped a spoon into the mixture then blew out the candle on the bench before leaving the kitchen.

She followed the path Dorran had led her down before, into the stone cathedral-like room that separated the main section of the house from the indoor garden. Bright, welcoming lights glowed through the garden's blurred window. Clare thought she could see Dorran's silhouette as he tended to the plants. She squared her shoulders and lifted her chin as she started to cross to the door. Her breath caught as a noise startled her.

What was that? She stopped moving. Sudden dizziness cascaded through her, making her stumble. She blinked. A rushing sound filled her ears. She tried to take another step, but nothing felt right. Nothing felt *real*. The bowl tumbled out of her hands, but she was only vaguely aware of the noise it made as it broke on the stone floor.

Clare shook her head. The motion made the dizziness worse, and nausea accompanied it. Her vision was hazy, and her heart raced, but she couldn't breathe deeply enough to get the oxygen her lungs needed. Pain moved through her stomach like a sharp, hot needle.

Light washed over her as the garden door opened. Dorran called to her, but she couldn't answer. Her legs were shaking. She fell, but before she hit the floor, Dorran caught her.

"What's wrong? What happened?" His hand moved over her forehead then her throat, checking her.

She tried to answer. The nausea became worse, clawing its way from her stomach to her throat, and she convulsed as she was sick over the floor.

Dorran dropped her. She couldn't see him. The room was a

swimming mess of colors and shadows. But she heard footsteps beating over the stone floor. Then a door slammed open. She hugged the ground. It refused to stop moving, tilting her over until she retched again. There was nothing left to bring up.

Then, without warning, Dorran was back. He skidded across the floor and came to a stop at her side. He flipped her over, keeping one hand under her head. The other plunged a needle into her chest.

Clare barely felt the sting. She couldn't tell if she was suffocating or hyperventilating. She only knew she couldn't breathe or stop shaking.

"Come on, Clare." Another needle stabbed into her thigh. Then Dorran pulled her close against his chest. "Fight it. Please. Fight for me."

She tried to speak. Her muscles spasmed, wrenching her head back and making her torso twist until it was painful.

Dorran didn't let her go. He pulled her closer as he began moaning under his breath. "Please. Please. Come on, Clare. Please."

She convulsed again. Stark, bleak fear wrapped around her. She tried to hold Dorran, the only real, solid thing in her world, but her hands wouldn't work. Her mouth was open, but no air reached her lungs.

He cradled her, one arm holding her up, the other running over her hair and her cheek. "Clare. Don't leave me. Please."

Darkness seeped around her, dragging her down, drowning her until she couldn't even hear the ringing in her ears.

CHAPTER 16

THE BED WAS WARM. The blankets were soft. The inside of Clare's chest ached, and her head throbbed. Between the fog of sleep and the pain of wakefulness, though, she was grateful that at least she wasn't cold.

Every part of her felt heavy, especially her eyelids. She left them closed and instead focused on the sounds and sensations around her. She heard a fire crackling. Wind whistled in the distance as it clawed its way through broken roof tiles and narrow gaps in the stone.

She lay on her side. One hand was tucked under the blankets, but the other was left out. It wasn't cold, though. Warm fingers rested over it. A thumb brushed across her knuckles. She squeezed lightly in response.

She heard an inhale, then Dorran's voice. "Clare?"

"Hi." The word came out slurred. She forced her eyes to open and blinked through the blur.

Dorran sat next to her. He looked ghastly. His normal skin color had been replaced by an ashen gray, and dark circles ringed tired eyes. He shuffled forward in his chair and bent closer. A cautious smile grew. "How are you feeling?"

"Great," she lied. She felt like death. If she hadn't seen the barely hidden panic in Dorran's eyes, she would have let herself fall back asleep. "What happened?"

He turned aside, and his expression twitched, but only for a second. When he turned back to her, his face was calm again. "You were sick. You ate something bad."

Even breathing felt like an effort. "Bad? The soup? It tasted fine."

"No, Clare. Not the soup." His fingers rubbed over hers. "Cyanide."

"Oh." She knew he was telling her something important, something that should mean a lot more to her, but she just couldn't muster the energy to be upset. "That sucks."

His head dropped, and his shoulders shook. When he looked up again, he was laughing, but moisture shone in his eyes. "Sleep for now. I will watch over you. You're safe."

"Mm." She didn't know what she needed to be safe from, but sleep sounded like the best idea she'd ever heard.

The next time she woke, light had vanished from the windows. The fire had been kept strong, though, and even though the wind sounded cold, it didn't chill her.

Dorran's chair was empty. She blinked at it then tilted her head to see more of the room. He stood by the fire, arms folded and head bowed. He swayed slightly as he watched the flames. She wanted to say hello to him, to break through whatever thoughts were making his posture so defensive, but her mouth was dry, and the words weren't loud enough for him to hear over the ambient noise.

The third time she woke, the fire had dropped lower in the grate. The sun hadn't yet risen. Dorran was pacing. Her heart sank at how haggard he looked. She reached a hand toward him, and his face brightened when he saw her move.

"Clare." He was at her side in an instant and took the hand she held out to him. "Do you feel any better?"

The aches had receded, and the exhaustion, while still there, seemed less pronounced. "Yeah."

Her voice was croaky, but he still smiled. "You'll want water. Here." Dorran lifted her and pushed pillows behind her back until she was supported upright. Then he held a glass to her lips and helped her drink.

Her headache throbbed every time she moved, but Clare hoped it would fade with hydration. When she'd finished drinking, she inclined her head back and closed her eyes as she tried to gather her thoughts.

Her recent memories were distorted so badly that they felt like dreams, but one part stood out. "Did you say I ate cyanide?"

"Yes."

Clare was awake enough to realize the implications. She

looked down at her hands and squeezed them. They seemed to work all right, albeit without the strength they normally had.

Dorran pulled his chair closer and sat so that he faced her. He looked gaunt, and she wondered if he'd eaten or slept. "Do you remember taking it, Clare?"

"No." She tried to shake her head, but that made the headache worse. "I remember coming home from the shed. I had lunch. I was going to bring you some, but I felt sick before I got there."

"Did you take a tablet? A round white one?"

"I…" She frowned. "I did. One of the painkillers."

He ran his hand over his face, and his expression tightened momentarily before relaxing again. "So you did not eat it deliberately. That is a mercy."

"You thought I poisoned myself?"

"I did not know what to think. This house is such a bleak place to live. And we had failed to reach the radio, which I know you desperately wanted." He shook his head. "But the fault must be mine. I am deeply sorry. I don't know how, but I left the wrong bottle out."

She narrowed her eyes. "How is that possible? Why do you have bottles of cyanide in the house in the first place?"

Dorran stared at his hands folded in his lap, seemingly lost in his mind, then he took a short, tight breath. "I suppose you should know."

Clare could tell the revelation was painful for him. She watched him even though he wouldn't meet her eyes.

"It is the reason I cannot leave Winterbourne. I tried, once before, when I was nineteen. I wanted to move to the city, to find employment and make a life for myself outside of the estate. My father supported my wish. My mother opposed it."

He'd never spoken about a father before. Clare pushed herself a little higher on the pillows as she waited for Dorran to collect his thoughts.

"My father married into the family," he said. "He never bought into the...*insanity* that had possessed my mother. He was tired of maintaining the old ways when it had no benefit. It was a constant tension between my parents for as long as I can remember, but in most instances, he eventually bowed to my mother's will. Not in this case. He was resolute in supporting me. He planned to help me find employment with one of his relatives."

Dorran's pose was steady, seemingly calm, but a pulse jumped in his throat. "It turned into a painful, drawn-out fight. Every family member took a side. Hold on to the old ways or open ourselves to change? It lasted for days. Every time it seemed to be dying down, someone would make a comment, and the house would be filled with yelling once again."

Very briefly, a smile flitted across his face. "I thought, for a few happy days, that we might be close to reformation, to *escape*." As quickly as it had appeared, the smile was gone. "My mother sensed she was losing. She was not powerful enough to keep us here against our will, and once the unrest started, it would be hard to tamp back down. She said she was prepared to compromise. She said she wanted to discuss it over dinner that night."

His hands tightened around each other until the knuckles

turned white. Dorran's face and voice were impassive, but Clare could see the guilt and grief in his eyes. They were eating him alive. "She poisoned them. Everyone who did not agree with her. My father. My uncle Eros. My aunts, Tabatha, Jayne, and Abigail. Two of my cousins, Henry and Peter. Cyanide tablets dissolved into their drinks at dinner. She proposed a toast. It took effect within minutes."

"Dorran…"

His breath caught. His eyes were moving, flicking from side to side, the only external expression of his agitation. "Convulsions. Coughing blood. Fits. Screams. They all fell in a matter of minutes, collapsing out of their chairs. I could do nothing for them. There was no cure and no respite. The others—the ones who had taken my mother's side—they must have known it was coming. They sat quietly and watched it happen. I held my father while he died. I saw the fear in his face. And when he was finally still, when he stopped twitching and his body stopped drawing breath, my mother placed her hand on my shoulder and whispered into my ear, 'Perhaps now you will remember your place.'"

Clare pressed her hand over her mouth. She felt sick.

He stood and crossed to the window. His shoulders were shaking, but he remained straight and tall as he clasped his hands behind his back. "I do not know why she spared me. Perhaps some misplaced favoritism. Perhaps I am just fun to torment. But she has made it clear—if I step out of line again, my nieces and nephews will suffer for it. They are only children, Clare. She considers them expendable. I cannot leave her. I cannot fight her. I cannot even die."

Clare tried to imagine what that must be like—being forced to live a life that wasn't his own, unable to stand up for himself because others would be forced to pay the price, all the while knowing that half of his family had died because of a risk he'd taken. She didn't think she could have survived that kind of existence.

Dorran turned. His breathing was still rough. "The doctor, at least, was somewhat sympathetic to me. He smuggled in an antidote for cyanide. And I never forgot the symptoms of acute poisoning. When I saw you…white—"

"Dorran."

He was back at her side in a moment, and his arms wrapped around her. Clare hugged him back, pressing her face into his chest, trying to find a way to tell him it was all right.

"Clare, I cannot forgive myself for doing this to you. I must have been tired. I must have made a mistake with the bottles."

"Maybe you didn't." She tightened her arms around him. His heart thundered under her ears. She steeled herself then said, "I keep hearing things around the house. And that woman I saw… Maybe the bottles weren't your fault."

"Clare." He sounded sad. "I wish I could believe that."

"Why *can't* you?"

"When you fell ill—after I brought you back here—I consid-ered every possible cause. I went through the house again. From the attic to the basement, methodically. I left no square foot of ground uncovered, and no hiding holes ignored. I made *certain*. The fault is my own. I must take responsibility."

He pulled back but ran one hand over her hair, as though he were reluctant to let her go. "I think we stopped it fast enough. With rest and time, I think it will be all right. But we must be careful. I cannot take any more risks with you, Clare."

There was something intense and desperate in his expression. Then he stepped back, and it was gone. "You need food. Try to rest. I will be back momentarily."

Clare waited until the door was closed behind him before pressing her hands over her face. So many emotions were swarming through her, overwhelming her. Hope. Despair. Fear.

There has to be a way to help him. She slipped her legs out of the bed then tested her balance. It was wobbly, but not too bad. She followed the wall along the room, holding on to it to keep steady as she made her way to the bathroom. *He needs to be saved from this house and this family.*

As she washed her hands, Clare heard the bedroom door creak open. She turned off the tap and shuffled back to the bathroom door. "It's okay, Dorran. I just..."

She stopped. The bedroom door was open, but no one stood on the other side.

CHAPTER 17

CLARE SHIVERED DESPITE THE fire. Her senses heightened, she moved toward the doorway. As she passed the fire, she took up the poker and held it tightly.

Cold air rolled through the open door. Clare was wearing only the dress, without shoes or a jacket, and she hated how quickly the cold eroded her sense of comfort. She stopped in the doorway. Her hands shook as she flexed them around the poker. The window at the hallway's end was covered, leaving the space nothing but a mess of shadows.

Someone exhaled, and Clare twisted toward the noise. There was an exceptionally dark patch to her left, where the intersecting hallways created a little nook. Clare squinted at it. *Is that a person? Or just the furniture?*

The longer she stared, the more convinced she became that she was imagining it…and the more her paranoia began to scream.

The dark mound wasn't quite as tall as a human, and it wasn't formed quite like one either. But the shape didn't seem natural. She stared, not even allowing herself to blink, as she waited to see if it moved. It didn't. But it wasn't resolving itself into something explainable either.

Curiosity wanted her to step into the hallway, to find the light switch and unveil the shape. Prudence, wearing Beth's voice, begged her to retreat into her room and lock the door. They warred for a second. Then Clare took a step into the hallway.

"Clare?"

She jolted and swiveled, holding up the poker. Dorran stood at the other end of the hall, at the top of the stairs, carrying a tray. She opened her mouth then closed it and turned back to where she'd seen the figure.

The space was empty except for shadows and the twisting, insane wallpaper.

"Clare, you shouldn't be out of bed." When he reached her, Dorran placed the tray on the ground and touched her shoulder. "You're freezing."

"I…" She swallowed, her voice failing.

He glanced past her, toward the empty hallway, and his eyebrows pulled together. "Did you hear something again?"

"Yes."

"Would you like me to search?"

She hesitated then shook her head. Dorran pulled her closer, and his arm slipped around her shoulder as he guided her back inside the room. She let him take the poker, and he placed it back beside the fireplace.

"I'll stay with you the rest of today," he said as she sat on the edge of the bed. His smile was reassuring, but his eyes were worried. "You won't have to be frightened."

He was true to his promise. After they had lunch, Clare fell asleep again. Distorted, confusing dreams plagued her, but whenever she stirred, she found Dorran was still beside her. Sometimes he napped, with his arm bent under his head in a pose that couldn't have been comfortable. Sometimes he stared into the distance, and the fire's glow played across his features. Sometimes he watched her. He always smiled when he caught her looking, and she smiled back.

When Clare couldn't sleep any longer, he read to her. The mansion had a well-stocked library, though none of the books had been published within the last century. Clare was starting to understand why Dorran's language was so formal, bordering on archaic. He'd had no TV or radio and very little contact with people outside his family. Since she'd arrived, he seemed to have been making an effort to talk more casually and match her tone, but he kept slipping back into the more old-fashioned style of speaking, especially when he was stressed.

She loved listening to him read. He had a good voice. It was deep and full of conviction. Sometimes she let the plot threads escape her and just listened to the way he pronounced each word.

He brought her servings of the soup four times that day. As afternoon aged into evening, they argued about whether Clare was well enough to sit by the fire. She eventually won. He wrapped her in blankets and watched over her as she stretched her feet toward the flames.

She compulsively looked to the windows, but the curtains had been drawn. "What's the weather like?"

"Just a lot of snow, I'm afraid." He folded one leg over the other and rested his hands on his knee. "It is nearly back up to its original height."

Clare shook her head. "How many days is this? Seven?"

"Eight."

"Yikes. It's starting to feel like it will never melt."

He gave her a grim smile. "We may have to consider the possibility that we will be trapped here for the remainder of the winter. I'm afraid that each passing day makes that possibility more likely."

Clare chewed on the corner of her thumb. She tried to imagine spending four more months in the house. She liked Dorran—a lot. He was kind and made for good company. But Beth would be beside herself. There was no way she could sit and do nothing without at least speaking to her sister. "How's our resource situation looking?"

Dorran hesitated before answering. "Firewood is fine. We're in no risk of running out of it. I'm using gasoline to keep the garden lights running but trying to be careful how much I use the generator."

Clare glanced up at the lights. She hadn't given it any thought before, but Dorran had left them on almost all day. "We should turn those off."

"No. I like them on."

She narrowed her eyes at him. "No chance, Mr. Skulks-Around-in-the-Gloom. You turned them on for me, didn't you?"

He shrugged, raising his eyebrows. "I have no idea what you're talking about."

"Don't coddle me. I'm not afraid of the dark."

"Of course you're not." He took up his cup of tea and blew on it. "I already told you I enjoy having the lights on. It is completely selfish, I promise."

She sighed. "All right. But at least keep them off while we're sleeping, please? I'll feel guilty if you waste fuel on me."

"We can do that."

"What about food?"

Again, he hesitated. "We will get by."

"How bad is it?"

"Well, I am thoroughly tired of soup."

"Ha, me too."

"The first sprouts are coming up. I can start mixing some mung beans into our food within the next day or two. That will help make it last. And we have kept the hothouse warm enough that the seeds have germinated. Things will be a lot less uncertain once the first plants are ready to harvest, and that will be as close as four weeks away."

"Maybe we should ration our food." Clare bit her lip. "We can live on half serves for a few days."

Dorran's expression flattened. "No."

"But—"

"Your body is trying to regenerate blood *and* cope with poisoning. It needs all of the fuel it can get."

She blinked as pieces of the puzzle slid into place. She'd only seen Dorran eat one meal that day. When she'd asked him why he wasn't joining her for dinner, he'd laughed and said he'd already eaten. "You've been rationing *your* food, haven't you?"

"That's not relevant to this discussion."

"Like hell it's not." She scowled. "I'm not going to let you starve yourself."

"I'm not."

"You've been doing all of the work lately. No wonder you're starting to look gaunt." She ran a hand over her face, feeling sick. "How long have you been skipping meals?"

He placed his cup on the coffee table with a harsh snap. "I am managing my own affairs, and I would appreciate it if you ceased trying to meddle."

They glared at each other. Clare felt emotions choking her and blinked furiously to fight back tears. Then she took a short, sharp breath. "Here's the deal. From now on, I'm not eating unless you eat with me."

He stood, muttered something she couldn't make out, then began pacing. "You are not in a position to give me ultimatums."

"So help me, Dorran, you need food. I eat when you eat. If that means we both starve, so be it."

He glowered down at her, his face full of unforgiving lines and sharp eyebrows. Then his expression softened. He lowered himself to the floor and laid his hands on her chair's armrest so that she was looking down at him instead. "Clare, I am not being reckless or endangering myself. I am trying to keep us *both* alive."

She couldn't stop the tears any longer. They rolled down her cheeks and dripped off her chin. "Either we both eat, or neither of us eat."

"Stubborn, infuriating woman." The words were said half-laughingly. "I have yet to win a battle against you."

"I let you keep the lights on." She rubbed the back of her hand over her nose. "Sorry, I don't know why I'm crying. I know I'm a mess—"

He settled beside her in the chair and pulled her close. She wrapped her arms around his neck and cried into his shoulder. He held her with one hand and stroked her hair with the other. Warm breath ghosted over her ear.

"We will be all right," he said. "I will find a way. Everything will be all right."

They both slept on the bed that night. Dorran lay on top of the blankets, close enough that he was always within easy reach when the nightmares woke Clare. She didn't know how much rest he'd gotten the night before, but he slept deeply.

She woke sometime in the early morning when the fire had almost burned itself out. She could make out Dorran's features in the snow-muted moonlight. Long eyelashes. High cheekbones. Deeply set eyes. Heavy brows. She'd never seen anyone as handsome.

She carefully, hesitatingly reached out and ran a finger over his cheek. He murmured something in his throat and adjusted his position. Clare pulled her hand back and smiled as he continued to sleep.

A hinge groaned. Clare's heart faltered. She closed her eyes and tried to ignore the noise. It was a windy night. There was no reason the sound had to be malevolent.

A floorboard creaked. The noise came from inside the room. Clare's eyes shot open. She sat up, clutching her blankets as though they might protect her.

The bedroom's main door was still closed. She let her eyes drift to the side, toward the bathroom door. Dorran had shut it before they'd gone to bed. It leaked too much of their warmth otherwise. But now it hung open. And the woman stood in front of it.

CHAPTER 18

MOONLIGHT GLOSSED OVER THE gray figure in strange ways, creating shadows where they didn't belong and refracting off the skin in ways that made it seem to glow. The woman's hair had fallen out in chunks. Her back was badly twisted. She hunched over, pelvis forward and hands dangling behind her knees. White ribs jutted out of the hole in her side, fanning out like spikes. Saliva dripped from the open mouth onto the tattered, grimy white dress.

A scream caught in Clare's throat. She blindly felt for the man beside her. "Dorran!"

The creature threw its head back, eyes narrowed, lips parting just far enough to release a hiss.

Dorran stirred. Clare yanked on his arm, trying to get him up, to face the creature, to *see* it. He lifted his head, squinting. The woman was gone, vanished into the shadowed doorway.

"She was there." Clare knew she sounded half-wild. "The woman. Watching us sleep. She was there!"

He blinked furiously as he tried to shake away tiredness. "What? You are certain?"

"Yes!" She clutched his arm. "She… Her…her ribs were poking through her skin. She's right there. In the bathroom."

Dorran's gaze moved from the open door to Clare, and she was horrified to see doubt in his eyes. She knew how she must sound, raving about a woman with ribs jutting out of her chest. She swallowed. "I know. I know it sounds insane. I can't explain it. I just know what I saw."

"I will search." He slid out of bed and crossed the room in four long strides. He didn't take a weapon this time as he stepped into the bathroom and turned on the light. A moment later, she heard another door open and another light switch as he moved into the second bedroom then the hallway.

Dorran was gone for close to twenty minutes. Clare stayed huddled in bed, her knees pulled up under her chin. She heard doors opening throughout the house. A sense of nauseating dread rose through her the longer the search went on. It was becoming an all-too-familiar pattern. He would find nothing.

Finally, the doors began closing rather than opening. Dorran re-entered the way he'd left, through the bathroom, shutting the door behind himself. His head was bowed. His expression was tense.

Clare couldn't stop shaking. Part of it came from the shock. But most of it was the fear of what Dorran's return implied. *If he can't find the stranger, what does that say about me?*

"I don't know where she goes." Clare crawled across the quilt toward him, pleading. "But she *is* real."

He sat on the bed, shuffled close to her, and took both of her hands in his. His voice was gentle. "You trust me, don't you?"

"Yes. Of course."

He rubbed her hands, his gaze imploring. "Know that I would not lie to you. There are no strangers in this house tormenting you. There are no phantoms hiding around the corners. You have to fight these fears. Don't give them any power. Don't let them drag you under."

Her hands were still shaking, and they wouldn't stop. *I'm not crazy. I'm not crazy.* She looked toward the bathroom doorway. *I can't be crazy. Not here. Not now. I'm already so much of a burden.*

"I'm fine," she managed, her voice tight. "It was probably just a shadow."

His fingers squeezed lightly. "You have been through a lot these past days, more than any person should be asked to bear. I will help you as much as I can, but the brunt of this fight will be internal."

She closed her eyes and nodded. She wanted to cry but refused to let the tears out.

"You are not alone." He tilted his head down, close to hers. His voice was soft. "I will do what I can to make sure you never have to feel that way. So stay with me and trust me. I will keep you safe."

Clare didn't sleep at all for the rest of the night, even though she pretended to. She was fairly sure Dorran was feigning rest as well. His breathing was a little too deliberate.

She felt a small spark of relief when morning light hit the windows. Dorran smiled at her as though nothing had happened as he helped her into the bathroom.

He'd said she wouldn't be alone, and he seemed intent on keeping that promise. While Clare brushed her teeth, she could hear Dorran moving around in the main room. Normally, he was as quiet as a wraith, but that morning, he never went more than a few seconds without making some noise. When Clare came back out, he'd boiled basins of water for her to wash with. He stayed in the bathroom while she scrubbed herself clean, and when she was done, he came back out and redressed her stitches.

"These are looking a lot better."

Clare lay on her back, blankets over her chest and lower half, while he cleaned the stitches on her stomach. It was easier to feel like things might be normal now that it was morning and they were back into a routine. She smiled. "Yeah? Think we can take them out soon?"

"A little longer. Maybe another week. But it is healing faster than I had hoped." He reapplied the bandage. "I'll get breakfast. Two minutes, and I'll be back. Will you be all right for that long?"

"Of course." She laughed. "Take longer if you want." She tried to sound carefree, but as soon as Dorran was out of the room, her smile dropped. She dressed as quickly as she could then stood close to the fire, watching both doors.

Is it possible this really is some kind of paranoia? Delusions manifesting? It has to be, doesn't it? Women with holes in their sides. Bones poking out. That can't be real. But if it's not, then what is it?

She chewed on her thumbnail as she paced in front of the flames. Believing that the building was haunted was a wild leap of logic, but at least it made a little more sense than the alternatives. If a house was going to have a ghost, Winterbourne would be an ideal contender. Old, opulent, full of horrible family secrets…

She'd read a handful of gothic books as a teenager. In one of them, the heroine had discovered that her husband-to-be was hiding his insane first wife in the attic. It had been a chilling scene. For a moment, Clare considered the idea that she might be living in a real-life recreation of the story. Maybe Dorran wasn't hiding a wife, but a family member could have been locked away for her own good and found a way to escape from her hidden room.

That theory didn't hold up, though. Dorran had been sincere when he'd told her they were alone. She was sure of it. There had been no hint of any lie in his expression. He was just as confused and concerned as she was.

Besides, no one should have been able to survive the disfigurement the woman endured. Not for ten minutes. And certainly not for days.

That left two possibilities—ghosts or delusions. *Dorran said he's never heard any rumors of ghosts. And if the house really is haunted, wouldn't someone else have seen the spirit? Surely I can't be the only one.*

She felt sick to her stomach. When the door clicked open, she reflexively flinched. But it was only Dorran. He'd promised two minutes, but she was pretty sure he'd returned faster than that. She checked that his bowl was full before she started eating.

It was easier to relax while he was around. He was reliable and safe, and he didn't try to belittle or pick at what Clare had seen. They sat by the fire and talked about the outside world while they ate. Dorran wanted to know what her life was like, so Clare told him about her work at a bookstore. Remembering her old job felt strange. She'd only been gone for a week, but it felt like a lifetime. She realized she was probably fired by that point. She hadn't turned up to work on Monday, and being uncontactable, they would eventually need to replace her.

"It wasn't a bad place to work." Seeing that Dorran had finished his meal, she drained the last of her soup. "I mean, every job has stress and annoyances, and some days you wish you could chase certain customers out of the building with a broom, but my coworkers were nice. And that makes the biggest difference."

"Good people can make a bad situation bearable," Dorran said.

"Exactly! There was one shift where everything went wrong. It was a Saturday, which is crazy to begin with, and then our terminal stopped working. I thought I was about to drop from exhaustion by the time I got home. But the other staff and I pulled together to get it done, and I felt kind of proud when I flipped the sign to Closed." She put her bowl on the coffee table and pulled her legs up under herself. "What about you? Do you get along with any of your family?"

He hesitated, and Clare instantly realized her mistake. The family members who'd supported him hadn't survived the fateful dinner. She pressed her hand over her mouth. "I'm sorry—"

"Some of the staff are quite nice." He smiled to let her know it was okay. "The doctor was good company, and I got along well with most of the gardeners. All of the staff supported my mother—she wouldn't tolerate subversive employees—but at least they were not as extreme as her. Most of them were friendly."

Clare lowered her hands. "I guess that must have helped."

"Yes. It made this home feel less like a prison. And I was able to learn skills from some of them. Not all of my time spent here was unpleasant."

He was more cheerful about it than Clare thought she would have been if their situations had been reversed. She followed his gaze to the fire. "Did you have any plans for today? I don't want you to feel like you have to sit with me constantly."

"I enjoy being with you. Enough that, yes, I am starting to neglect some very necessary work." He chewed on his lip. "The garden needs to be a priority."

Clare grimaced. He'd spent more than an entire day at her side without even looking at the plants. And she'd been selfish enough to welcome it. "You'd better go. They'll need water."

"Come with me. I can make you comfortable in the garden, and you will not have to be alone that way."

She was desperate for a chance to get out of the room and began to rise. "Yes!"

"Steady." Dorran came up beside her and put one arm around her shoulders. The other slipped under her legs, and in an instant, he'd lifted her off the ground.

Clare grabbed at his sleeve. "I can walk!"

"It is a long way. This is safer." Unfazed, he plucked a blanket off the bed, then he used his shoulder to push the door open and carried her toward the stairs.

Clare kept her hold on his shirt as Dorran smoothly moved through the maze of passages to reach the lowest floor. It was impossible not to feel the way his body pressed against hers. His muscles shifted under his shirt with every breath, warm and firm. She kept her head down so he wouldn't notice the color spreading across her face.

The wind continued to beat at the house, clawing more holes in the ceiling. Even with the blanket thrown over her, Clare felt the chill. Their breaths plumed in the frosty air.

When they reached the hothouse, Dorran shifted his grip on her to unbolt the door. A gust of warm air rolled over them, and he stepped through and shut the door before more could escape. He carried Clare to where a little reading chair had been placed in one corner and carefully set her down.

"Are you comfortable?"

"Yes."

"Warm enough?"

She grinned and gave him a light shove. "Don't fuss."

He smiled back then turned toward the plots of dirt. Clare couldn't resist. She pushed the blanket off her shoulders and approached the nearest bed.

Tiny green leaves poked out of the earth. She bent to read the marker at the end of the row and was thrilled to see they were the tomatoes she'd planted.

"They're coming along nicely." Dorran had fetched a watering can and was trickling liquid over green sprouts in a different row. "If I can keep it at an optimal temperature and leave the lights on a few hours longer each day, we should be able to beat the estimated growing times."

"Good." She gently caressed one of the bright-green leaves. It was tiny and delicate, and Clare felt her heart swell with hope and nerves. Their survival most likely relied on those sprouts. She was painfully aware of how easily they could be broken—the green shoot, barely thicker than a thread, seemed horribly close to disaster. A misplaced hand, too much water, or even a strong wind could be enough to kill it.

She tried not to focus on how vulnerable they were. Dorran knew what he was doing. He moved from garden bed to garden bed, watering the plants that needed it and checking every row. A small, content smile grew as the plants met his approval.

"I'm going to add more fuel to the furnace." He placed the watering can back onto its bench and dusted his hands on his pants.

"What can I do?"

"Can I convince you to sit and rest?"

She pulled a face, and Dorran laughed.

"All right. I'd like to have a few new rows of spinach. Could you make a start on that?"

"Yes, definitely!" She rounded the bed to the shelf of seeds and began shuffling through them while Dorran left. She found the jar full of tiny brown seeds and scoped out an empty plot of dirt for them.

She had only just started digging a trench with her fingertip when a sense of unease broke through the calm. Her pulse kicked up. Her scalp prickled. Slowly, she turned to face the door.

A shape stood on the other side of the frosted window. Clare's smile died as she stared at it. The figure lifted one hand—its fingers knobbly and far, far too long—and pressed it against the glass. Its head tilted to one side as they stared at each other through the blurred screen. Then it stepped back, fading into obscurity again, leaving Clare clutching the jar against her chest as she fought for breath.

CHAPTER 19

A WAR WAGED THROUGH Clare. Instincts screamed for her to stay where she was, to keep hidden in the greenhouse with its thick metal door and warm, comforting light. But that would leave Dorran alone and unaware in the basement.

It's not real, her mind whispered. *There is no need to run to Dorran because he's not in any danger. He wants you to fight this stuff. Resist it. Don't give it power.*

But the small risk that she might be wrong—that Dorran could actually be in real peril—was too sharp to ignore. She took a breath and, still holding the seeds tightly, pushed on the garden's door.

She was alone in the room. Dreading the loss of light but knowing the plants needed their warmth preserved, Clare shut the door behind herself and shuddered as the gloom flooded around her.

A lit candle rested on a holder on the opposite wall. It was the only light in the space. To Clare's right, the gaping archway led to the wine cellar. As she watched it, she began to imagine she could hear whispers floating out of the darkness. The longer she stared, the louder the echoes grew. They dragged through her mind like nails on a chalkboard. She didn't realize she was biting her lip until she tasted blood.

Clare backed away from the arch. The whispers began to fade. She turned to the door in the opposite wall. It was smaller and narrower, but she could feel traces of warmth drifting out from under the wood. She gave the wine cellar one last wary glance then stepped through the basement door.

The metal stairs were steep and narrow, and the wall had no railings. Clare walked with one shoulder brushing against the stone to her left and a hand reached in front of herself. Refracted light highlighted the edge of each curving step. The staircase led her deeper and deeper under the house, so deep that her legs began to shake and her lungs burned. She began to worry that the stairway might never end. Then it leveled out and opened into an enormous cavern.

The room was made of bare rock walls. Five huge, funnel-like furnaces were spaced through the area, with large stretches of bare ground between them. One of the furnaces was lit. Clare gripped her coat tightly as she approached it.

Dorran had taken off both his jacket and shirt as he fed wood into the furnace. Sweat shone on his muscles and ran down his back. In the red light and dancing shadows, he almost looked like something mythical.

His bruises were starting to heal. They had darkened but no longer looked as raw. He crouched as he checked the furnace's glowing insides.

"Hey," Clare called, trying to sound cheerful.

Dorran jolted at her voice then stood and crossed to her, his eyebrows heavy. "Are you all right? You weren't supposed to leave the garden. Did something happen?"

"Oh, no, just…" She swallowed thickly. "Wanted to see the furnace."

His eyes flicked to the seed jar in her hand, and she knew he'd guessed the lie. He was quiet for a heartbeat then beckoned her forward. "Of course. You haven't seen it yet. Let me show you."

He gestured to the furnace he'd been working at then the other four scattered about the cavern. "These were designed to heat the lower levels of the house. This one, of course, directs heat up to the garden's floor. The others go to the dining room, the library, the foyer, and the main sitting room."

"It's hot." Even twenty paces away, Clare could feel the heat radiating out of the fire. It was no wonder Dorran was sweating. A bead of liquid trickled between strongly defined shoulder blades, and Clare hurriedly averted her eyes.

"It's not the most economical way to do things," he admitted. "It heats slowly, but once the warmth has seeped through the floor, it holds for a long time. Normally, the fire wouldn't be this intense, but we're playing catchup."

He wiped his forearm across his forehead then beckoned for her to follow him back toward the stairs. "See that chute in the wall? That connects to the back of the property and lets the staff drop chopped wood into here without having to climb the stairs."

A small mountain of logs had developed below the metal opening. They all seemed to have come from the same tree type, and Clare guessed the family had been cutting into the pines that surrounded them.

Dorran stopped next to a bucket of water near the stairs, drenched a cloth, and began to wash off. Clare was caught between the impulse to turn away and the irrepressible temptation to watch. She'd never met a man like Dorran before. He was fascinating. Strong neck muscles merged into wide shoulders. As water dripped over his back, Clare was reminded of one of her earliest impressions of him: that he had been carved out of stone by some master artist.

She realized she was staring again and abruptly turned to admire the vast space instead, her face hot. "Does this go under all of the house?"

"Not quite, but nearly." He didn't seem to have noticed her awkwardness and motioned toward the ceiling. "There are no furnaces for the staff areas except, of course, the gardens. The house's footprint is a bit larger than this. It was designed almost as an extravagant waste of money. So much space, so much effort, just to make the floor in a room warm. I believe it was installed to create a luxurious experience for any guests. Since the family doesn't winter here, we almost never use the furnaces. The normal fireplaces work faster and are easier to control."

"I guess sometimes people have things just so that they can *say* they have them."

"Precisely." He slipped his shirt on and buttoned it up. That was a relief and a disappointment all at once. "I'm about done here for now. Would you like to go back to the gardens? Or I could take you to your room."

Awed by the space and the massive brick structures, Clare had almost forgotten about the figure she'd seen outside the hothouse. She guessed that had been Dorran's intention: to talk until she didn't feel scared anymore. It had worked.

She looked down at the jar of seeds. "We still have more work to do in the garden, don't we?"

"I can take care of it later if you prefer."

"No. I want to help. Just as long as you stay with me."

He dipped his head. "Of course I will. Let me help you up the stairs."

The rest of the day passed quickly. Dorran didn't leave Clare alone again. When he went to make lunch, she followed. When she needed the bathroom, he waited outside the door, where she could still hear him.

By the time they returned to the bedroom, they had planted dozens of rows of seeds. Some of the plants that had sprouted would grow quickly. Others wouldn't be ready to harvest for four or five months. Even though they likely wouldn't need them by that point, Dorran had wanted to plant them anyway as a precaution.

Clare slept well that night. Occasionally, she thought she heard scraping, scrabbling noises chasing her through her dreams. But whenever she woke, she found Dorran not far away—either sleeping on the other side of the bed, pacing near the windows, or reading in one of the wingback chairs.

He kept the fire hot through the night. When Clare got up the following morning, she didn't feel how cold the day was until she approached the windows. The bite of winter still seeped through, hard and angry. She thought the temperature might still be dropping. Snow continued to fall from heavy dark-gray clouds.

They slipped into something like a routine. Dorran was unbelievably patient. Clare didn't think she would have had the stamina to revolve her life around another person, but he did it almost automatically.

They alternated their time between the garden and the bedroom. There were dozens of rooms in the house that Clare wasn't familiar with—libraries, ballrooms, smoke rooms, and parlors—the kinds of spaces that rarely existed in modern houses but seemed perfectly natural at Winterbourne Hall. Their excursions into those other areas were infrequent, though. With just two of them, there wasn't the time or any reason to try to heat the whole house. If Dorran wanted to pick up a new book from the library, they would don their jackets, leave the warm, safe rooms, and brave the near-freezing temperatures in the rest of the house for the shortest amounts of time possible.

Clare still saw the phantoms and still heard them. They followed her in her mind if not in reality. She could hear their soft, patient scratching whenever she listened, as well as their rasping, gasping breaths. And sometimes, especially when she was tired or confused, she would look up and see the shadows lurking in the hallways or hidden in the rooms' corners, watching her.

She never said anything to Dorran, but she thought he guessed. He'd developed a habit of distracting her whenever she stared at one of the clumps of darkness for too long. He would pull her attention to something solid and concrete, such as a book, a task, or even just easy chatter.

And he kept the lights on for her. Wherever they went, he turned on lights, chasing out the shadows and leaving the space bright and clear. Clare tried to argue. There was no room for wastefulness when they needed the fuel to power the hothouse. Dorran's response was always the same. "It isn't a waste."

She could see worry in his eyes. Desperation, even. She hated being a burden. He never said or did anything to make her feel like one, but she knew what she was. The poison's effects were slow to recede. She grew tired easily and couldn't handle long flights of stairs without becoming breathless.

Clare did what she could to be useful. She chopped herbs while Dorran diced and fried the frozen meat to mix into the soup. She matched him in tending to the garden, monitoring humidity and heat levels, and holding his ladder steady when he needed to replace a blown bulb. When she grew too tired to do that, she would sit and read for Dorran while he worked. The days almost always ended the same. She would doze off in the seat in the room's corner and wake up later that night in her bed, with the book—its place marked with a bookmark—lying on her bedside table, and Dorran within reaching distance.

The weather outside varied. Some days, sleet would pound at the house and leave a frosty coating over the chilled stones. Other days, snow fell. Twice, there were more thunderstorms and even a small smattering of hail, though it didn't grow as large as the day they'd been trapped in the cottage. She preferred the days with sleet. It tamped down the snow, reducing the drifts and making it look almost possible to walk over the field again.

There was only one clear day that week. Sunlight glittered off the endless blankets of white. Clare had the impression that the sun felt a bit like she did—dazed and disoriented. It warmed the air's temperature enough to start melting the snow, but more dark clouds rolled in that afternoon to undo the effort.

On the sunny day, she broached the idea of trying to reach the car again. Dorran crossed to the window and stared across the field of white for several minutes. Clare, sitting by the fire, knitted her hands together while she waited.

After an agonizing pause, he said, "I don't think we can risk it again yet. You're not well enough to travel that distance. Not safely."

She bristled. "I'm doing better."

"You are." He turned back from the window and smiled. "I'm happy. But those snowdrifts are going to be challenging, even for me. And if we're caught out by another storm…"

She understood. The weather had been unpredictable, bordering on insane. One minute, the air outside the house could be still and silent. The next, freezing, screaming gusts swept through, catching up flurries of snow and assaulting the already-damaged manor.

"I could try to go alone." Dorran scratched the back of his neck. "But even that's risky. If something happened to me out there, you would be trapped here alone."

She stood, crossed the space, and rested a hand on his arm as she tried not to laugh. "If something happened to you...*I'd* be lonely? That's what you worry about? Not the fact that you'd be—you know, dead?"

She could feel his chuckles reverberating out of his chest. "All right, that wouldn't be good either."

"You worry about me too much."

"I'm more selfish than you give me credit for." He patted her hand. "I think being *alone* could be worse than death in some situations."

She closed her eyes. "Yeah."

"But I feel that as long as we stay together, as long as we stay a team, we will be all right."

Clare smiled. "I'd better get stronger, then. And the sun had better spend some more time melting the snow. Because I don't think I could stand ignoring that radio for much longer."

"I know."

CHAPTER 20

WHEN CLARE WOKE THE next morning, Dorran was still asleep beside her. He'd stretched out, one leg hanging off the edge of the bed and his forearm over his eyes to keep out the sunlight.

She moved gently to avoid disturbing him as she slipped out of bed and approached the window. The sun was out again. That seemed like a good sign. She shivered as she leaned close to the glass and tried to guess how deep the snow was. Another layer had been applied the night before. The sun might have been working to cut through the cold, but it had a long way to go.

Clare stepped into the bathroom and splashed icy water over her face, trying to shake off the last cobwebs of sleep. A door farther down the hallway creaked open. She kept her eyes fixed on the basin as she brushed her teeth.

Dorran thought that ignoring the phantoms would make them go away. Clare had hoped it would get easier the more she shut her eyes and ears to them, but the paranoia seemed to be growing worse.

Her hands shook as she ran the toothbrush under the stream of water. She still couldn't control her reactions. Fear was always present, lurking just under the surface, waiting for the smallest disturbance to rise up and wreak havoc. A creaky door. A whistle of wind. A floorboard flexing. They were simple, harmless noises, but they made her pulse race and her throat dry.

It was better when Dorran was around. She could look at him, and he would smile back. That was enough to often stop the hairs from rising and her breath from quickening. He thought they were safe. And that meant they were. *Didn't it?*

She left the bathroom and stopped at the edge of the bed to watch Dorran's chest rise and fall. She'd woken early that morning.

Something that might have been a cricket or a closing door latch echoed from the floor below. Clare closed her eyes and squeezed her hands together as her breath hitched. She could wake Dorran. He would blink lazily then stretch, like he always did in the mornings, and she would feel safe again.

But that wasn't solving the problem. Ignoring it wasn't making anything better. Keeping the lights on, staying close to the man she trusted, and backing away from anything threatening weren't fixing her.

Will confronting it change anything? She had asked herself that question repeatedly over the last few days. Bethany had never been part of the face-your-fears camp, but Clare knew it worked for some people. They would meet the phobia head-on, embrace it, and learn to live with it. And then it would stop being frightening.

But what she had was more than a phobia. She still didn't know what it was. She didn't want to believe it might be insanity. But there were very few other explanations that made sense.

If there is something wrong with me...something that's been knocked loose in my brain...will confronting it make it better or worse?

Clare carefully, silently plucked her coat off the chair beside the bed and slipped her feet into the oversized boots. They couldn't keep on the way they were—wasting electricity and wasting Dorran's time. The radio, Clare's only other hope to escape the phantoms, was just as far out of reach as it had ever been. So it was time to try the other option.

She turned the door handle gently. It had been kept oiled and didn't make a noise. She gave Dorran one final look before she stepped out of the room and shut the door behind her.

The air bit her exposed skin. Her knees were already shaking as she tugged the jacket over her back and zipped it up. It had a thick, fluffy collar, and Clare tucked her chin in so that her neck would stay warm.

She waited for a moment, arms folded, as she listened to the house. The wind was calm that morning. The sense of hollowness about the space seemed to reverberate tiny noises back at her. They were maddening.

Simply being alone in the corridor made the back of her neck prickle. But it wasn't enough. She needed to face it, to see it, to stare it down and win. Whatever *it* was. That meant traveling into its territory.

An image popped into her mind: the wine cellar. Clare reflexively stepped back then forced herself to hold still and not shiver as the fear enveloped her. She didn't want to go to the cellar, which meant she had to.

The frantic voice of caution begged her to tell Dorran where she was going. But she couldn't do that. He wouldn't want her to go anywhere alone. He wouldn't want her stepping into the dark.

It's just a cellar. She reached the staircase and ran her hand along the banister as she descended. *One large, dark room at the foot of the house. There is nothing sinister about it, nothing dangerous. You'll walk into it and spend a minute or two in the darkness, surrounded by old bottles that probably cost more than your car. Once you've acclimatized and realized there's nothing to be afraid of, you can come out again. Run back to your room, slip back into bed, and you'll be a step closer to conquering this.*

She tried to cling to that thought as she passed through the foyer. There was nothing dangerous about a cellar. It wasn't like going outside, where one bad footing could leave her stranded and freezing. The phantoms—whatever they were—existed only in her mind. She would be safe. She might not feel it, but she would be.

She entered the stone chamber. The familiar garden door stood ahead. The lights hadn't turned on yet that morning, but they would automatically power on soon. She glanced to her right, at the small, innocuous, and familiar door to the furnace room.

To her left, the cellar's archway seemed larger than she remembered it. The opening was huge, its insides a swirl of moving black and infinite possibilities, none of them friendly. The stones were old, almost old enough to start cracking, but somehow, they managed to look eternal. She knew the steps would be much the same way. Solid. Unyielding. Unforgiving.

The table at the back of the room held candles and matches for when Dorran ventured into the basement. Clare found one that was half-melted and lit it. The flame started small but quickly grew as it softened the wax and fed itself more fuel. She picked up the old bronze holder and turned toward the cellar.

It's just a wine room. The temperature dropped noticeably as she approached the entrance. *A place for fancy people to store expensive drinks. Nothing more exciting than that. Don't give it any power.*

Her candle flickered as she passed over the threshold. Clare stared at the light, her heart hammering and her palms sweaty, but the flame righted itself within a second.

She almost backed out. The thought of her bed upstairs was painfully tempting. She could lie there, warm and comfortable, swaddled in soft sheets, as she watched Dorran dream. She didn't *need* to push herself that day. She didn't *need* to face her demons as long as Dorran cared enough to stay at her side.

But that was the problem. He was giving by nature. He would do what it took to make her feel safe. And she couldn't keep asking him for that, absorbing his time and energy, wasting resources, and slowing him down at every turn. He didn't need an obligation. He needed a partner.

She stepped down. The chill had been bad at the top of the stairs, but it grew worse with every step. Clare began to imagine shuffling footsteps ringing out of the eternal blackness. When she stopped walking, the shuffling noise stopped too.

Echoes. That's all. Echoes in the fancy people's wine room. Don't give it power.

She kept descending. Her heart kept hammering. She didn't remember the stairs going down so far. The hallway was wide—wider than the flight of stairs into the basement—and made of slabs of solid gray stone. Her candlelight caught on uneven scraps of rock, and the shadows it created ran in circles around her.

Something rang out in the blackness ahead. Clare froze, and she clenched her teeth to keep quiet. She thought the sound was caused by something being dropped.

It's an old house. Things fall sometimes. Maybe there was a chip of rock on the wall, and the reverberations from your footsteps knocked it free.

She'd come too far to turn back. Clare forced her legs to work, to carry her lower. After three more steps, the staircase leveled out on the stone floor.

Shelves surrounded her. Dorran had said his family had squandered most of their wealth, and she could see some of the symptoms in that cellar. The shelves were less than a tenth filled. Empty brackets ran for rows sometimes before the pattern was interrupted by a bottle. She supposed good wine was expensive, and having good wine delivered into the middle of nowhere must be even more so.

Clare waited, forcing her back to be straight as she faced the room. It was large. The shelves continued on farther than her light could manage, disappearing into the inky gloom. The stones under her shoes were well worn from countless feet pacing over them in search of the bottle that had been requested. Clare focused on those details, on the elements of the room that were mundane and normal, grounded in reality. She tried to use them to push out the panic in her mind and silence the soft scrabbling noise she imagined coming from the room's unseen corner.

Stay for two minutes. That's all. Then you can get out of here. She swallowed. The cold stung her throat and made her nose water. She blinked her eyes rapidly as she stared toward the nearest wall.

There was something dark there. It looked like a stain of some kind, like a liquid that had sprayed over the stones and soaked into the porous material. *Blood,* her mind whispered, and Clare clenched her teeth. It obviously wasn't blood. She was in a wine cellar. Bottles would inevitably, eventually be broken.

Maybe I am *delusional. My flames of paranoia are being fanned by an unwelcoming mansion. How long has it been since I've spoken to someone other than Dorran? It has to be weeks.*

The scrabbling noise wasn't going away. In fact, she thought it might be coming closer. She steeled herself, knowing that running would only make the fear worse in the long term. She was nearly at the two minutes she'd assigned herself. She would spend the last few seconds approaching the other side of the room—the unseen side—and once she'd conquered her imagination, she could leave.

She walked forward, each step slow and measured. The delusions were realistic. She could pinpoint the exact space the sound seemed to be coming from—ahead and a little to the right, near the ground, close to the space she'd imagined seeing the figure days before. Fingernails on stone.

Each step revealed more of the space. The soft golden glow of her candlelight poured out like a liquid, running over the stone floor and stone wall to give her a little dome of light. Then the candle guttered as moving air disturbed it. In those brief seconds when the flame trembled and fought to hang on, Clare thought she saw two round, yellowed eyes staring out of the darkness.

CHAPTER 21

CLARE STOPPED MOVING. THE candle stabilized. Her throat was dry, and her hands shook, but she knew what she had to do.

It's not real. There's nothing there. Step forward. Prove it to yourself.

Her shoe scraped across the stone as she lifted it. As the candle moved forward, its light cut into the blackness. There was a shape there. The huddled, filthy figure was almost invisible on the absolute outer edge of her light.

It's not real. It's not real.

She lifted her other foot. The limb felt heavier than stone. It barely moved forward, but when it did, the light that splashed across the shape became a fraction brighter.

Vertebrae had cut through the skin on its back. The bones were jutting out and poking up like a spiny ridge. The skin surrounding the protrusion was a dark red, almost black.

It's not real. It's not real!

She couldn't breathe. She wanted Dorran. He would erase the fear and make her feel safe. He would make her believe nothing in the cellar could hurt her.

Dorran. She clung to the thought of him. *Dorran is why you're doing this. Dorran needs you to be better.*

Her foot scraped forward again. The creature moved. Its gaunt face turned toward her. It was a woman…but only just barely. Strands of long gray hair hung about its face. Its jaw was too long and projected out. Deformed. Bony fingers tipped the arms that didn't fit properly at its sides. It took Clare a second to understand what she was seeing. The arms were far too long. They had an extra joint each, making them jut out at bizarre angles.

It's not real.

The creature had been scrabbling at the stone wall, in the same place Clare had seen the first woman. Its round, lidless eyes stared at her as it rose out of its crouch. A narrow, pale tongue darted out to taste its bottom lip. Then one of the three-jointed arms reached toward her.

It's not real.

Her legs shook. Her body shook. Her hands jittered so badly that the candlelight shimmered.

Elongated teeth filled the gaping maw. The arm kept reaching, stretching closer and closer, aimed at Clare's outstretched hand that held the candle.

A memory rushed through her. It was vague and gone in an instant, but the emotions associated with it were sharp enough to make her breath catch. Claws digging into her. Claws just like the overgrown nails protruding from the woman's fingers.

Clare turned and ran. The creature made a noise, something between a hiss and a rasping, gurgling inhale. Then its nails began scraping over the floor as it gave chase.

All rationality had fled. Clare only cared about one thing—reaching the top of the stairs. Her shoulder hit one of the shelves. It shook her, and she stumbled. The enormous wooden structure creaked and swayed. As Clare swiveled, she saw the creature two paces behind her, jaw stretched wide and spines glistening in the light. Then the candle went out.

Clare yelled. She lurched forward, toward where she knew the stairs had to be. She hit another shelf. Bottles clinked and rattled. Clare used shaking hands to feel along the structure's edge, guiding her forward. Her lungs were starved for air. Her throat was too tight. Then she hit the first step of the staircase and tumbled forward.

Sharp rock hit her jaw, jarring her and making her taste blood. She barely felt the pain, though. She clambered up. The clawing, scratching noises were almost on her. She could hear more of them. They came from every corner of the cellar, clicking over stones, scrabbling around the shelves as they converged on her. With every heartbeat, she expected to feel the sharp pain digging into her ankle. She ran, pure adrenaline driving her up, closer and closer to the archway of light in the distance.

She burst through the archway and made it four more steps into the room before she collapsed onto the stone floor. Sobs wrenched out of her, each one aching as it forced its way past the lump in her throat. She pulled her legs up under herself and wrapped her arms around her knees. She couldn't run anymore. But the creatures didn't seem to be chasing her.

Light came out of the garden's open door. It wasn't enough to fully illuminate the space, but it wasn't darkness either. Clare lay there, curled into a tight ball. Her head throbbed. Her limbs all felt like they were made of stone. And the inside of her chest ached from where her thumping heart had bruised it.

Very slowly, she lifted her head. She'd been aware of the light around her, but it had taken a second for the relevance to sink in. The garden's door was open. That wasn't normal. It wasn't right. Dorran was always careful to keep it shut tightly and preserve the warmth their precious plants needed.

Clare glanced toward the cellar archway. It remained empty. Then she looked toward the door leading back into the main parts of the house. It was shut, the way she'd left it when she'd come into the room.

"Dorran?" Her voice was a croak. Perfect, undisturbed silence was her only reply. Clare pushed herself to stand and staggered forward.

There was no one inside the garden room, no one she could see at least. Clare squinted through the fog of stress as she reached the entrance and leaned on the open door for support.

She'd spent so much time in the space over the recent week that she could picture the scene by heart. Snow peas were stretching tendrils up their trellises. They were small, but enthusiastic. The tomato sprouts were still tiny. Their delicate, fuzzy green leaves reached toward the artificial lights above them, not seeming to notice or mind that it wasn't the sun. The lettuce had three leaves apiece, and Dorran had said they would need only two more weeks before there would be enough to start picking.

Clare stepped through the doorway, and a moaning wail wrenched from her chest. Their beautiful garden—their love, their pride, their *survival*—was dead.

The plants had been dug out of the ground. Not eaten, but uprooted. What had been perfectly smooth beds the day before were now mounds and valleys of dark-brown soil. Bruised leaves poked out. Exposed roots withered in the lights' heat. Not a single plant had been spared.

"No, no, no." She clutched at the sides of her head as she shook it. "This can't be real."

It's a delusion. It has to be. Please, let this be all in my mind.

She reached toward the closest plant, a small tomato. Its stem had broken when it had been dug up, and clumps of dirt still held to its delicate, hair-like roots. Its leaves had started to wilt. She touched the sap that had beaded at the bent section of the stem. She felt how limp the foliage was and how crisp the delicate roots were.

"No." This was real. She couldn't imagine such detail. She couldn't imagine such nuanced sensations. The garden was gone, churned up, destroyed. "No!"

This can't happen. They can't die.

She lifted the tomato plant back upright and gently, carefully scooped soil around the damaged roots. When she let it go, the top flopped back over where its stem had broken. Clare moaned. But she didn't stop. *There might still be time to save some of them.* Some of the plants hadn't been shredded in the massacre. *If I can just stop the roots from drying out…*

She darted among the beds, trying to right the plants she could find and scooping soil back around them. Tears ran down her cheeks, and Clare didn't try to stop them. She wasn't being as delicate as she knew she should be. Her hands shook. Crumpled, torn leaves flecked the soil. There was too much to do. And the remaining plants were withering with every passing moment.

"What have you *done?*"

The familiar voice cut through her. She turned. Dorran stood in the garden's open door. She didn't know how long he'd been watching her, but he was sheet white. His dark eyes, normally so comforting, were wide as he stared at the carnage.

Clare took a step toward him. "We can…we can save them."

He looked at her, but there was no affection in his face any longer. He sounded like he was in pain. "What have you *done,* Clare?"

She looked down at her hands. They were filthy with dirt. It clung under her fingernails like blood from a crime scene. She cowered back. "This wasn't me. I didn't do this."

"You didn't—" He pressed his hand over the lower half of his face and closed his eyes, seemingly trying to swallow words he knew he would regret. When he took the hand away, he was trembling. "This was important. You *knew* how important it was. We will *starve* without this."

"I know! I know!" Fresh tears ran, and she was powerless to stop them. "I didn't do this! There are people in the house. Monsters. They look human, but they—"

His fist slammed into the door.

Clare flinched as the sound of the jarred metal echoed around her.

Dorran spoke slowly, but there was a deep, burning ferocity in his words. "There is *no one* here."

She couldn't meet his eyes. She clenched her dirt-caked hands at her sides as she tried not to crumple to the ground. "I didn't do this. *They* did it."

"Were you so desperate to convince me of your delusions?" His eyes were colder than the ice outside. "You would damn us to make me believe your lies."

"No! Dorran, I swear!"

He took a pace toward her, and she stepped back. Her eyes burned from the tears. She didn't know what else she could say.

"I gave you everything." He whispered, but each word hurt her more than if he'd screamed them. "Wasn't that enough?"

"Please. I...I..."

He towered over her. She'd never felt the height difference as acutely as then. His lips shook, but his eyes were steady and unyielding. "Get out."

She ducked and ran past him. He didn't try to stop her. Clare's legs gave out as she neared the door, and she clutched at the structure to stay upright. When she looked over her shoulder, Dorran wasn't watching her. He was staring at the ruined gardens, his shoulders bowed.

She got her legs back under herself and kept running. The tears blinded her, but she didn't slow down to see her way. She burst through the door into the long waiting room, then into the foyer. There, she collapsed onto the cold marble floor and wrapped her arms around her head.

Her chest ached as she strained to breathe. She wished she could die. Then, maybe, she wouldn't be able to cause any more damage.

A little voice was whispering in the back of her head that maybe Dorran was right. Maybe she *had* destroyed the garden. Out of the two of them, he was the sane one. She trusted what he said, didn't she?

Maybe she'd never gone into the wine cellar at all. Maybe the twisted, broken woman wasn't the only delusion. Maybe the encounter had been all in her imagination while she had mindlessly clawed out their precious plants.

A wail choked in her throat and fell silent. She smacked a fist into the side of her head. The shock helped her think, at least a little. She lifted her eyes. The front door stood twenty paces away, bolted but easy to open.

Beside it, in the foyer's corner, next to the carefully crafted side tables and coatracks, were their snowshoes and coats.

CHAPTER 22

NOTHING TRIED TO DISTURB Clare as she buckled on the snowshoes. She already wore the thick, puffy jacket Dorran had given her, and she zipped the spare over the top then pulled on the gloves. She didn't have time for all of the other precautions she'd worn the previous trip—the extra layers of socks, the second pair of pants, the hat—but that didn't matter. She only needed to get to her car.

The door was immensely heavy. She leaned her weight on the handle to wrench it open. On the other side, the snowdrifts were up to her shoulders. Clare found a chair along one of the foyer's walls and used it to climb out.

Cold wind buffeted her as soon as she tumbled down the embankment. Clare squeezed her eyes closed and took a moment to let herself acclimatize. In some ways, the freezing sting was nice. It distracted her from the way her insides felt like they were tearing themselves apart. She gave herself a second, then she got the snowshoes under herself and stood.

She remembered the way to the forest. When Dorran had led her out there, he'd taken her down the main driveway then speared off to pass the groundskeeper's cottage. She followed the same path, struggling up one side of the dunes and skidding down the other.

Her body was worn down. Even though she'd been awake for less than two hours, she felt ready to collapse, close her eyes, and never open them again. The forest's edge looked impossibly far away. The sun was nowhere near as warm as it had seemed from the windows. A hazy fog had spread over the sky, reducing visibility and giving the environment a sense of impending twilight.

She pushed the weariness down and instead grasped the kernel of pain and fear inside of herself. She squeezed it, making it hotter, and let it fuel her as she hiked toward the forest.

The groundskeeper's hut was visible. The snow had abated slightly compared to the day she and Dorran had taken shelter in it, and more of the stone walls were exposed. The little tunnel they'd dug to the door had been thoroughly filled in.

Walking past the structure was painful. She tried not to relive that night when they'd shared the mattress and huddled in front of the fire as the elements assaulted them from every direction. An internal assurance had told her they would be fine if they just stayed together. That memory hurt too much. She thought it would hurt for a long time to come.

Past the groundskeeper's cottage, the ground leveled out. Clare guessed it was a clearing ahead of the forest. She fixed her eyes on the tree trunks, which were nothing but a blur of gray and shadows through the snow, and kept her numb, shaking legs moving.

The sky seemed to be growing darker. Clare watched it with one eye, but she didn't know what she would do if it swept over her. She wasn't going back to the house. The groundskeeper's cottage would be locked. If she could get to the forest, it would help protect her from some of the elements. But she could survive outside for only so long.

Her plan was simple—reach the radio and contact Beth. Then she could see if there was any way someone could reach her. Even if it took a few hours, she could sit inside her car—assuming the crash hadn't fractured it too badly—and be protected from the worst of the cold.

It was a poor, broken plan with many opportunities for failure. The radio could be wrecked from water damage. Bethany might have given up and turned off her half of the pair. The car might be buried under six feet of snow if the crash site was in an area where the trees funneled the flakes. It was the only plan she had left, though. Her one lifeline.

Not that she deserved it. Under the gloves, her fingers were still caked with mud. The farther she walked from Winterbourne, the more convinced she became that she was responsible for destroying the garden. *What other explanation is there without reaching into the realms of fantasy?*

Tears ached as they turned to frost on her eyelashes. Dorran hadn't deserved that. He'd never raised his voice with her or even been irritable before. He'd been nothing except kind and patient. She owed him her life. And in return, he'd lost his only source of food.

She felt sick. Clare hoped, with one less person in the house, his stores would last until he could regrow the garden. Or maybe she could convince someone to go and check on him. They would need a helicopter to reach the property. She wasn't sure if she could talk a search-and-rescue team into dropping off supplies to a house that almost no one knew existed and that was otherwise uncontactable.

The forest's shadow passed over her, and she half-closed her eyes as the temperature fell even lower. Every breath felt like it was burning her lungs. At least the wind would be gentler once she was among the trees.

She stepped over the first bank of roots and staggered as the snowshoes threatened to upend her. The massive, many-layered pines had largely protected the forest floor from the incessant snow. It still clumped there, often in enormous drifts, but patches of clear ground were visible too. Clare couldn't wear the snowshoes any farther without risking breaking them. She unfastened them and left them propped against a tree at the forest's edge. One of the estate's gardeners might find them there eventually and return them to their little closet.

She stepped into the forest and relished the feel of bark under her gloves. The insides of Winterbourne Hall had been almost entirely devoid of life. She, Dorran, and the garden had been the only living things there.

Banksy Forest was an incredible expanse. Some of the oldest trees had died, collapsing over and slowly rotting to feed the next generation. What was left was ancient and gnarled. The trunks were immense and often twisted by wind, other plants, or simply their own weight. Several trees had split down the middle but still grew pine needles on both halves.

As Clare climbed deeper, she was able to appreciate the generational difference. Younger trees had grown in between their forbearers. Sometimes they were fully grown, as large as their sires, but discernible because they didn't conform to the straight rows of the previous generation. Others were small—the perfect size for someone to move into their living room for Christmas. A few tiny trees struggled to survive in the low-light environment of the forest floor. The younger plants tended to be spindly unless they'd been lucky enough to grow in the space left by one of the fallen first generation. Shrubs, winter-hardy vines, and the occasional fungus had made their home in between the pines.

Once, Clare saw a flurry of motion in the distance as some animal—probably a rabbit—fled. She didn't know which direction led to the road. All she had was Dorran's mention that it lay straight ahead. She kept walking, struggling through the snow and over exposed roots, breathing heavily and unstable on her feet.

She hadn't expected the walk to be short. There would be no way for the manor to be so unknown if it were too close to the road. But the farther she hiked, the deeper her anxiety set in. The frightened little voice in the back of her head asked what she would do if she'd gone in the wrong direction and completely missed the road. She didn't have much of an answer beyond wandering around until she either found the street or the manor again.

Or die of exhaustion.

Her feet ached, and thirst began to make its presence felt. She'd had a drink that morning when she'd brushed her teeth, but nothing since, and the stress had dehydrated her. She ran her dry tongue over parched lips. The forest's interior was, at least, a few degrees warmer thanks to the trees' insulation. Her face still stung from the cold, but her core was warm. She tried to focus on that.

The ground tended down suddenly, and Clare staggered into the snow-filled valley. The dirty white powder came up to her knees, and she began struggling through it to reach the next hill.

Then she stopped and looked to her left. The valley continued on for a hundred meters before gently bending out of sight. "Oh," Clare whispered. The layer of snow hid the asphalt, but the even, straight edges were unmistakable. She'd found the road.

She managed a shaky smile. Her life was a mess, but at least she'd been able to do one thing correctly. She looked to the right then back to the left, trying to guess which direction her car might be. There were no visible signs. She chose left.

The snow was hard to wade through, so Clare climbed back into the forest. She clutched at low branches to help her navigate around the trees. It was surprisingly hard to recognize the road when it was full of snow, but she thought she might know the bend ahead. It was about halfway through the forest, if her memory served.

She tried to pick up her last memories of driving. She'd entered the forest. It had been snowing furiously, and she'd breathed a sigh of relief as the ancient growths gave her protection. After that...

Clare blinked and shook her head. She thought she remembered hearing some kind of noise. She reached for the sound, but it was gone before she could grasp it. She visualized the scene. Her phone had been in the cup holder. Her bag had been in the passenger's seat. Had she packed anything else? If she was visiting Marnie, she usually tried to bring some supplies that her aunt couldn't get easily at the tiny nearby village. That usually meant paints and watercolor pencils. Marnie loved art, but the general store didn't sell anything better than crayons.

Clare was almost certain she hadn't brought any art supplies that day, though. She remembered glancing into the rearview mirror. There had been something in the back seat, something large. *A box, maybe? What kind of box was I bringing?*

Like the rest of her memories, it faded almost as soon as she clutched at it. Frustration took its place. Those were the last few normal hours of her life. To be denied them felt painfully unfair.

She reached the corner and followed the bend in the road. Something large and red lay up ahead, curled in between two trees. Clare took a quick breath and began jogging. She'd found her car.

CHAPTER 23

CLARE HAD BOUGHT THE little red hatchback secondhand a year before moving to her cottage. The car had been good to her. Beth had always worried when Clare drove the car on ice or snowy roads, but all it needed was good-quality snow tires, and it handled the winter conditions well. It had been a reliable beast that had taken on a bit of a personality and started to feel like part of Clare's tiny family.

Seeing it broken hurt her deep inside. Its hood had crumpled. Lumps of bright-red metal, softened by layers of snow, twisted up toward the sky. As she neared it, Clare could see the tree she'd hit was one of the forest's originals. The giant had been tilted back from the impact. The damage to the roots was most likely bad enough to kill it.

Clare pressed one hand to her throat. It was hard to see her car like that. Harder still was knowing she'd been the one to cause the damage. The Banksy Forest route was one of the safest in the area. The road was wide and gentle with no sharp turns and good visibility all around. She was practiced at driving in snowy conditions. Clare couldn't understand how she'd gone off the path so drastically.

She ran her hand along the car's body as she circled it. Fuel had leaked out of the engine, though it had long mixed in with the snow. The driver's door hung wide open. The bend in it told Clare that the impact had popped it out. The windshield had a massive crack across it, though the safety glass had stayed in one solid lump.

Clare looked down at her stomach, where the bandages hid nearly healed cuts. She'd come to believe the glass from the windshield had sliced into her. But seeing it still in one piece, she had to assume maybe metal had poked through into the driver's seat and done the damage instead.

She reached the back door and pulled it open. Like she'd thought, there was a shape inside. It wasn't a box, though. Two travel cases rested on the seat. She unzipped the closest one. Inside were clothes—enough to account for half of her wardrobe. A sewing kit had been nestled into the back, along with two novels.

Confused, Clare rounded the car and climbed back in among the trees to open the other back door. The second travel case was full of food.

She carefully, wonderingly, sifted through the tins and boxes inside. She recognized her nonperishable food collection that she kept locked in a spare cupboard in case she was ever snowed into her home. She'd designed it to give herself enough food to last for nearly three weeks in a worst-case scenario. She'd managed to cram it all into the oversized case.

Her emergency pantry also contained water. Clare, suspecting where she might find it, retreated to the trunk and pressed on the latch. The car was unlocked, and the hatch popped open. Sure enough, six massive jugs weighed her car down. The water inside had frozen, and the plastic bulged but hadn't split.

Clare dragged her hand through her hair. She'd packed up for the trip to Marnie's, but not any normal kind of packing—emergency packing. *Wait…no…it wasn't a trip to Marnie's.*

Clare had been driving toward Marnie's, but she hadn't been planning to stop there. She was picking up her aunt on the way to Beth's.

"Why was I doing that?"

Because Beth called you. She was worried about…about…

The memory danced away again. Clare closed her eyes and pressed her fingers to the bridge of her nose.

Beth had a bunker. She wanted Clare and Marnie to stay with her. And Clare had brought her emergency supplies because once the three of them reached Bethany's, they wouldn't be leaving for a while.

Clare suddenly felt chilled to her core, more so than the weather allowed for. She swallowed thickly as she returned to the trunk. The two-way radio was there, as she'd known it would be. The small black box had traveled with her for more than a year. She hadn't ever needed to use it before.

She lifted it out and checked it. The batteries were still all right. She turned it on, adjusted the frequency, and pressed the button to transmit her voice.

"Beth?" She held her breath, waiting, terror pounding through her veins. Static answered. Every passing second ramped up her fear. She pressed the button again. "Bethany, it's me, Clare. I'm all right. Please answer."

The box replied with ceaseless static. Tears burned even though she'd thought she didn't have enough moisture left in her to cry. She began pacing, her breaths ragged. "Please, please, Beth, if you're there, if you can hear me, answer me. I need to know you're okay."

As the box continued to play white noise, Clare sank down with her back against one of the trees. She dropped her head to rest it on top of the box and scrunched her face up as short, gasping breaths cut through her. She knew Beth kept the box in her kitchen so she could hear it from every part of the house. And Beth wasn't likely to leave it, not if Clare was missing.

What happened? Why was I running? She turned the questions over in her head a dozen times, fear making her nauseous.

If Beth had retreated to her bunker, like Clare's supplies seemed to suggest, she would have taken the radio with her. It was considered a necessity, not just for communicating with Clare, but for talking with anyone else in the outside world.

She tried again. "Beth, it's me, Clare. Please answer me."

Clare shivered as the static played around her unrelentingly. The longer she sat still, the more the cold seeped into her, making her muscles stiff and her body tired. At last, Clare forced herself to stand before she froze. She placed the radio, still turned on, onto the car's roof. Its tuneless static song played over her as she stared up and down the path.

Banksy Forest Road wasn't a major highway, but it connected two small towns. The council was always prompt about clearing it after a snowstorm. If the towns had been hit by the same sort of erratic weather that had assaulted Winterbourne Hall, the snowplows were probably busy elsewhere. Still, it seemed strange that *no* effort had been made to clear the path. The snow was pristine. There were no mounds of it on either side of the road to indicate the plows had moved through. There were no tire tracks from brave—or brazen—citizens who had forded the road in their lifted trucks. No footprints. No sled tracks. Nothing.

Clare turned in a circle. She wasn't having any trouble breathing, but the oxygen didn't seem to be reaching her limbs. She felt cruelly, horribly isolated. The radio continued to play static behind her. She snatched it down and swiveled the dials, moving through other channels. The radio was capable of picking up commercial stations as well as other amateur broadcasters. She moved steadily, winding through every number. They all played static. Every single one of them.

Clare turned off the radio and tucked it inside her coat. She leaned forward, her gloved hands braced on the car as she gasped desperately and tried not to fall apart.

There has to be an explanation for this. Something normal and laughably mundane. Something simple. Because I need simple. I don't think I can deal with complicated anymore today.

The memories tangled over each other, too confusing and jumbled to focus on. Clare shook her head as noises and images assaulted her. It was too much, too fast. She staggered around the car's side, toward the passenger's door, looking for somewhere to sit down.

Then she saw the damage inside. The door had been left open. The dashboard was remarkably intact. The car had been designed to protect the driver in case of a crash, and it had done a good job.

Clumps of snow littered the floor and the passenger's seat. Clare's mobile was no longer in the front. She guessed it must have gone flying during the impact and was probably lost somewhere in the back, between the travel cases or under the seats.

Blood had been splashed across the front of the car. Specks of it had sprayed over the dashboard, the steering wheel, and the ceiling. Gluts of it had soaked into the driver's seat and dribbled onto the floor. It was old and dry. It still smelled, but not as badly as Clare thought it might have. Instead of being red, it had turned a grotesque black-brown shade.

And there were three lines gouged into the side of the seat. Clare reached out to feel them, but she hesitated before touching the marks. They looked like the swipe of a claw, like something a bear or a wolf might make. Banksy Forest didn't have any animals that large, though. The worst it had were foxes, and they shied away from humans.

Clare pressed her gloved hand over her mouth as the memories, lost and tangled for so long, slid together into one clear image.

CHAPTER 24

CLARE STRETCHED THEN EXHALED as her back popped. Standing in front of her coffee maker was one of her favorite parts of the day. It was right next to the window overlooking her garden, and for the two minutes it took the water to boil and percolate, she didn't have to think or do anything except enjoy the view.

Winter had technically started, but the day was still warm enough that she only needed a light jacket. The deciduous trees in her garden had all finished shedding their leaves, and their dead branches stretched into the sky.

"Sunday," she mumbled and rubbed her sleeve over her eyes. Sunday was the best day of the week, no contest. Weekdays were spent working so that she could afford to enjoy her Sundays. Saturdays were for everything else she'd neglected during the week. Errands. Shopping. Cleaning. Visiting friends who were overdue for catchups. Sunday was for relaxing.

The coffee was ready. She took the mug out and inhaled. It was sharp but not too strong. She saved the really strong stuff for Mondays, when she needed energy. She didn't mind waking up slowly on Sundays.

Clare made her way into the small study. The space wasn't really big enough to be called a full room, but it was the most comfortable space in her house. She'd positioned a beanbag opposite the full-length window to take advantage of the view over her garden. Clare flopped into the cushioned seat and reached for the thriller novel that waited on the little table beside her. She held her coffee close to her chest, where it acted as a miniature heater, as she opened the hardback to the bookmark.

Her phone buzzed. Clare pressed her lips together, looking mournfully at her novel, then placed the coffee to one side and rolled out of the seat. It was always tempting to ignore phone calls on Sundays, but she never did. The only people who had her personal phone number were very close friends and family. If they were calling at eight in the morning on a weekend, chances were it was important.

Unless it's a telemarketer. Oh boy, for their sake, it had better not be.

She brushed loose hair out of her face as she picked up the phone. "Hello?"

"Clare?" Beth often sounded stressed, depending on how difficult her work was being and whether anything had broken or gone wrong. But she sounded unusually strained that morning. "Clare, are you okay?"

"Of course I am." Clare rested her hip on the kitchen counter so that she could stare out the window. "What's wrong?"

Beth took a sharp, tight breath. "You haven't turned on the TV this morning, have you?"

"No. It's a Sunday." Clare grinned. "And Sunday is for reading."

"Not today, sweetheart. Turn the TV on."

Bethany hadn't called her sweetheart in years, not since Clare had fallen out of a tree as a teen and ended up in the emergency ward with a broken arm.

A sense of uncertainty caught up to her. She crossed into the cramped living room and began searching for a remote control among the cushions. Beth took another sharp breath and said, "I think maybe you should come and stay with me for a couple of days. Just in case."

"Why? What's happening?"

"I don't know." She sounded like she had started to cry. "No one knows. But...but..."

Clare gave up trying to find the remote. She jumped over the chair to press the button on the TV then crouched down in preparation to change the channel. She didn't need to. Even though that station was supposed to be playing kids' shows at that time in the morning, news coverage was splashed across the screen. Still holding the phone to her ear, Clare backed up until she could slide onto the couch.

The emblem in the corner of the screen identified it as a news stream from another station. The anchors sat pin straight, their faces holding no sign of amusement or lightheartedness. Clare knew the expression. It was the one they wore during serious segments like terrorist attacks, natural disasters, or war.

The man was speaking. Clare's TV wasn't large enough for her to be certain, but she thought she saw a bead of sweat on his forehead. "…in Denmark. We have also been advised that now large parts of Quebec have gone dark. Our own reporter, Greg Harrelson, is currently uncontactable. We are going to re-air the last footage we received from him. But we would like to caution viewers that what you are about to see may be distressing. Viewer discretion is advised."

The screen changed. The new view showed a snow-swept city road lined with cars. Harsh orange light from streetlamps illuminated the scene. The image jostled violently as the person carrying the camera jogged.

"Beth?" Clare rubbed at the back of her neck. "What's going on?"

She could hear what sounded like a different news broadcast in the background of Beth's call. Beth was definitely crying now. "I don't know. I don't know. Cities are vanishing. I mean, they're still there—we can see them—but no one can contact the people living there. Anyone who drives into them isn't heard from again. They don't know why yet, or what happened to them, or—"

Beth's voice faded into the background as Clare focused on her screen.

The reporter came into view. He was running, his gray hair sticking to his sweaty red forehead. "Up ahead is the so-called quiet zone." He yelled to be heard over his pounding footsteps and ragged breaths. "Civilians in surrounding areas are being evacuated to Toronto. We are told that—"

He broke off as an explosion boomed in the distance. The camera jerked back as its bearer stopped running, and the screen swiveled away from the reporter's shocked face and toward the skyline.

Flames bloomed above the silhouetted buildings. Red, gold, and ribbons of thick black smoke rose into the night. The reporter's voice was uneven. "That—I think that was a plane. A plane just fell out of the sky. I, uh, the city's power is gone. There may have been some kind of bombing. We are not sure yet. We're going to try to—"

He looked over his shoulder. He seemed frozen. His body seized up as he stared at something beyond the camera's view. Then he began backing away, motioning urgently to the cameraman. The frame swung to encapsulate the street behind them. Something was moving between the cars.

Then the frame changed again, this time exploding into a block of white as something bright arced across the sky like lightning. The reporter yelled incoherently. Then the camera tumbled, catching distorted fragments of the damp street and lightless buildings. A jagged line appeared across the screen as its lens broke.

Clare heard irregular footsteps followed by a cry. Then the streetlights above flickered and died, one by one, plunging the image into near darkness. That scene lasted for another thirty seconds. All Clare could see was starlight catching on the roofs of cars and the side of one building. Then the feed abruptly cut out.

The screen returned to the two stony-faced newsreaders. Neither spoke for a second, then the woman exhaled. "We are still waiting to reconnect communication with Greg Harrelson. Everyone here at QBC hopes for his safety and speedy extraction, as well as that of Thomas Strokes, who was operating the camera."

Another stretch of silence filled the room. The woman shuffled, lifting herself an inch higher, and began speaking in a more energetic tone. Clare guessed someone must have been barking instructions into her earpiece. The man's attention stayed fixed on the papers on his desk, his eyes dull.

"Some have speculated that this may be the beginning of World War III. However, no country has claimed responsibility for the attacks at this time. We now have an updated list of quiet zones, as reported by social media and our sister stations in other countries."

A map displayed on the screen. Large patches of red had been painted across it, signaling the dead areas. Clare bit her knuckle. The color was spread across the globe—the US, the UK, Australia, Russia, Africa, East Asia. Some patches were small. Some would have covered tens of thousands of kilometers.

The woman began reading the names of areas that had lost contact. Clare finally realized that Beth was still talking into her ear.

"Clare, please, are you there? Say something."

"I'm here." She swallowed, leaning closer to the screen, trying to pinpoint the areas where she and Beth lived. She found their nearest city. It was red. But mercifully, the color hadn't encroached into the countryside yet.

"The uncontactable areas are spreading." Beth's voice was thick with tears. "And new ones keep appearing. Two news stations have already stopped broadcasting. The hosts were talking one minute, then the next, it was just static. I thought it was a joke at first. But Clare...maybe my bunker..."

"Yeah. Okay." Clare rose out of her seat. "I'm on my way."

She put the phone on speaker and tucked it into her front pocket as she jogged through her house. She hauled two large travel cases from her closet then began throwing clothes and toiletries into one. Her brain felt as though it were buzzing, and she struggled to think through what needed to be brought. Clothes would be important. A couple of novels, too, to stop the boredom from setting in. She grabbed two off her shelf indiscriminately. She left her technology—laptop, kettle, and hair dryer—where they were. The bunker's power supplies would be limited. She couldn't afford to bring things that would drain it. All the while, the humming living room TV blended into the fragments of news stories floating through the phone.

Clare hauled the luggage—one empty, one full—out into the living room. She then flipped the spare case open in the kitchen and began dredging her nonperishable supplies into it. "Have you spoken to Marnie yet?"

"No." Bethany's voice crackled, and Clare had to strain to make out what she said. "I phoned you first."

"Call her. Let her know what's happening. I'll pick her up on my way through. There's room for a third person in the bunker, isn't there?"

"Yes. But she's nearly two hours away from you."

"It's fine. It's not even really that much out of my path. Call her. Make sure she'll be ready."

"All right." The phone beeped as it was disconnected. Clare had filled the luggage case with as much food as it would hold and hauled it through the front door.

Her little red car waited outside. She hadn't changed its wheels yet. There had been traces of frost and even one thin dusting of snow, but nothing significant. The sky was clear. She didn't think she would encounter any difficulties on the road to Bethany's.

Both sets of luggage went into the back seat. She opened the car's boot then ran back inside for the water. As she passed the TV, she kept one eye on the reports. The anchors were discussing the likelihood of chemical warfare.

She wanted to stay and hear what they said, but Beth had sounded frantic. The drive to her sister's house would take five hours if the roads were clear. She could listen to the news on the way.

Clare dragged two large water jugs outside. As she nudged the swinging screen door open, she was assaulted with a blast of chilled air. She looked up. The sky had been blue when she'd made her coffee. It had since turned a bitter gray.

She frowned at it as she heaved the water into the boot, then she returned inside for another lot. She *probably* wouldn't need the snow tires, at least not on the way to Beth's. If she ended up staying for a while, a few days or a few weeks, she might need them to get home.

Clare warred with herself as she brought out the second set of water. Changing the tires would waste time. But it might be a wise precaution, depending on how serious the situation turned out to be.

It felt surreal. She still held on to the idea that it might be some kind of misunderstanding. Some sort of elaborate April Fool's prank at the wrong time of the year. Or maybe there was a simple explanation for it all. Broken communication satellites. A solar flare. *Something.* Because entire cities couldn't just *vanish.*

Give it a couple of hours, and it will all make sense. You'll regret buying into the hysteria.

But something inside her told her she wouldn't. She could overprepare and look like an idiot when the whole thing turned out to be a mistake, or she could underprepare and risk regretting it later. The consequences of one were so much worse than the other.

As she slammed the last two jugs of water into the car's trunk, a speck of water hit her cheek. It was cold in the way that recently melted snow felt. The gray sky was turning thunderous.

Play it safe, Bethany's voice whispered. *Put the snow tires on.*

She'd gotten pretty efficient at changing the tires since moving to her cottage. Clare hauled them out of the shed and set about the task in something that looked like a frenzy. Dirt scuffed over her clothes, but she barely noticed.

By the time she'd fastened the final tire, snow was starting to fall in earnest. It had taken precious minutes, but it was better than becoming stranded in the middle of nowhere. She ran through a mental checklist. Clothes. Food. Water. Beth would provide the shelter. She just had to pick up Marnie on the way.

She slid into the driver's seat and turned the key.

CHAPTER 25

THE WINDSHIELD WIPERS MADE a rhythmic thumping noise as they fought to keep her front window clear. They were on the fastest setting, but it wasn't helping much.

The snowstorm had risen in what felt like no time at all. Even with the snow tires, the car was barely coping. Clare coaxed it along as quickly as she dared in the near-zero visibility.

She'd tried listening to the news reports on the radio until the distortion made them impossible to hear. No one could agree on what was happening. The quiet zones were spreading, with new ones appearing every minute. Anyone who was brave or foolish enough to go into them wasn't heard from again. A small handful of people were reported to have stumbled out of the affected areas, but they were delirious and incoherent. Beth said there was footage of a man being carried into a hospital by people in hazmat suits. He'd been writhing and screaming words that made no sense. Shortly after that footage was broadcast, the hospital's power had died and the people inside had stopped answering calls. It was declared a new quiet zone.

The phone in Clare's cup holder crackled, and Beth's voice came through, thin and broken. "It's too danger—s. Turn ba—"

"It's going to be okay." Clare prayed she was right. "I'm picking up Aunt Marnie. I'll be there before noon as long as none of the roads are closed. We'll phone you and make a new plan then."

Some people on the radio had claimed the stillness event was some kind of chemical warfare mixed with electromagnetic pulses. The attacks seemed centered on the largest cities. The few brave souls who lived on the edges of the quiet zones and refused to be evacuated shared videos of explosions and flashing lights. No airborne missiles or foreign planes had been detected, though. Most of the experts seemed to agree that it wasn't active bombing. But the most bizarre thing was that no one claimed responsibility. Every country capable of an attack on such a large scale had been affected.

Some people said it was end times, that the good were being sifted from the sinful. They said those who didn't believe would be left to suffer on earth. Others thought it was an alien invasion. Rumors were rife in laymen's circles. Beth had been repeating some of the tweets to Clare over the phone before the social media sites had gone down.

New information still dribbled in, but it was becoming harder and harder to verify as communication networks failed. Many claimed the military had been mobilized, but no one seemed to know against *what*.

The emergency response lines were begging people not to call them unless there was a life-threatening injury. Their lines had been swamped, and several of their operating centers had been swallowed by the quiet zones. The ones still operating urgently repeated that they were prioritizing life-and-death situations and were powerless to look for lost family and friends in the uncontactable areas. They weren't even responding to the mass lootings or rioting that was spreading through the remaining cities.

A dark, hulking shape emerged from the white on the side of the road, and Clare squinted as she tried to make it out. It was only when she was nearly beside it that she realized she was looking at two cars, parked end to end, with their doors open.

"Dangerous—" The phone's static was growing worse. "Don't—as—safe!"

Clare slowed to a crawl as she passed the cars. They were empty. The internal lights created a soft glow over the flecks of white and the children's toys bundled into one of the rear seats.

She pressed down on the accelerator to get back up to speed. The steady *thd thd thd* of the windshield wipers matched her heart rate. The phone's crackles no longer played in the background.

Clare reached for her phone blindly, not prepared to take her eyes off the road, and tried redialing. It refused to place the call.

"Come on," Clare whispered. She had a terrible mental image of Beth's suburb being swallowed and turned into a quiet zone.

Beth was smart. She would have run to her bunker at the first sign of danger. More likely, though, the phone lines had been overwhelmed, and the telecommunications networks had gone down.

She, Bethany, and Marnie should be safe, at least for a little while longer. The attacks—if that really was what they were—seemed to have been concentrated on cities and heavily populated areas. Clare's small family all lived on remote properties. There were no houses near Banksy Forest. They should still have time.

Something darted past the car, moving low to the ground. Clare reflexively twisted the steering wheel and barely managed to correct her course before the car began to spin. She pressed a hand to her thundering heart.

What was that? A fox?

She didn't have the luxury of time to focus on it. Shadows appeared in the distance, and Clare let out a sigh as she recognized the formation. She'd reached the edge of the Banksy Forest. And that meant safety…from the storm, at least.

As her car coasted into the trees, Clare took a fortifying breath. *We can do this. As long as the storm lets up before the roads are too choked. As long as there are no accidents blocking the streets. We can do this.*

She reached for the phone again but stopped before her fingers touched the metal. A strange noise surrounded her car. It sounded like the whirr of helicopter blades. Clare leaned close to the windshield and tried to look up, but she couldn't see anything through the forest's canopy.

Maybe that's the military response. Though what they're doing in this part of the country, I don't know.

Something darted across the road. Clare reflexively hit the brakes and grunted as the seat belt bit into her. She rocked back into her seat, breathing quickly, her heart galloping.

That wasn't a wolf. Or any other kind of animal.

She could have sworn the shape had been human. But he hadn't *looked* like any man she'd seen before. Wispy yellow hair hung to his bony shoulders, which jutted out strangely. His torn shirt had hung around his waist. And he'd been running on all fours.

Clare tightened her fingers on the steering wheel. Her mind was spiraling out in a hundred different directions. She'd been frightened that the call with Beth had cut off because Beth's home had been sucked into a quiet zone. But maybe that had been the wrong way of looking at it. *What if I'm in a quiet zone?*

Her heart hammered. She put pressure on the accelerator, making the tires dig through the thin layer of snow that had drifted through the canopy.

Something heavy slammed into the side of her car. Clare screamed. Bloodshot eyes pressed against the glass on the passenger's door. Long, scabbed fingers scrabbled at the glass. Terror overrode Clare's wits. She stomped on the accelerator. The engine screamed and shot her forward. The creature tried to cling on but dropped away within a few feet. Then another one hit the other side of her car.

There wasn't enough time to correct. Her car rose up onto the side of the road. A massive pine tree blocked her path. Clare tried to brake, but the tires had left the ground. She was powerless to do anything except hold on.

The front of her car crumpled in a wail of twisting metal and breaking pipes. Clare's jaw hit the edge of the steering wheel, then she was forced back into the seat as the airbag deployed.

It was all over in seconds. She was left gasping and shaking, staring over the deflating bag and through the cracked windshield at the mangled remains of her car's hood.

"No…" Clare's hands shook as she unclenched her death grip on the wheel. She felt dizzy. Shock blurred her senses, and it took a moment to feel the aches develop. Her neck hurt where her head had been wrenched forward and thrown back. A rib stung, and her jaw felt sore. But there was nothing worse. It was a small miracle, considering the state of her car. She looked down at her legs and confirmed they were still intact.

She turned to look through her side window. She could see the road in both directions. Her car's wheels had left imprints in the soft snow, clearly marking her trajectory where she'd veered off the path. There was no sign of anything else.

What was *that?*

She ran her trembling hand over her face then felt for the key. It turned in the ignition, but the car didn't respond. She tried twice more before letting the key go. Her car was dead. Even if she could walk out of the forest, she was miles from any kind of civilization. She needed some kind of rescue, but with the emergency response hotlines all busy, that could be a long time coming.

She had food and water in the car and would normally be

prepared to hunker down for however long it took for someone else to drive down the road. But not that day. Not with that *thing* out there.

Beth would come for her. Clare shuddered at the idea of asking her sister to leave her bunker in the middle of a global collapse, but Beth wasn't just the most reliable option—she was the *only* option. Clare looked for her phone. It had flown out of the cup holder during the collision. She doubted it would help anyway. It hadn't picked up any kind of signal since before she'd entered the forest.

She still had her shortwave radio, though. Tucked into its pouch in the trunk, it would still work even if every phone in the area was dead.

Clare pressed close to the driver's side window, scanning her environment. There was nothing on the roads. She couldn't see anything in the trees. She hated the idea of opening the door, but she doubted the situation would improve if she sat still. She set her jaw, braced herself, then threw open the door.

The temperature had dropped alarmingly since Clare had left home. She barreled into the snow, skidded, and caught her balance on the side of the car. The only thing she could hear was her rasping breathing and the whistle of the storm as it ripped at the upper levels of the forest.

She turned toward the trunk. Being outside the car left her feeling exposed and vulnerable. But she just had to grab the radio, then she could duck back inside into the car's relative warmth and safety.

A noise jangled through the frigid air as Clare passed the rear door. She felt her heart plummet as she looked up. A shape crouched on top of the car. The man's curly blond hair was bloody from where he'd smashed his head. His fingers were splayed across the cold metal, seemingly without feeling it. His bloodshot eyes bulged, and a trickle of red ran from his nose and across his bared teeth.

They made eye contact for a fraction of a second. Then Clare lunged back toward the open driver's door. He swiped at her, his fingers catching her jacket and yanking her back. Clare screamed. She hit the ground and rolled away reflexively. An instant later, the man landed where she'd just lain, his bare feet thudding into the snow.

"No." Clare scrambled back. A second figure emerged from the forest on the other side of the road. A woman. Her jaw hung limp as if dislocated, and it swung with every staggering step she took. Her head tilted to one side as she stared at Clare, and the drooping lips curved into a smile.

The man darted toward her. Clare threw out a foot. It connected with his chest but wasn't enough to throw him back. His fingers dug into her leg. The nails were long and sharper than Clare had expected. Her pant leg tore, and Clare shrieked as nails shredded her skin.

She rolled and kicked her other leg. This time, it hit the man's arm, bending the elbow in the wrong direction. He thrashed back, releasing her, and she crawled toward the car.

Her leg was on fire. The cuts weren't deep, but the pain was intense. She reached the driver's seat and used her arms to haul herself inside.

They were coming after her. Thundering through the snow, bodies contorted as they scuttled on all fours. Clare pulled her legs into the car and wrenched the door closed.

She was too slow. One of the man's bony hands caught on the door's edge, stopping it from shutting properly. Clare screamed and pulled harder, slamming the door on the hand. The fingers bulged and spasmed as she fractured bones. The pain didn't seem to reach the man, though. His face pressed close to the glass as he hissed and smeared his lips across the window.

The twisting, spasming fingers horrified Clare. She leaned back in the car, half into the passenger's seat, as she tried to use her body weight to pull the door closed. She couldn't take her eyes away from the broken digits that still seemed to reach for her.

The second creature slammed into the driver's door, and the impact nearly shook Clare's grip on the handle. The woman and the man jostled for space as the woman began worming her fingertips into the gaps left around the seal.

Clare shook her head, silently begging them to stop, begging them to leave. The woman adjusted her grip on the door. Then she pulled on it. Clare didn't stand a chance. The metal bent, distorting, as the two ghouls pried it open. Clare held her arm out ahead of herself, trying to shield her face, as they poured in through the opening.

There were fingers everywhere, scrabbling at her stomach, digging into her throat, and shredding her arm. Clare screamed and couldn't stop screaming as the pain blazed through her like wildfire. Blood gushed. Dripping down her arm. Soaking her clothes. She beat at the creatures, but they didn't seem to notice the blows.

Then a loud crack in the distance made them freeze. They turned their heads toward the sky, teeth bared in a snarl as they watched something Clare couldn't see. A steady *whmp whmp whmp* floated into her consciousness. *Helicopter blades.* They were growing nearer.

The creatures wailed. Their heads swiveled, and panic filled their wide eyes as they tried to escape the sound. Then they scuttled back, disappearing into the trees, leaving narrow trails of Clare's blood in their wake.

She slumped across the steering wheel. Pain blurred her vision. She felt sick and dizzy. She tried to lift her arm, but it wasn't responding properly.

For a brief second, she imagined the helicopter might be coming for her. Maybe Beth had realized what had happened. Maybe she'd managed to convince someone to look for Clare.

The delusion didn't last long. The noise passed overhead then receded. Clare closed her eyes. The pain was fading as shock set in properly. She could feel the blood dripping, though. Dripping over her seat, over the floor, and running into her shoe. That upset her more than it really had any right to. The shoes were only a few weeks old. She'd been trying so hard not to let them get muddy, but she'd ruined them with a bit of careless bleeding.

A strangled laugh gurgled out of her. Then she scrunched

her face up as she battled tears. *I don't want to die like this. Beth will worry.*

Through the fog of pain and fading consciousness, she thought she saw a light in the distance. It bounced as it moved down the road, slowly growing nearer. She vaguely wondered if that was death coming for her. She'd thought it would be more dramatic.

A figure appeared behind the light. A tall man, too far away to make out any features. He slowed down as he saw her car then increased his pace to a jog. His flashlight jostled with each step.

Clare couldn't keep her eyes open any longer.

CHAPTER 26

CLARE RESTED HER FOREHEAD against the car's roof. She was shaking but, in spite of the cold weather, felt far too hot.

The missing hours had come back to her, but that didn't mean they were easy to accept. She couldn't visualize the images on the TV or the shapes running through the snow without feeling like she was reliving a feverish dream.

But then she remembered what she'd seen in Winterbourne. The woman with the hole in her side, ribs poking out like feathers, and the figure with the broken spine that jutted through her skin. They looked less human than whatever had attacked her in the snow, but she was certain they were the same breed.

Clare moaned. She had spent the past week afraid that she was delusional. But as her memories resurfaced, she thought she would have preferred insanity. Because being right—seeing what she had seen and piecing it together with what Beth had said and what had been on TV—created a reality that she wasn't sure she could exist in.

Dorran. Her heart missed a beat. He would have been traveling to Gould in his family's convoy at the time of the stillness event. His mother refused to let them listen to radios. He'd never heard the news reports.

And he was still in the mansion, trapped with the creatures. They had found a way to hide, and they were clearly reluctant to be seen. But they were there, and it was only a matter of time before they turned on him. She had to go back. Even if she couldn't convince him of what she'd seen, she needed to find some way to keep him safe.

Clare turned toward the forest separating her from Winterbourne Hall. In the space between the closest trees, two round, bright eyes stared at her.

The world seemed to slow down. A fleck of snow spiraled past, twirling in the gentle wind, taking an eternity to reach the ground.

The man from her memories crouched among the pines. His eyes were huge and staring. He'd lost the remainder of his clothes, but he seemed wholly unaware of his nakedness and the cold that had turned his fingers and toes black.

One hand was spread on the ground, fingers splayed for balance. The other was balled into a clawlike fist. It reminded Clare of a pigeon she'd seen with a broken foot—and a moment later, she realized that was exactly what it was. The fingers were broken from being slammed in the car door. They'd curled into a twisted mess of flesh and shattered bone, but he still walked on the hand.

That wasn't the only change. The tips of his collarbones had jutted out from his hollow chest wall. His ribs seemed to have sunken in. When he moved, his hip bones strained against the thin layer of skin covering them, seemingly threatening to split it.

There was no way he should have still been alive. But he was. And his lips pulled back from receding gums as he stared at Clare.

No. Please. Not again.

She ran, kicking up a plume of snow as she plunged back onto the road and aimed for the bank of trees opposite him. A horrible clattering noise rose from the forest. Clare looked up. Two shapes moved through the trees, leaping from bough to bough—a large one with long hair and something small. A child still wearing the scraps of a brightly colored shirt.

Clare twisted away and tried to run along the road. It was bare except for the endless expanse of snow. She was too exposed. She had to get to the forest—either side—and find something to use as a weapon. Something to shield herself with.

A noise came from her side. The man raced parallel to her, moving on all fours like a broken cat. He lunged at Clare, his mouth open, and she gasped as she pulled back, out of his reach. He skidded on the snow, trying to right himself, as the woman leaped out of a tree.

Clare had no choice—she reversed her direction, racing back to the car. She could hear the creatures chattering behind her as they followed. Weariness dragged her down. Her mouth was so dry that every breath felt like swallowing sandpaper. But fear kept her moving. The healing cuts on her stomach and leg ached, a threat of what was to come if she was too slow. She hit the open car door, swung around it, and barreled inside.

The car jolted as the creatures impacted it. The door was already bent and wouldn't close. Clare just tried to pull it as near to shut as she could. Then she leaped across the bloodied driver's seat and fell into the passenger's side.

Metal cried as the door was wrenched back open. Clare grabbed the passenger's door handle and shoved. She tumbled through the hole then kicked at the door, smacking it shut in the creatures' faces.

Both the man and woman had tried to follow her through the car. They pressed against the closed door, fingers and teeth clacking against the glass. Neither tried to use the handle. Like she'd thought, they'd lost their humanity and, with it, their intelligence.

Clare struggled onto shaking feet and clutched at the closest tree. Her heart felt ready to burst, but she couldn't rest. The car wouldn't contain the creatures for long. She checked that she still had the radio tucked into her jacket then turned.

Deep snow covered the forest floor in that part of the woods, and Clare struggled over trees and between trunks. She passed a low, dead branch, half-detached from its tree, and gave it a wrench to snap it off. It was heavy and unwieldy, but it would work as a weapon. Her main priority had to be getting back to shelter as quickly as she could.

A shriek made her freeze. She looked back to where the car was barely visible through the forest. It no longer rocked as the monsters tried to free themselves. She couldn't see through the window, but she thought it was empty.

They had gotten out faster than she'd hoped. Clare started running, praying she was moving in the right direction to reach the clearing and Winterbourne. She was struggling, though. And she thought she could hear more noises—more of the creaking, scratching sounds of branches being bowed as a creature clambered through them.

Something grabbed her foot, and Clare yelled as she fell. She rolled onto her back. Bones rippled under the man's emaciated skin as he clawed at her leg, shredding her pants with his too-sharp nails.

Clare swung her branch at him. The blackened wood hit him squarely on his jaw, and his head rocked back. It didn't stop him, though. He kept digging at her torso. Scrabbling. Tearing. Clare felt the sting of cut flesh and swung her weapon again.

That time, the contact was vicious enough to knock him off. His broken hand spasmed as he tumbled back. Clare tried to rise to her feet so she could put some distance between them, but another figure hit her before she could move.

Long hair caught in Clare's face. She gagged as its rancid scent choked her. The creature bit into her wrist, and Clare screamed.

Then, suddenly, the pressure was off her. Clare was vaguely aware of a heavy cracking sound and a blur of motion. Then a voice yelled something.

"Ah!" Clare hissed in pain as she tried to open her eyes. A hand touched her shoulder, and she thrashed away, trying to escape it.

"It's all right! It's just me!" Dorran crouched over her, one hand on her shoulder, the other holding a bloody shovel. His eyes were wide with fear, and his breathing was ragged. Then he looked up, and his expression tightened as he swung the shovel again.

It hit the man, who had been crawling over the closest snowbank. His head snapped back then rolled as the neck broke.

Clare waited for him to drop. But he didn't. The man's head had tilted completely back. It faced the sky, his eyes wide and jaw slack. The back of his head rested between his shoulder blades. The skin on his neck, stretched taunt, quivered as he tried to make a noise. But he stayed upright, arms and legs spread wide to hold himself up, and began scuttling toward them.

Dorran made a horrified choking noise. He stepped over Clare and swung again. The shovel hit the man's shoulder. The opposite shoulder blade finally cut through the skin, unleashing a glut of dark blood. The bone had grown sharp, almost knife-like, and the skin flaps jiggled around it like gory jelly.

A chattering noise made Clare turn. The woman was coming back. Her broken jaw still hung loose, and the black maw of her mouth stretched horribly wide. Her hair had fallen out, save for a few sparse clumps, and like the man, she had grown bone thin. All that remained from her prior identity was a scrap of floral dress dangling from her neck.

Dorran still faced the man. The second creature was almost

on them. Clare grabbed her branch, but instead of swinging, she pointed it straight ahead and pushed it forward to meet the woman.

The sharp tip plunged into the woman's chest, between her breasts, making sickening cracking noises as the brittle bones broke. The impact forced the air out of Clare as she was knocked to the ground.

The woman lurched back, standing tall, her lips widening then pursing again. The stick protruded from her chest like a pole. Then her eyes locked on Clare, and she pitched forward. Clare yelled and lifted her feet to protect herself. The stick hit the sole of one shoe, and Clare kicked as hard as she could.

The branch made a ghastly sluicing noise as it cut through the woman's body. The sharpened end poked out of her back, drenched in blood. The woman staggered then righted herself. Clare felt a moment of sheer horror as she thought even that would not be enough. Then the woman tumbled and fell facedown onto the snow. Her body twitched twice then went still.

Clare turned. Dorran stood a few paces away, panting. His own assailant lay crumpled on the ground. What had once been a head was a bloody paste. Bone fragments and brain matter mixed into the snow.

Dorran dropped the shovel and turned to Clare. He took an unsteady step toward her then dropped to his knees, holding out his hands.

She crawled to him and tried not to cry as he pulled her close against his chest. One hand tightened around her back, clutching her desperately, and the other stroked her hair. "I am so sorry," he whispered.

Clare held him in a fierce embrace. He was sweaty and shaky, but so was she.

"I am sorry for doubting you." Desperate words tumbled out of him, and she thought he might have been practicing them on the walk through the forest. "I am sorry for yelling. And I am especially sorry for telling you to get out. I did not mean to make you leave the house. I did not *want* you to leave. I was not thinking rationally."

She shook her head, trying to tell him it was all right. Words had become choked in her throat. The argument in the garden felt like it had happened half a lifetime ago. She didn't care about it anymore. She was just grateful Dorran had come after her.

He pulled back. Dark eyes searched her face. One hand brushed over her cheek then ran over her neck, which was scratched. Then he looked down and saw the blood dripping off her wrist, and his eyes tightened. "You're hurt."

"Not bad." She tried to hide it under her jacket sleeve. "I can't really feel it anymore."

He picked up her hand, gently peeled back the jacket, and examined it. Then he looked around them, first at the impaled woman then at the man he'd killed. His composure wavered, then he blinked rapidly, and it was restored. "We need to get back to the house."

"Yes." The shock was starting to fade, and Clare was beginning to feel the implications of what had happened. "Yes—quickly. These two aren't the only ones."

He tightened his arms around her and lifted her as he stood. "Can you walk?"

She thought so. "Yes."

"Stay close to me." Dorran scooped the bloodied shovel off the ground. Clare's radio had fallen out of her jacket during the scuffle. She picked it up and prayed it hadn't been damaged as she tucked it back into place.

Dorran then put his spare arm around Clare's back. He paused for a moment, his eyebrows pulled low as he listened to the forest. Then he nodded to her and began leading them between the trees.

CHAPTER 27

THE AIR FELT UNNATURALLY still. All Clare could hear were the crunching footsteps and their gasping breaths. She tried to move quickly to keep up with Dorran, but her legs weren't obeying her commands properly. Dorran matched her pace, though. When she started to struggle, he looped his arm under hers so that she could lean on him. His eyes never stopped scanning for movement among the patchy white-and-black landscape.

Clare's mind began to make connections. Shortly before driving into Banksy Forest, she'd passed the two cars pulled over onto the side of the road. The doors had been left open, and the rear seat of the larger car had held an assortment of toys. One had been a distinctive caterpillar-like creature suspended from a hook above the window. She was sure the same design had been emblazoned onto the monstrous child's shirt. It had been discolored and torn in the weeks spent in the forest, but it was unmistakable.

Nausea surprised Clare, and she stumbled to a halt as she tried not to be sick. Dorran supported her, one arm around her and the other rubbing her shoulder as she regained her composure.

"All right?" he asked.

She nodded and fixed her eyes on the path ahead.

The creatures were like something out of a fever dream. But it was a hundred times worse to know that they had once been real people not much different than her. They had been in their car, trying to travel to safety, to seek shelter from the events sweeping the world.

Clare didn't know why they had been caught and she had been spared. She had the awful idea that it came down to dumb luck. They had just been on that stretch of road at the wrong time.

She wished she knew how it had happened. Whatever *it* was. A gas, maybe. A beam. Some kind of radiation. She didn't know. She wasn't certain she would ever know. All of those thoughts could be saved for later when they were out of the forest.

The trees creaked. Clare's heart dropped as she looked behind them. Dorran had heard it, too, and he craned his neck. The environment was still and quiet. He waited a second, then he tucked the shovel under his arm, bent, and picked Clare up.

She gasped as the earth was pulled away from her feet. The dizziness grew worse, and she had to squeeze her eyes closed until it abated. "I...I can still walk."

"Faster this way," he muttered.

He was right. Clare knew it must be taxing him, but he increased his speed to a jog. The motion was smoother than she'd expected. He loped through the forest, his steps even and reliable, his head ducked to avoid the lowest branches, and Clare tucked tightly against his shoulder.

She thought she could see some lightness ahead. Inside the forest, even the snow seemed to take on a dingy shade. They had to be facing the clearing surrounding Winterbourne.

The creaking noise grew louder. Clare looked up and saw a spindly shape scuttling through the boughs. Its limbs were far too long. Its arm span must have been nearly eight feet, and it was using its increased reach to lurch from branch to branch like a deformed monkey.

"Dorran—"

"I see it." He kept his head down but tilted to the side, one eye on the trees above them. Each breath sounded painful and raw, but his speed didn't slow.

They broke through the trees at the edge of Banksy Forest. Winterbourne Hall sat ahead, huddled in its blankets of white. Its dead, cold windows followed their movements like eyes. The distance between them and the mansion seemed immense.

Dorran staggered as the snow thickened, and he sank into it up to his knees.

"I had snowshoes," Clare said.

"Yes." Each word was punctuated by a gasp. "Me as well. Where?"

She scanned the forest's edge, trying to pinpoint the place she'd entered. Tracks marked the clear blanket of snow, arcing from Winterbourne across the field until they terminated at the forest's edge nearly forty paces away. "There!"

Dorran still watched the woman above them. She'd stopped moving and was crouched in one of the trees above their heads. Bony knees jutted out wide, and her arms dangled as she watched them. Clare couldn't see her expression, but her eyes flashed in the low light.

She was more cautious than her companions had been. That worried Clare. The woman seemed to have retained at least part of her mind—whether it was intelligence or purely instinctual, Clare didn't know. But it made the woman unpredictable.

Clare could feel Dorran weighing up the risk of going for the snowshoes versus trying to run across the field. The battle lasted for only a second. He turned and stepped back into the woods, where he could walk along the edge more easily than wading through the snow.

The woman followed them. A tremor ran through Clare as she realized the long-armed creature wasn't alone. Chattering, whispering noises echoed out from between the trees. A new pair of eyes glistened from around a trunk. She tried to count the creatures, but it was hard to follow the motion in the tangle of black branches.

Dorran re-emerged from the forest's edge. He'd judged the distance well and came out almost beside the snowshoes. There was only one pair, though. He lowered Clare to the ground then swung the shovel around to hold it defensively. "Put them on."

"What about you?"

"I need you to trust me." He didn't move, but his eyes

continuously roved across the forest. "I can keep you safe. But you will need to run for the house."

She swallowed. "Who will keep *you* safe? You can't fight those things alone."

"We do not have time to argue."

"Then let me help."

The corners of his lips twitched. "Ah, Clare. I will let you win as many arguments as you like once we are back in the house. But you *must* trust me, just this once. Put the shoes on. Run. Do not look back."

Despite the smile, she could sense how tense he was. Sweat glistened on his forehead as he faced the forest. The denizens were creeping closer, growing bolder. There were at least five of them. She threw the shoes down and began strapping them on.

"You have to promise you're going to make it back." The words choked her as she struggled to tie the shoes with shaking hands. "I'm not living in that house without you. I'm not dealing with…*this* without you. So you've got to be safe. Okay?"

He stayed facing the forest, his feet braced, standing between her and the chattering in the trees. "I will. Now go. *Run.*"

Clare pulled on the last of her energy to race across the field. The snowshoes were unwieldy. They threatened to tangle her, to trip her, and she kept her eyes fixed on her feet as she ran.

Snarling noises came from behind her, but when she tried to turn her head to see what had happened, she nearly lost her balance. The *thwack* of a shovel hitting something solid echoed through the cold air.

He wants me to trust him. I can. I will. She put her head down and focused on moving toward the house. In the distance, the sky had darkened as another storm developed. It would be the second in two days.

Please be safe, Dorran. Please, know what you're doing.

She heard the crack of breaking wood followed by a scream. That was almost enough to stop her. But the scream had a guttural, animalistic undertone that told her it hadn't come from Dorran.

Clare reached the end of the field and leaped into the snow-coated courtyard. Her head buzzed from the exertion, but she was close. The dark front door was visible ahead, half-buried under the snow.

Thunder crackled in the distance. When she'd left her old home, the news reports had talked about erratic weather. She guessed that was what had come over the property the past few weeks—unpredictable switches of storms, hail, and snow, all encapsulated in abnormally low temperatures.

She clambered up the slope created by the front stairs and collapsed as she reached the door. Her lungs ached. Her throat burned. But she'd made it. Dorran had left the double doors open when he left. Clumps of snow dotted the marble floor in the foyer.

Clare finally allowed herself to look back. Dorran was slowly weaving his way across the field. But so were a cluster of dark, twisted shapes.

"Oh…" Using the stone walls for support, Clare stood.

Dorran backed toward the house, moving cautiously but steadily. Anytime one of the creatures drew too close, he swung his shovel at them. Twice, he hit his mark and knocked them down. More often than not, he missed.

Clare realized he wasn't trying to hit them. There were eight of the creatures. Trying to battle all of them at once would have been suicide. Every time he swung the shovel, though, the crowd would back off, allowing Dorran to gain another few feet.

Clare pressed a hand to her throat. If Dorran could just get to the front door, he could drop inside the house, and they could slam the wooden slabs shut. The creatures would still be outside, but she and Dorran should be relatively safe in the building. At least for a few days...until their food ran out.

She tried not to think about that. Dorran's tactic was risky. He was slow, trying to move through the thick snow and keep the creatures at bay at the same time. They weren't as mindlessly obsessed as the first two monsters that had attacked Clare, and they weren't rushing forward recklessly. Occasionally, one would try to creep around the group to get at Dorran's back, and he had to dance away to keep them all within sight. She didn't know if he had the energy to ward them off until he reached the house.

"Come on," she whispered. Once he got closer, she would be able to help. She could find a weapon or distract the creatures by throwing something at them. But he was still too far out for her to do anything, and he was drifting away from the front door.

Clare took a step forward, confusion and panic catching in her throat. Instead of aiming for the house's front, Dorran had speared off to the side. She couldn't tell if the creatures had managed to herd him off course or if he'd become disoriented. As far as she knew, there was no entrance to Winterbourne in the direction he was moving. Just endless windows, all locked. *And the pond.*

When Clare craned her neck, she could see the hollow in the snow. Dorran had told her to avoid the area. The excess warmth from the garden room was piped outside near the pond. The ice would be unstable.

Clever, Dorran.

He passed behind the snow-frosted hedges. Clare, unwilling to let him out of sight but also conscious of her promise to stay in the house, slipped through the open doorway. Her sore feet ached as they jarred on the marble floor. She pushed the doors closed so that passing eyes wouldn't think there was a way into the house but left them unlocked in case Dorran needed to make a hasty retreat. Then she kicked off her snowshoes as quickly as she could and jogged through the house.

Despite the time she'd spent in the manor, she still wasn't familiar with its layout. She thought she could visualize the path she needed to take, though. She burst through one of the doors and into the dining room. The immense space stretched along one side of the house, overlooking the front gardens. And, like Clare had hoped, it had a view of the pond.

She ran across the room, pressing close to the tall, narrow windows as she watched Dorran's progress. He seemed to be flagging. His broad shoulders shook, and when he swiped the shovel, the movements lacked their earlier intensity. But he'd managed to lead the monsters on without letting any of them circle around him. Clare bit her thumb as she watched.

The snow dipped down over the pond, and Dorran let himself skid down the side. As he came to a halt in the basin, his movements slowed and became much more cautious. He lowered his body and used a hand to help disperse his weight as he crept back toward the building.

It was a gamble. He was banking on the idea that the ice was melted enough to crack when eight emaciated bodies weighed it down but wasn't thin enough to drop him in too. He'd asked her to trust him. He wasn't making it easy.

Clare pressed close to the window. Dorran moved incredibly slowly. The humanoid creatures were gaining on him. They didn't seem to realize what he was doing, and in their eyes, it must have looked like Dorran's energy reserves were gone. One of them got near enough to bite at his leg. He jabbed the shovel at it, and it backed off, teeth bared.

Now that they were closer, Clare could see the malformed bodies. They were walking nightmares. The closest one, the one who had tried to bite Dorran, had meters of excess skin. The flaps hung loose, like a blanket wrapped around the body and pinned at strange places. Whenever the creature moved, the flaps swung like pendulums. Holes pocked the skin. Clare thought she saw maggots squirming inside one of them.

Another creature scuttled closer. Its lower teeth had grown horribly long. Three of them had pierced its upper jaw and poked out through the cheeks. The skin around them trembled every time the being breathed.

Dorran had passed the halfway point in the lake. He looked down then back up. Clare felt her stomach drop. The monsters gathered together, keeping in a group, but their combined weight wasn't enough to break the ice.

Maybe he miscalculated. Maybe the vent wasn't hot enough. Maybe the lake is still frozen solid or has five feet of ice that won't crack, no matter what.

Dorran stood. Clare guessed what he was about to do. She yelled and banged her open hand on the window. He turned, looked at her, and gave her a very small smile. Then he lifted the shovel and slammed its edge down onto the ice.

Clare heard the cracking noises even through the window. Dorran took a step back as the frozen surface under his feet lurched.

The creatures sensed their moment of opportunity and swarmed forward. Shards of ice burst upward as the lake's surface broke, showering little specks of snow across the scene. Then they all, monsters and human, plunged into the lake.

CHAPTER 28

"NO!" CLARE BEAT HER fist against the glass. Jets of water sprayed up as the nine bodies disappeared into the lake. Dorran wasn't surfacing.

The front door was too far away. Clare tore off her gloves. Numb fingers scrambled along the window's edge and found the latch. It was fused closed from disuse and cold. She wrenched on it until the glass cracked and the latch finally gave way. Then she kicked at the window frame, forcing it open, and climbed onto the sill.

Dorran surfaced, black hair plastered over his face. He coughed violently, reaching for the shore. The ice, already fractured, broke under his hands.

Hold on. Please, please, hold on.

She wouldn't be able to get close enough to pull him out without being sucked into the lake as well. Desperation pulsed through her as she searched for something—anything—she could throw to Dorran. The serving tables were too large and heavy. The chairs were too short. The curtains...

The curtains might just do.

The windows were massively tall, and the curtains had been designed to match. The vivid red cloth had to be close to fifteen feet from floor to ceiling. Clare grabbed the nearest bunch. It was thick, heavier than was ideal, but there was no time to look for something better. She yanked on it. The curtain rods were well-made and barely bowed. Clare wrapped her arms around the fabric and leaped off the windowsill, using her weight to pull them down.

The wooden rods cracked and broke, and Clare tumbled to the ground in a flurry of fabric and clatter of metal rings. She rolled, regained her feet, bundled the cloth up, and threw it through the window.

Dorran clawed at the edges of the lake. Icy water surrounded him in a maze of blue and fractured blocks of white. Every time he gained an inch, the snow gave way and dropped him back in.

Clare ran, struggling through the thick snow and dragging the curtain with her. She stopped where the snowbank sloped down to the water's edge and bundled the curtain up.

"Dorran!" She didn't know if he could hear her, but she threw one end of the fabric. It spiraled out, unraveling as it tumbled, and slapped into the water near Dorran. He grabbed it. Clare tightened her grip on the other end then leaned back and pulled.

Slowly, agonizingly, Dorran began to emerge from the lake. He kicked to help push himself out while Clare tilted backward. Her tired muscles screamed. She stumbled, dropping Dorran back by half a foot. Then she collected herself and redoubled her efforts.

He coughed, hacking up water as he gained solid ground. Once he was free, he fell to his side.

Clare let go of her end of the cloth and scrambled down to Dorran. He was shaking uncontrollably, and his eyes were closed. He looked completely spent. She dropped to her knees at his side, gripped his wet shirt, and shook him. "Dorran. Dorran. You have to get up."

His eyes cracked open.

"Please." She ran her fingers across his forehead, pushing the drenched hair away from his face. He felt like ice. "I can't carry you. You have to get up. The house is close."

"I am sorry." The words came out as a gasp through chattering teeth. "I am sorry. I tried. I...I am sorry."

"Dorran?"

His eyes lost their focus. Terror hit Clare, thick enough to choke her. She grabbed Dorran's collar and shook him hard, trying to keep him awake.

A hissing, clicking noise came from the lake behind them. One of the creatures had reached the shore. It clawed at the snow mindlessly, its fingers frozen stiff.

Clare's throat closed with panic. Moisture stung her eyes.

Dorran was breathing thin gasps that sounded raw and painful, but he wasn't moving. The water leaking from his clothes was turning to rivulets of ice among the snow.

"*Dorran!*" She screamed his name, her voice breaking. "*Get up, get up, move!*"

He took a ragged breath, and his eyes opened. They were dull, exhausted, and resigned. He didn't *want* to fight anymore.

No. Don't leave me here. She pulled on his shirt, trying to drag him toward the house. "Please. Please. Get up. I need you. Please."

"Nh." He pressed one hand into the snow and tried to rise but collapsed back down.

Clare wrapped her arms around him. He felt like winter. Her hands turned numb as she grasped fistfuls of his shirt and tried to lift. "Come on. Again."

He lurched onto his knees. Clare tried not to gasp. Icy water drained from his clothes, seeping into her jacket and turning to frost on the zipper. She tightened her hold.

"A bit more. I won't leave you. Just…just keep trying."

A grunt of pain escaped him as he staggered onto his feet. Clare kept her arms wrapped tightly around him, carrying as much of his weight as she could. She dragged him toward the open window. One of his hands gripped her shoulder hard enough to leave a bruise. He didn't know how tightly he was holding her, and Clare didn't try to stop him. The ache lent her focus.

"Just a bit more." Her voice cracked. She didn't know how she was going to get Dorran through the window. The door was too far away. But she *had* to get him inside.

Think, Clare!

Dorran unexpectedly let go of her. He reached forward and grasped the sill then pulled himself onto it.

He had no strength left to climb, so instead, he fell. He hit the floor of the dining room with a horrible thud. Clare followed him, clambering over the sill, shaking. She slammed the windowpane shut behind them. In the distance, the lake edge shimmered in the pale light, a sheet of ice already reforming. The sole surviving monster clung to the shore, its arms coated in ice and cemented to the ground. Its head continued to move, though, as its jaw twisted and gnashed.

"We did it. We're okay." Clare bent and touched Dorran's face. He didn't respond. Her smile faded, and she shook his shoulder to rouse him. "Dorran?"

He was still breathing, but he wasn't moving. Her heart squeezed, the relief vanishing. He needed warmth. Clare looked toward the dining room door. The bedroom was heated, but they were separated from it by two flights of stairs.

The dining room had its own fireplace, but it was stone cold. Clare had no other options, though. She ran to the hearth and shoveled the kindling inside. Numb fingers struggled to light a match, and it took her three attempts to get the fire started. Mist rolled away from her lips with every breath.

It won't be enough. Come on, Clare. How do you treat hypothermia? You know this.

She returned to Dorran. He lay beneath the window, his clothes dripping water across the tile floor. She rushed to pull his boots off then unbuttoned his jacket and shirt. She couldn't lift him high enough to get the clothes off his arms.

The nearby serving table had a cupboard underneath. She

crawled to it and wrenched the door open. Inside were utensils, including a carving knife. She flexed her grip on the handle as she moved back to Dorran.

Be careful. Your hands are shaking. Don't cut him.

She pressed the blade against his throat, near the collar. He flinched. It was a small movement, but Clare took a shuddering breath. She began cutting.

The fabric was a thick weave, but the blade was sharp. Clare sawed through the shirt's sleeves then turned to Dorran's pants. She didn't dare touch his underwear, but everything else came off.

"Okay. Okay." Clare dropped the knife. The scraps of fabric lay underneath Dorran. His skin, still damp, was an unnatural white-gray color, the same shade as a corpse.

Get him off the tiles. Clare dragged her fingers through her hair as she looked around. Her lips trembled as she fought to keep frightened tears inside. The fireplace had a rug in front of it. The mat was thick and covered in a twisting pattern of blues and golds. Clare grabbed it and dragged it back to the window to position it at Dorran's side.

She got her arms around him again, fighting her impulse to recoil from his cold flesh. He was heavy, but Clare didn't give up until he was fully off the tiles. He fit on the rug without much room left. Breathing heavily from the exertion, she let him go then tilted his head back, ensuring that his airways would be open.

What next? What does he need?

"Heat," Clare whispered. The fire's blaze was still young but growing. Clare gripped the rug's edge above Dorran's head, then leaned back, gasping and struggling as she pulled it across the tiles. She got him to the space in front of the fire, as close as she could manage, then dropped down beside him, exhausted.

Don't stop. Find blankets.

She winced as she returned to her feet. Her fingers were burning as exertion forced hot blood into her cold hands. Her mind was scattered, pushed to breaking from fear and exhaustion, but she pressed it to work, to remember what she needed, as she crossed the foyer and climbed the stairs. She found blankets in the upstairs bedroom and towels in the bathroom. She filled a pot with water and snatched their dressing gowns off the bedroom door on the way out.

The water sloshed and threatened to spill, and Clare's teeth began to ache where she was clenching them. She stumbled down the stairs, too frantic to be safe, and made it back to the dining room. As she closed the door behind her, she craned her neck to see Dorran by the fire.

He's not breathing.

A metallic tang flooded her mouth as she bit her tongue. She staggered forward, the pot's water dripping over her arms as it tipped. She left her burdens on the floor and knelt next to Dorran. Her fingers shook as they pressed against his chest. If there was any warmth left in him, she couldn't feel it.

"No, no—"

He drew breath. It was shallow and weak, but not yet gone. Clare rocked forward, gasping from relief.

Heat. Hurry.

The fire was gaining momentum as it consumed the kindling. Clare shoved small pieces of wood onto it and set the pot of water beside the flames to heat. Then she grabbed one of the towels from the pile beside her. She dug it into Dorran's long black hair, squeezing to get the water out. He made a small noise in the back of his throat.

"You're okay." Clare leaned over him, her face above his. Dark shadows framed his closed eyes. His lips were blue. "I'm here. You're going to be okay."

Clare turned toward the pot in the fire. It wasn't quite boiling, but steam rose from the surface. She picked up a fresh towel and dipped it into the water, heating it, then draped it over Dorran's throat, where the warmth would reach his core faster. She held it there until it started to cool, then returned it to the pot to heat again.

Please, this has to be enough.

Images of frostbite ran through her mind. She wanted to wrap Dorran's hands and feet in warm towels, but Bethany's sharp voice rang through her mind. She'd heard that lecture many times: heating extremities too quickly would cause more damage. The best she could do for him was to get his core warm first.

Shivers racked Clare. The fire's heat kissed her skin, but her own clothes were still damp. As she left the heated towel on Dorran to warm him, Clare shuffled back and quickly undressed down to her underwear. She wrapped one of the gowns around herself, tied it tightly, then took the wet towel away from Dorran's throat and dabbed the skin dry.

It wouldn't help to cover him yet. The fire's glow was warming him better than the blankets could, so she left him exposed to it. But his right side, the one facing away from the fire, was left cold.

Clare shook out the blankets then carefully lowered herself to the rug beside Dorran. She wrapped the blankets around her own back, then shuffled forward to share her body heat.

Embarrassed, but too afraid of what would happen if she didn't, Clare undid the dressing gown and pressed herself against him. His arm lay along her stomach, the cold fingers resting on her thighs. She resisted the urge to move away from his chilled body and curled forward, resting one leg against Dorran's and placing her hand on his chest. She could feel him breathing under her fingers.

She closed her eyes and whispered against his shoulder, "Please don't leave me."

He was still cold, but she thought she was starting to feel traces of warmth beneath his skin.

Clare didn't mean to fall asleep. But as a storm moved in over Winterbourne and the patter of hail began to drift through the stone walls, she found she had no more strength to keep her eyes open.

Finally giving in to the weariness, she let the noises of the house flow around her. The crackling fire. The sharp pipe of the wind funneling through gaps in the roof. And the clattering as the windows rattled, which sounded far too much like overgrown fingernails tapping to be let in.

CHAPTER 29

"HMM." CLARE SQUINTED HER eyes open. Straight ahead, her fire roared. More wood had been fed into it since she'd fallen asleep, and the heat was enough to not only warm her, but most of the dining room as well.

The curtains had been drawn over the windows, blocking the view of the gardens. Only the window with the broken curtain rod was uncovered. The storm battered snow against the glass, the white flecks half-hidden by fallen night. The dining room lights had been turned on, and the room felt safe and comfortable.

Clare tilted her head back. Dorran sat by her head, wearing the gown she'd brought him. His long legs were stretched toward the fireplace. He looked like himself again. Symptoms of exhaustion lingered in the lines around his mouth, but the color had returned to his skin, and the alertness was back in his eyes.

His hair was nearly fully dry, and he'd pushed it back from his forehead, leaving the sharp angles of his face clear. He smiled down at her. "Hello. How do you feel?"

"Hey. I'm good." Relief ran through Clare, burning her throat. She tried to sit up but stopped as she realized her dressing gown was still undone. Dorran had draped a blanket over her to cover her. She hurried to tie the gown, heat blooming across her face. She hadn't meant to fall asleep. Or for Dorran to wake while she was still lying next to him.

"I owe you thanks." Dorran turned away while she fastened her gown, and leaned toward the fire, stoking the coals. He either hadn't noticed her embarrassment or was pretending he hadn't. At least she could always count on him to be a gentleman. "I would not have made it back inside without you or survived the cold without your help."

"I didn't do anything special." Clare shuffled onto her knees and wrapped her arms around herself.

"On the contrary." Dorran moved back to sit at her side, close enough that their shoulders would have brushed if she leaned toward him. A small smile lifted the corners of his mouth. "You were incredible."

Clare suddenly felt too warm. Dorran held a bowl toward her, filled with water from the pot by the fire. She hadn't realized how thirsty she was until then. She drank until she felt sick. As she lowered the bowl, she realized Dorran was still watching her. His lips parted a fraction, as though he were on the edge of speaking, but he exhaled and looked away instead.

A vicious gust of wind screamed around the house. The windows shook, their frames clattering. Dorran's expression darkened.

Clare felt her uneasiness return. "Is something wrong? Are you hurt?"

"No. I am fine." He tried to smile again. "Just…attempting to reconcile myself to a world where monsters exist."

The gust faded, and the eerie silence returned, lying thick through the house. Still fogged from sleep, Clare's mind balked at the memory of the creatures. It felt more like a distant nightmare than reality. She closed her eyes and forced the words out. "I remembered what happened on that last day. The day you found me. I was driving to my sister's. She has a bunker."

Dorran inclined his head to show he was listening, but he didn't try to interrupt her. He must have sensed how difficult she was finding it to recount her experience.

"Something happened that morning. I don't know what, but it was all over the news. Areas were becoming uncontactable. They called them 'quiet zones.' Phones stopped working, Wi-Fi stopped working, and people who went into those areas didn't come out again." She pulled her knees under her chin and watched her toes curl on the rug. "They don't know what it was, whether it was a war or a natural phenomenon or what."

"So you were traveling to your sister's to be together, to be safe."

"Right. But on the way there, I think I entered one of the quiet zones. My phone disconnected. And then…" She took a breath and dragged her fingers through her hair. "Those things drove my car off the road. Whatever happens in the quiet zones, they were caught up in it. I guess it changed them somehow. I don't know into what. They're not human anymore, though."

Dorran let the silence rest over them for a moment. When he spoke, his voice was hoarse. "Do you remember what areas were affected?"

"Lots of places. All across the world. And they were spreading fast. Unless they stopped…" *The whole world will be gone.*

He closed his eyes and exhaled through his nose. "While I was walking home, when I was in the forest, I thought I heard a noise. I dismissed it at the time. But it must be related."

"I heard it too. Some sort of crackling noise. Then something that sounded like a helicopter. I don't know if it was the military or what caused the quiet zones or something else. At least seeing the car brought my memories back." Clare chuckled weakly. "So now we know why the phone lines are still down. And possibly why the weather has been so bizarre."

"And what happened to the garden."

Clare's stomach turned. She leaned her head forward so that her hair would help hide her face.

"I owe you every apology for doubting you all this time." Dorran's eyebrows had lowered again, and his lips were pressed tightly together as he stared at the fire. "All this while, I have been trying to tell you that what you saw and heard were figments of your imagination. When you described the figures you saw—women with holes in their sides—I couldn't reconcile that with reality. I thought you were seeing waking nightmares. It took me to see it with my own eyes to believe you, and for that, I am deeply sorry."

Clare shrugged, heat spreading over her face. "You were trying to help me. If our positions had been reversed, I don't know if I would have been able to believe you either."

"Regardless, I made you doubt your own mind. And that is a cruel thing to do." He shook his head. "You trusted me when I asked for it. And I want to give you that in return. I will not doubt you again."

"What if I try to tell you something really crazy, like dragons made their nest in the attic?"

He smiled. "Not even then."

"Thank you." She chuckled as a painful kind of happiness filled her stomach. The best word she found to describe it was *bittersweet*. She didn't know what was happening to the outside world or if there even *was* an outside world any longer. But she had Dorran. He was alive, and he didn't hate her. And that counted for a lot.

Dorran inclined his head toward her, and when he spoke, his voice was soft. "I also wanted to apologize for what I said in the garden. I never wanted you to be afraid of me, and I never meant to grow angry. But I did. And I regretted it immediately. I should have followed you when you left, but I allowed myself to stay in the garden. To calm down, I told myself. When I finally went after you to apologize, you were gone."

A log in the fireplace broke, sending a shower of sparks dancing into the chimney. Dorran faced the fire but glanced at her. Guilt and grief hung about his eyes.

"I didn't realize you would leave the house. When I saw your snowshoes were missing and the door was open, I was terrified. If you had become lost in the forest or succumbed to the snow…" He drew a shallow breath. "I thought I had sent you to your death."

"You can't get rid of me that easily." Clare leaned a little closer, nudging his shoulder with hers, trying to break him out of his melancholy.

He smiled. "Ah, Clare. *Never* leave again without at least giving me a chance to beg you to stay."

Clare's throat ached, but she smiled. "All right."

Gale-force winds shook the windows. They both looked up at the noise, and Clare pulled her knees closer to her chest. Even though the fire was warm, she still felt cold.

"I think it is safe to believe we are not just waiting out the snow any longer," Dorran said. "We must turn ourselves toward both short-term and long-term survival."

Clare thought of the destroyed garden and tried to breathe around the rising dread. "How much food do we have left?"

He didn't answer for a moment, and when he did, Clare thought he was trying to sound optimistic. "We have some. And the garden was not a complete loss. You managed to save some plants. And after you were gone, before I realized you had physically left the house, I did what I could to replant the remainder. Some will not survive. Growth will have been stunted in most of them. But it is significantly better than starting from scratch."

Remembering a detail that had been lost in the scuffle in the forest, Clare took a sharp breath. "There's food in my car. I was bringing it to my sister's. There's enough to last two people at least a couple of weeks."

"Good! That will make a difference." He chewed his lip. "The only issue that remains is *retrieving* it. I don't know how many of those creatures are still in the forest, but there are at least several. They seemed reluctant to leave the trees. The eight that followed me to the pond were just the ones I could coax out."

"They looked thin. They might starve if we leave them alone for long enough." Clare felt uneasy just saying it.

"We will hope for it. But there is another, slightly more pressing matter." Dorran looked toward the ceiling and the dozens of rooms hidden out of sight. "Some must have found a way inside the house—the ones you saw. I do not know how. The doors and windows stayed locked this whole time, but they are in here with us."

"I've seen three. One with a hole in her side. One with a twisted back. And one with a spine that pokes out of her skin."

"Heaven help us," Dorran muttered under his breath. "I would rather face death than a fate like those creatures."

She shared his sentiment. The thought of being twisted, losing her mind, and having her body broken was unbearable. Clare's wrist was stinging. She glanced at it and saw a smear of dried blood where the skin had been broken. Her heart skipped a beat. "Do you think it's—"

"It is not contagious." Dorran took her chin and turned her

head so that she looked him in the eyes. His voice and expression held conviction. "It is *not*. You will not turn into one of them."

She nodded, but frightened tears stung her eyes.

Dorran's hand moved from her chin to stroke the side of her face, and his voice softened. "You were badly scratched when I found you. At the time, I thought it had come from the crash, but I can guess now it was the creatures' doing, correct?"

"Yeah."

"If it was contagious, I think we would have known about it well before now. Do not let it frighten you. That matter aside, the bite looks painful. Wait a moment. I will take care of it."

He rose, and Clare knew he was going to fetch the first aid kit. She grabbed at his dressing gown to keep him in the room. "No. If those creatures are in the house, we can't split up."

"Hm." He rubbed at the back of his neck. "We cannot stay here forever either. Soon we will need water and food. Plus, the garden will need additional care if we are to save what we can."

"I have a theory." Clare rose so that she could stand at Dorran's side. Together, they faced the closed dining room doors. "I don't think they like light."

"No?"

"Anytime I've seen them has been in shadow. Either at night, when the lights are off, or when natural light was blocked out."

"They were reluctant to leave the forest's shelter," Dorran said. "You may be right. And it might be why they came into the mansion in the first place. The building was darker."

"When I saw one in the wine cellar, she reached for the candle. I think she wanted to snuff it out."

"Which means light doesn't hurt them, but they are repulsed by it. So having the lights on helped keep them away." Dorran laughed. "Well, I did one thing right by you."

She moved a little closer to him. "You did a lot of things right. Where do you want to go? The bedroom?"

"It might be the safest location. The bathroom will give us water, and it has only two doors to defend. The windows would be too high for them to reach, unlike the rooms on the ground floor." Dorran nodded at the curtains he'd drawn over the dining room's windows. "I tried to hide our presence, just in case. The creatures seem broken, but they are unnaturally strong."

"They bent the door on my car." Clare squirmed at the memory. Dorran was right—she didn't think windows would present much of an obstacle if the monsters wanted to get through.

"The bedroom will be farther from the foyer's door in case we need to run," Dorran said. "But I don't feel that is a huge disincentive. Where would we run *to*?"

"Exactly. The bedroom, then?"

"It seems to be the best choice to me, for the short term, at least. Once I have made sure you are safe there, I will secure the garden and fetch some food to tide us over."

"Or," Clare countered, "we stay together, visit the kitchen and garden together, and I don't have to spend twenty minutes imagining all the ways you could die."

He lifted his eyebrows. "I would prefer knowing you were safe."

She retorted by lifting her own. "You said you'd let me win as many arguments as I wanted if we got back to the house."

"Of course I did." He sighed. "Evidently, I should not make promises in dire situations. We will go together."

CHAPTER 30

CLARE GATHERED THE THINGS they would need: Dorran's wet boots, the blankets and pillow, and the radio. They were an armful, but she balanced them against her chest as Dorran took up a fire poker and approached the door.

"If anything comes at us, try to get your back against a wall or into a corner. I don't like the idea of fighting these things inside the house. If we're attacked, our preference will be to retreat to safety and regroup. Agreed?"

Clare nodded aggressively. "Yes."

Dorran sent her a fond smile, then his face darkened as he opened the door. Cold light dripped through high windows to illuminate the space. Ahead, the staircase hung like a dark ribbon along the back wall. To their right, doorways led deeper into the building. The sense of hollowness that Clare had begun to associate with the foyer washed over her again. It was too sparse.

Dorran led her across the space in an arc to avoid straying too close to any of the doors. As they passed the stairs, he picked up a ring of keys hanging near the phone. Moving quickly and quietly, they went through the narrow doorway at the back of the foyer and stopped in the stone chamber while Dorran lit a candle.

Clare found it impossible not to stare at the gaping wine cellar archway as they passed it. At least one of the creatures had its nest down there. But there was no way to barricade the opening. The archway was tall and wide, and it had no door. Even if they managed to drag furniture into the space and build a blockade, there was nothing to secure it to, and Clare suspected the creatures wouldn't have a hard time beating it down. That meant the archway would be left open. And she could do nothing about it.

Clare inhaled deeply when she stepped under the garden's warm lights. The space, full of the musty smell of damp earth and with a gentle heat rising from the floor, had always felt like a sanctuary. Dorran shut and locked the metal door, and they turned to face the gardens.

Dorran had done good work in rescuing the plants. Most of them were wilting as shock set in, but he'd replanted them all into neat lines. Clare noticed he hadn't disturbed the erratic, desperate planting she'd done before he arrived.

He filled the watering can from the tap and began moving through the rows, tending to and examining the plants one at a time. Some would die, and others would be stunted, but it could have been a lot worse.

Dorran nodded to her. "If you feel up to it, would you plant some new rows? It will help replace the lost crops."

"Right." Clare placed her luggage on the chair in the garden's corner then crossed to the seed bench and chose several bottles. While Dorran watered, she populated a new patch of ground. They worked efficiently. Clare had nearly finished a row of snow peas when a scraping noise made her look up. Dorran righted his watering can and stared at the frosted window in the door.

A silhouette lurched past. It moved erratically, twitching, and was gone before Clare could even flinch back. Dorran placed his watering can on the bench and crept toward the door.

"No," Clare whispered as he reached for the handle. He looked back at her and must have seen the dread in her face because he withdrew his hand. The window remained empty. After a few moments of silence, both she and Dorran returned to their work.

Clare tried to keep her head down but couldn't stop herself from watching the door out of the corner of her eye. She sensed that Dorran's attention was divided too. It wasn't possible to see far through the window. The glow from the candle on the other side of the stone room gave her a sense of space, but every distinct detail had mixed into one solid blur. The creature could be hidden anywhere out there, waiting, holding its breath, knowing that she and Dorran would have to leave their shelter eventually.

When Dorran returned the watering can to its shelf, Clare knew they couldn't delay their journey back into the main parts of the house any longer. She licked dry lips as she stacked the jars of seeds back onto their shelves. Then she gathered her bundle of bedding material while Dorran picked up his fire poker.

"Into the kitchen next, yes?" he asked.

She tried to look more confident than she felt. "Yes."

He must have shared some of her misgivings. When he opened the door, it was an inch at a time, with his weapon held at the ready. As the metal swung open, Clare saw the candle at the opposite side of the room. It acted as a beacon, its flame spluttering in the air that traveled through the hallway. Dorran hesitated inside the doorway for a moment, running his eyes from the wine cellar to the basement door. He finally nodded for Clare to follow him out and shut the door behind them.

Instead of turning back to the main part of the house, Dorran led her deeper into the stone chamber and toward a nook beside the garden. Shelves full of equipment lined the walls. He stepped beside them and sorted through the knickknacks until he came up with a padlock. They returned to the garden doors, and Dorran bolted it shut, using the ring of keys from the foyer to lock it.

"Not a perfect defense, but it will have to do." He offered the key ring to Clare, and she tucked it into her gown's pocket. "Those were the housekeeper's. They can get into most rooms. I don't know if those creatures are smart enough to use keys, but it would be wise to keep them with us regardless."

They stayed close to each other as they re-entered the hallway. Dorran moved into the kitchen, turning on the lights as soon as he opened the door.

The visit was brief. Dorran found a crate under one of the

benches and funneled supplies into it with quick precision—
plates, cutlery, the jars of sprouts that hadn't already been eaten,
and most of the food from the pantry. He lifted the crate and led
her toward their room.

Once they were on the stairs, they picked up the pace. Dorran
was clearly battling with the idea of using light to ward off the
creatures and the need to conserve precious fuel. He turned out
lights whenever they left an area but always waited until the last
possible moment.

Once they reached the third-floor landing, they had a straight
run to their room. Dorran hit the switch beside the stairs. The
bulb directly above them flickered on, but that was the only one
that did. Dorran made a soft noise in the back of his throat and
gently nudged Clare behind himself.

"That's not a bad fuse, is it?" Clare asked.

"No."

The closest light washed over them and lit the highest few
stairs. Its sphere of influence ended just meters ahead of them.
The remainder of the hallway was swallowed by shadow, with
a sliver of light coming from under the curtain covering the
window at the end of the hall. Between its refracted light and
the traces echoing from the first bulb, Clare could pick out the
corners where the cross paths intersected. Glittering fragments of
broken lightbulbs were scattered over the carpet.

"Do you want to keep going?" Dorran asked. "Or would you
feel safer turning back?"

Clare bit her lip. The door to their room was halfway along

the passageway, before the intersection. "You know the house better than I do. What do you think?"

He took a slow breath. "My preference would be to continue. The room is still more easily protected than the dining room or kitchen. But I do not want to place you somewhere you will not feel safe."

"Let's go on, then. I'll feel as safe there as anywhere." *As long as you don't leave me alone.*

Dorran shifted his crate and held it under one arm. Then he adjusted the fire poker in the other hand and began moving again.

A floorboard groaned as they passed over it. Clare alternated her attention between the closed bedroom door and the end of the hallway. The sliver of light trembled as the curtains moved. Clare tried to tell herself it was just an air current, nothing more.

Dorran pulled up short, and Clare nearly walked into him. She bent forward, around his arm, trying to see why they had stopped. He stared toward the intersection. Dim light ran over the hallway's corners. One of the edges was straight. The other was ragged.

Clare's heart missed a beat. She could just barely make out the edge of one long, limp arm. The stranger was horrifically tall. Its head nearly grazed the ceiling. A ringlet of stringy hair trembled as it breathed.

Dorran flexed his grip on the metal poker and took a step forward. As he did, the figure leaned farther around the corner, its elongated arm swinging.

It gave Clare the impression of a predatory animal. Its hunger drove it forward while fear anchored it. As Clare and Dorran drew closer, it began to lose restraint over its impulses to hunt.

The door was only ten paces away. Dorran spoke in a whisper. "We will run for the bedroom. If we cannot make it, return downstairs instead."

She nodded. He reached into the crate then moved forward in three long paces.

The creature reacted instantly, lurching around the corner. Gangly arms swung aimlessly, but its legs were capable of phenomenally long strides that ate up the distance between them.

Dorran pulled the flashlight from the crate and let the box drop. It created a deafening bang as it hit the floor. The creature paused midstride. Dorran pressed the switch and lifted the flashlight in one motion. Harsh light burst down the hallway.

The creature came into sharp relief. It filled the passageway, its head grazing the ceiling. Its face was stretched painfully, an effect emphasized by its slack jaw. The thin, curved neck seemed wrong, as though it had been an accident to stick it between the jutting collarbones. Its eyes were round and shocked. It looked confused. The arms swung like giant pendulums as their momentum went unchecked.

"Go," Dorran called.

Clare ran for the door. The creature had hesitated in the face of the light. It took a shuffling step forward, massive feet scraping over the carpet, but its eyes stayed fixed on the torch. Dorran followed Clare, holding the flashlight at arm's length and directing it at the monster's uncomprehending face.

Clare reached the door and wrenched it open. She threw her armful of necessities through, praying the blankets would buffer the radio enough to keep it safe, then she reached back out to grab the crate of food. As she dragged it inside, she called, "Okay!"

Dorran kept the torch up as he sidestepped into the room. He slammed the door, turned the lock, then stepped back. With one hand resting on the wood, he listened. The hallway outside was silent, almost quiet enough to make Clare believe they were alone.

But she only had to look at Dorran's expression to know she hadn't imagined the monster. Dorran's eyes were tight, and his jaw was tense. He stepped away from the door, crossed to the fireplace, planted his hands on the couch, and began to push. Clare guessed what he was doing. She dragged the crate out of the way then joined him, and the couch's feet scraped across the carpet as they pushed it across the room. It thudded to a stop as it hit the door, barricading it.

Clare, her pulse galloping, sank onto the seat. Dorran slid down beside her and ran his hand over his forehead. He looked ashen.

"She was hungry," Clare said. She wrapped her arms around her chest and rocked gently. "She was frightened of us, but she was starving."

Dorran rested his hand on her shoulder. A moment later, chills ran through Clare as something brittle scraped against the other side of the door. The sound started high then moved lower, digging into any crevice it could find.

Dorran's hand tightened over Clare's shoulder. The creature kept clawing, digging around every seam and crack. Clare held her breath. A moment passed, then the noise faded, replaced with heavy, thumping footsteps moving back down the hall.

CHAPTER 31

DORRAN EXHALED AND LET his eyes fall closed. He looked exhausted. Clare didn't feel much better. The bedroom had been their choice, and it was supposed to be their safe haven. But with the creature prowling the hallways, it felt closer to a prison.

Then Dorran's head snapped up. A look of alarm flashed over his features, and before Clare could ask what was wrong, he darted away. Clare rose onto aching feet to follow him as he moved into the bathroom. As she entered, she saw the second door in the room's opposite wall, and her stomach flipped. She'd forgotten the bathroom connected them to the hallway through the second bedroom.

Dorran was already at the door. The lock made a muffled clicking noise as he sealed it, then he backed into the bathroom and closed its door, as well. The closest wall held a heavy cabinet, and Dorran put his shoulder against it and pushed it over the tiles until it covered the door as an added precaution. He sighed heavily as the cabinet ground to a halt. "There. Now they cannot get in…at least without making plenty of noise to alert us."

Clare tried not to think about what they would do if it came to that.

"Would you start the fire, please?" Dorran's smile was tired but resolute. He stepped past Clare and back into their room. "I will make fully certain that we are alone."

Clare lowered herself to the rug in front of the hearth. She kept one eye on Dorran as he searched the room, opening wardrobes and checking under the bed. She'd managed to get the kindling lit by the time he returned to her. He carried their crate of supplies and placed it on the edge of the hearth before sitting at her side.

"We are alone as best as I can tell." He flexed his shoulders and winced. "But if you ever feel that we are not—if you hear something or sense something—please tell me. I will not doubt you again."

She nodded and poked more sticks on top of the little flaming pile. Dorran fished supplies out of the crate and used a knife to cut through the top of a can of soup. Once the fire was large enough, he set the pot at the edge of the flames to heat, bending forward to stir it every few seconds. They didn't try to talk. Clare was wrapped up in her own thoughts, and she knew Dorran was as well.

Whatever had changed the people in the forest had been spreading across the world. That had been two weeks ago. The last experience Clare had with the outside world had been on the day of the crash when the helicopter passed overhead and disturbed the monsters gathered around her car. Since then, the sky had been bare. No planes. No drones. Nothing that could hint at a military operation. That made it a challenge not to assume the worst.

Marnie was probably gone, either killed by the creatures or swallowed by the quiet zone. That realization hurt like a fist slamming into Clare's stomach, and the ache was excruciating. Clare had been responsible for picking up Marnie. Beth had called their aunt to make sure she knew Clare was on the way. She would have waited—probably by the front door, with her luggage at her feet, wearing her favorite floral shirt and knit cardigan—for a rescue that would never come.

The pain was almost unbearable. Clare choked on it.

A second later, Dorran's arms were around her, and he pulled her against his chest. "Here," he murmured as he stroked her hair. "I have you. Let it out."

Burning-hot tears came like a wave. Dorran held her and brushed his fingers over her hair as she gasped and shook.

Marnie had deserved better. Beth deserved better, as well. She, at least, had a better chance of survival. Her bunker was reinforced and stocked with food. As long as she'd made it there on time, as long as she'd locked the door as soon as she saw the storm clouds building on the horizon, she might be safe. But her existence couldn't be a happy one. She would think Clare was dead. The last time they'd spoken, right before the call dropped, she'd been yelling at Clare to turn back. She must have been watching the news reports and seen a quiet zone appear over the road between them. She'd tried to save Clare.

If Beth was still out there, she would have spent the past two weeks alone in her bunker, grieving and terrified. Clare couldn't stand to think of her like that or of how much longer the state might continue. She pulled out of Dorran's arms and stumbled across the room to find the radio among the bedding. Dorran let her go, but he watched her closely. She brought the radio back to the fire and wiped tears off her cheeks as she turned it on. The crackling noise floated around them as she adjusted the signal to pick up Beth's frequency. There was only white noise.

Dorran silently divided the soup into bowls while Clare fiddled with the radio's settings. He placed a bowl at her side but didn't try to interrupt her. She continued turning the dial, trying to find anything except incessant static.

There has to be someone else out there. We survived. We can't be the only ones. Please, please, let us not be the only ones.

As she scrolled through the frequencies, something organic rose out of the static. Dorran took a sharp breath and moved closer as Clare rewound the dial. She held the radio between them and pushed the volume up as they tried to pick out the words. It was a man's voice, deep and rough, buried inside the never-ending white noise. Clare had to strain to make out the words.

"…and now my gasket's blown, so I'm scavenging through cars, trying to find one that will fit."

Silence stretched for a moment. Clare tugged on Dorran's

sleeve. "He's talking to someone else, but we can only hear his side."

"Ah, yeah, I'll give that a shot. Gotta wait 'til morning. Hollow ones are everywhere." After another stretch of silence, he said, "Hell if I know. If I can get to Clydesdale, I might try to make a permanent refuge. Or I might keep moving. Depends on how occupied it is. They're starting to rove, though, so even the middle-of-nowhere places aren't so safe anymore."

Clare and Dorran exchanged a look. The audio was nearly impossible to make out through the static, but Clare guessed *hollow ones* referred to the infected creatures.

The man exhaled a long, drawn-out swear word. "Ain't seen a dead one yet that wasn't deliberately killed. If they can die from sickness or hunger, they're taking their sweet-ass time about it." A short pause. "I don't buy that. It's a growth stimulant, one that affects the bones. A disease won't do this."

Clare pressed the volume a fraction higher. The man's voice became less and less clear as he and his companion delved into an argument, both trying to talk over the other. "Nah…nah… it's man—I said it's man-made. Get your hippy-ass theories out of here. How's a fungus doing this? Nah, listen. Something like this— it's chemicals. Government bombing. Hell if I know. Population control gone wrong? But I'm telling you, this ain't no virus."

The silence lasted a very long time. Clare desperately wished she could hear the other side of the conversation, but she didn't dare risk losing her current feed looking for it. Then the man exhaled a deep, weary sigh.

DARCY COATES

"Whatever. I'm heading in for the night. Got a lot of driving to do in the morning if I can get a new gasket. Talk tomorrow, same time, assuming we're not dead?" His laughter was raucous. "All right. All right. Be safe, buddy."

Clare lowered the volume as static replaced the voice. She sat back on her heels and bit her lip. "We're not alone."

"No," Dorran said. "But it doesn't sound good."

Clare knew the location the man had talked about—Clydesdale. The tiny village was a six-hour drive from her home. He'd made it sound like the place would be unoccupied by humans. Like *everywhere* would be unoccupied. That didn't bode well for the human population. She was suddenly very, very grateful for having found Winterbourne Hall. The building might not be the coziest or the most inviting she'd ever visited. But it was safe...relatively speaking. It was safe enough that she and Dorran had survived before they even knew what kind of threat they were facing.

She wound the radio back to Bethany's frequency and waited, holding her breath, for any noises coming through. If Beth was still alive and still had her radio, she wasn't using it. Clare turned down the volume and placed the box on the ground beside the fireplace, where she could continue to listen for noises, then pulled her knees up under her chin.

"Eat," Dorran murmured. "You'll feel better with food."

She knew she should be grateful for what she had. A home. Company. Food. Warmth. They were all luxuries she might otherwise have had to live without. But as she picked up the bowl and stirred the medley of vegetables inside, her stomach

266

revolted against the idea of eating. She put it back down. "What are we going to do?"

"I have been considering the same question." His expression was strained as he stared into the fire. "It would not be safe to leave Winterbourne."

"No," she agreed.

"And if we did, where would we go? Until the world is returned to some kind of order...until there is a safe haven that offers better chances of survival than Winterbourne..."

"We're better off staying here." Clare ran her hands through her hair. "Yeah. At least we have the garden and water." She blinked as she watched the crackling fire. Her throat still ached from crying. She was exhausted, physically and emotionally, but her mind wouldn't let her rest.

Dorran's dark eyes lingered on her, then he turned to the crate of supplies and fished out the doctor's medical equipment. Dorran sorted through the bottles, pulled out a roll of bandages, then held out his hand. "Let me see your wrist."

"It's not so bad." She tugged the sleeve over it again. "You're tired. You must be ready to drop."

"Hah." He shuffled closer, worked his fingers under her hand, then gently coaxed it out from where she cradled it against her body. "I won't rest easily if you're in pain. Let me fix it first."

He eased the sleeve back and hissed as he saw the red skin. He tilted it, examining it, then placed it back into Clare's lap as he went to fetch water from the bathroom. As he set it to boil over the fire, he laid out his supplies on a clean towel. "Does it hurt?"

"Not much." That was true. The torn skin still burned whenever Clare moved it or touched it, but otherwise, it had dulled to a steady ache.

Dorran still gave her two of the pain tablets then adjusted his position so that Clare could lean her head against his shoulder as he worked. He dipped a cloth into the boiled water and touched it, very gently, to the edge of the cuts.

"We cannot remain locked in this room forever." His warm breath ghosted across her temple as he focused on his work. "Somehow, we will have to either kill the creatures or drive them out of the house."

"Do we have any kind of long-range weapon? Guns?" She squinted against the pain as he washed blood out of the cuts. "Or, uh, crossbows?"

He chuckled. "That would make for an exciting encounter. But I'm afraid not. My family did not approve of guns in the house. We have kitchen knives and bludgeoning weapons."

"That's not ideal."

"No. But I don't think we have a choice. Somehow, we must find a way to secure the house. Otherwise, we might be surviving, but we certainly won't be living."

She agreed. Winterbourne had been her home for only a few weeks, and she already felt the squeeze of being restricted to the bedroom. For Dorran, who had lived there his whole life, it had to feel like an invasion. This was his home. He might not have loved the building, but having his sanctuary infiltrated had to smart.

"We will wait until morning. Right now, these creatures are in their element in the dark. They will be easier to find—and fight—during bright daylight. I don't think they enjoy noise either."

Clare closed her eyes as Dorran finished washing the cuts and moved on to the antiseptic. "We can open the curtains to let extra light in as we go."

"The house will need to be scouted systematically. Once we've searched a room and confirmed it is safe, we will lock its doors and find a way to ensure the seal stays untampered, perhaps with a thread tied to the handle so that it will snap if something opens it. If I start on the highest level and work down, the noise and disturbance might be enough to funnel them outside."

"And once they're out, we can lock them out."

"Exactly." He finished cleaning her wrist and unrolled the bandages. "This isn't bad enough to require stitches, thankfully. But try not to strain it."

"I can wrap a scarf around it or something for the fight tomorrow."

"Hm…" He glanced at her. "No. I will search the house. You'll stay here, where it is safe."

"That's not happening." Just the thought was enough to turn Clare's blood cold. "We had an agreement. We're in this together, and no one is leaving anyone else alone."

"But I also made a promise. To keep you safe."

"Well, tough." She tried to pull her hand out of his, but he tightened his grip on her, holding her still.

This time, when he looked at her, his expression was sharp

and didn't invite argument. "You are hurt. Tired. You have been under more stress in these last few days than any person should have to endure."

"And you nearly froze in a lake. Besides, I can hold my own. I did in the forest."

"You did." He exhaled a shuddering breath. "But we were lucky as well. Clare, if I was not able to keep you safe…if you were hurt…"

He tied off the bandages as his voice failed, and Clare imagined what would happen if she lost to the creatures. She pictured the too-sharp nails and teeth digging into her, tearing through the skin and muscle in their desperation to sate their hunger. She shivered. "Well, we won't let that happen. For either of us."

There was something in his expression. She couldn't read it. He'd always been a challenge to understand, but at that moment, it was harder than ever. His hand rested around hers, holding her lightly enough that she could easily pull away.

"I have never cared about anything as much as this," Dorran finally whispered.

Clare frowned lightly. "What do you mean?" *Survival? Defending the house? Is he talking about the garden or—*

His eyes met hers for a brief second then glanced away again. "You."

The world had grown muted. The wind, the house, even the fire faded into the distance until all she could feel was contained on that small fireside rug. Dorran. His halting, hoarse voice. The soft, barely-there touch.

His head was down, his eyebrows low. He watched their hands, and she realized why he was holding her so lightly. He expected her to pull away. He was ready to let her go as soon as she showed reluctance. Clare thought she finally understood him.

He had always put her first—with their food, with their resources, and with his time. He'd thought she had destroyed their garden, but he'd followed her to apologize before he even knew she was blameless. He had done what he always did—he had tried to help her, selflessly, wholeheartedly, no matter the cost to him.

And he was kind, not in the way that expected anything in return, and not that he was even *trying* to be kind. He just *was*. She hadn't been able to see it at first. He had hidden it away behind formality and cool impassiveness, like a shield, guarding the parts of himself that could be hurt.

As they had spent time together, he'd begun to pull back his walls to let her see inside. It couldn't have been easy for him. Those walls had been built over a lifetime, reinforced to protect him from a family that had given more cruelty than love. Lowering his defenses made Dorran vulnerable, and he dreaded vulnerability more than anything else.

But at that moment, as he knelt beside her, he was completely open, completely exposed. His breathing was shallow, his head was low, and his eyes couldn't meet hers even though he seemed to be trying. He was afraid, she realized. *He's learned that vulnerability leads to pain. It's all he's ever received. It's the only outcome he thinks he can expect.*

Yet in defiance of that, this man was offering himself to her, giving up his power to her. This beautiful, kind man.

She wanted to answer him, but she didn't know the words. She wrapped both of her hands around his and lifted it. The skin was warm under her lips as she kissed the knuckles, one at a time. Dorran's breath hitched. She pressed the back of his hand against her cheek, holding it there, hoping he would feel some of what she felt. The emotions were running through her in a flood, overwhelming her, almost painful in their intensity. They had to be spilling out, a tangible thing he could sense.

He breathed her name. The space between them was gone. His forehead touched hers. Clare sank into the sensations—the heat from his skin, the soft rush of his shallow breaths. He was so close. Long lashes framed his dark, intense eyes. His black hair mingled with hers. His lips were barely parted. She wanted to touch them, to know what he felt like.

He finally met her eyes. Another wall came down. She could read the emotions inside. Uncertainty. Shame and fear in equal measures. Hope—not much, but enough. And through that bewildering medley of emotions was adoration. It shone brightly, stronger than everything else.

It had always been there, she realized. It had been hidden carefully, disguised and smothered, but it had been growing with every day they spent together. He adored her.

Words were impossible. In their place, touch would do. She pressed into him, tilting up until her lips grazed his. A tremor ran through him like electricity. He moved to taste her again, cautiously, still expecting the sting of pain, but unwilling to withdraw. She held his hand to her face, and his fingers fanned out to touch her, to pull her into him. His lips were gentle and sincere, the taste exquisite. Everything about the kiss was so perfectly Dorran.

She was falling, losing herself in him, drowning but no longer afraid.

CHAPTER 32

SLEET ASSAULTED THE WINDOWS. Ice-fueled gusts rattled loose tiles and stones. But it was warm in the bedroom with the fire's heat spreading over them.

They sat on the rug, nestled close to each other. Dorran's arm was around her back, and his other hand was holding hers, their fingers entwined. They fit together well. Clare's chest was full of raw happiness, a strange, intense sensation. Dorran's chin rested on top of her head. When he exhaled, it was contented. She closed her eyes and smiled as Dorran's thumb traced over the back of her hand. Clare tilted her head back to kiss his throat. A happy murmur rose from him, and she felt him smiling against the top of her head.

"So beautiful," Dorran murmured. His guards were down. The normal hesitation had vanished as he opened himself to her. "You are so, so beautiful."

She chuckled, pleased heat spreading over her face. "I'm nothing special. You should see my sister—" Her voice broke. She couldn't believe she had let it fall from her mind. Marnie, Beth, and everyone she had ever known and cared for were lost out in the stillness. The radio waited beside the fireplace. Its static was barely audible. Beth's frequency remained unused.

Dorran's hand rose to touch her face. His dark eyes were filled with sadness as he watched her. "Clare—"

"I'm okay." She tried to smile. The muscles ached. "It's...it's okay."

"My dearest Clare." He said it hesitantly as though he weren't sure he was allowed to. It helped, though. The bittersweet sensation was back, a sad kind of joy mixed in with pain. Dorran lightly pulled her back against himself, and his lips brushed her forehead in a tender kiss.

"Thank you," Clare whispered.

His reply was equally soft. "I am sorry I cannot do more."

She looked toward the window. It was still dark, but each passing moment brought them closer to dawn. And dawn meant the horrors of the house would have to be faced. She licked her lips. "I want to go with you tomorrow."

"Ah." He exhaled then dipped down to kiss her cheek. The expression was gentle and almost painfully sweet, and Clare's heart ached as he moved away again. "I know how much this worries you, but you must trust me. Stay here, where it is safe. I will return as quickly as I can."

She swallowed. Her throat ached. "I'll be useful. I can watch your back."

"I am sure you would. I have no doubt that you would make a strong partner. But still, I am unrelenting." He kissed her neck.

Clare leaned into his touch, relishing him, but her mind wouldn't stop spinning. The mansion was so large. It had so many rooms, so many places to become trapped, so many places to be ambushed. And Dorran had been worn down over the last week. She'd nearly lost him to the lake. He would fight hard, but there was too much for one man to do.

"I can't—" She took a gulping breath as she tried to put her feelings into words. "You're all I have left right now. And…and I need you. I can't do this without you."

He looked at the door. She could feel the conflict running through him as he grazed his thumb over the back of her hand. At last, he said, "We can compromise. Perhaps there is a way for us to venture out together—not deep into the house, but somewhere nearby to assess the situation."

"Okay."

"But let us leave the details to negotiate until tomorrow. It must be near midnight, and we are both tired. We will benefit from some rest."

That was the truth. Clare reluctantly nodded.

"Forgive me." Dorran pulled back. "I forgot you haven't eaten yet. Sit a moment while I reheat your soup."

She tangled her fingers in his shirt. Even letting him move away to reach the bowl felt like too far. She was afraid if she tried to say anything, she would start crying again.

Dorran's expression fell. He brushed his fingertips over her face, running them over her cheek and her lips. When he spoke, his voice was tight. "We will be all right, my darling. We can make this work."

Clare nodded and let Dorran slip away. He reheated her soup then nestled her at his side while she ate it. She stared at the crackling flames, but her mind was on her other senses—the steady heartbeat and even breaths that moved under her ear, the distracting and entrancing feeling of his fingertips tracing over her arm, and the feel of his shirt under her cheek.

I can't let anything happen to him. He needs to be safe.

She'd had those exact thoughts days before. Back then, though, it had been over something very different: the family that refused to let Dorran go.

A wash of cold moved through Clare despite the warm soup. She'd been so caught up in grief over her family that she hadn't thought about Dorran's. He was dealing with his own loss. His entire family, the staff he'd become friends with, his dog—every person he had ever been close to—were gone. She clasped her hand around his and held it tightly. "Your family—"

"Are most likely dead, yes." He nudged her hand back to the bowl. "It is all right. Eat, my dear."

"Are you…okay? I mean, I know your mother was horrible, but…"

Emotion flitted across his face, but he hid it quickly. When he spoke, the words were measured. "I regret losing many of them. The staff were not all bad. My nieces and nephews especially did not deserve it. And yet, for the first time in my life, I am free. I do not quite know how to feel about it. It is…a lot."

"If you need to talk…"

He smiled. "Thank you. For now, I am looking forward, to our immediate priorities. Securing the house. Making sure you eat enough." He pressed her hand toward the spoon again. "Once we are safe, there will be time for everything else."

As Clare chewed another mouthful of dinner, she thought Dorran's perspective might be the sanest they could adopt. Grief and guilt couldn't protect them. They needed to stay alive, stay together. And that meant staying focused.

They fell asleep like they had previous nights: together on the rug, huddled close for warmth, with Dorran's arm thrown over Clare. She was tired enough to sleep for a full day, but her subconscious kept her dreams light and never let her stray far from wakefulness. She snapped to awareness when Dorran moved to add more wood to the fire. He lay back down, and she let sleep reclaim her again.

The second time Dorran stirred to keep their fire alive, Clare lay still and kept her eyes closed. She thought the sun was starting to rise. Even through her eyelids, the darkness felt less oppressive. Dorran's movements were slow and near silent as he added new logs to the grate. Then, moving cautiously, he draped a spare blanket over Clare.

A feather-light kiss grazed her cheek. She felt his presence move away and heard the muffled scrape of the chair being pulled back from the door. A moment later, distant hinges ground against each other, then the latch clicked as the door was shut again.

He actually did it.

Clare rolled over and sat up. The room felt painfully lonely with just her in it. The bed had clean sheets but hadn't been slept in for days. The wallpaper, which had seemed maddening when she'd first seen it, now felt familiar. Like she'd thought, the sun was just starting to rise. It was too early for it to breach the tips of the forest's trees, but the deep black of night had faded.

She shivered as she stood and folded her arms around herself. The fire's heat couldn't keep her warm as she crossed to the door. She knew Dorran would have locked it, but she still had to try. The handle was unyielding, as expected.

Clare had guessed Dorran's plan when he'd suggested they postpone making any decisions until the morning. He'd sensed that she wasn't going to give ground, and he had let her fall asleep and tried to leave before she woke so that she couldn't stop him. He probably hoped she would still be asleep when he returned from searching the house. The door was locked, sealing her in the room, just in case.

And Clare had let him go. She didn't want to argue with him again. It would be easier to ask forgiveness later. She pressed her lips together as she crossed to her dressing gown draped over the wingback chair. *It was a good try, Dorran. But you forgot something.*

Inside the gown's pocket were the housekeeper's keys Dorran had given her for safekeeping the previous day. The heavy metal ring was slightly rusted and held at least forty keys—some large and ornate, others tiny.

Clare sorted through the tangle of keys as she returned to the door, looking for one that would match the bronze handle. The fourth key she tried slid neatly into the slot, and a quiet clicking noise told her it had worked. She opened the door a fraction and peered into the hallway.

Dorran had already removed the curtain at the end of the hall, and stark-white light flooded the space. As far as Clare could tell, the halls were empty. She slipped back into the room and changed hurriedly, rushing to put on clothes that would keep her warm in the freezing building and protect her at least somewhat from bites and scratching claws. Winterbourne's clothing options for her size were limited to dresses, but she wore sturdy boots under the skirt and pulled on a heavy jacket with thick sleeves and a set of leather gloves. A knit scarf would protect her throat. Then she knelt by the crate. Dorran had already taken weapons from it, but he'd left a paring knife, which she tucked into her pocket. Then she picked up the fire poker and gave it an experimental swing. It was hefty and solid. Though not sharp enough to work as a sword, it would still do some damage in a pinch.

She returned to the door and hesitated at the opening as she listened for signs that she might not be alone. Everything was quiet. Clare took a moment to focus, sucking in a deep breath, and stepped through.

Dorran had said he would start on the highest levels and see if he could push the creatures downstairs. Clare didn't know the house's layout well, but Dorran had planned to funnel the creatures down and outside, so she guessed he would have started in the rooms farthest from the stairs. She followed the hallway, treading lightly, her senses on high alert.

The intersection split her path into three options. Clare stopped and turned in a slow circle. Everywhere she looked was a confusing mesh of high walls, dark wallpaper, and clusters of expensive furniture. The left passageway was still shrouded in shadows. Sunlight spilled through the window straight ahead, but none of that passageway's doors were open. Clare didn't think Dorran would lock himself in a room he was searching so she looked to the right. The tall hollow one had broken the hall's lightbulbs the night before. Shards of glass were scattered over the carpet, glittering like diamonds. And at the end of the hallway was an elongated, dark shape.

Clare took half a step back. Her heart missed a beat then thudded too hard, making her shudder. She wasn't looking at the stretched woman. She was looking at a ladder.

The house has an attic.

She flexed sweaty fingers over the poker and marched down the hallway. Glass shards crackled under her boots as she stepped over them. The light coming through the window at the end of the hall wrapped around the stairs and slipped through the slats, making Clare squint. She tried to listen for noises above her, but the wind was sharp that day, and if any subtle sounds permeated the air, she couldn't hear them.

She stopped at the base of the ladder and looked up. Through the square opening in the ceiling, she could see a light flicker over wooden beams high above. Her angle was too low to see into the room, so she cast one final wary glance about herself then began to climb.

The rungs, rarely used, creaked. Clare paused partway up the ladder with the top of her head peeking through the hole. The attic was immense. Temporary walls had been constructed at odd intervals. Some sections looked like they might have been modest bedrooms, though the furniture was nowhere near as grand as the rest of the house. Cheap metal bed frames held old mattresses and simple sheets, and wardrobes that looked like castoffs stood beside them. In other areas, the attic seemed to have been turned into storage. Crates, building material, old furniture, and dozens of thick cardboard boxes were scattered about. She couldn't see Dorran from her angle, but the light—a soft gold rather than the harsh white of outside—came from behind one of the walls twenty feet away.

She climbed off the ladder and followed the edge of the attic, close enough to touch the slanting roof. Insulating material had been placed in the ceiling to conserve heat, but she could tell where the wind had torn away tiles. The padding was sagging and discolored and had even split in some places, spilling piles of snow into the attic. The house's highest level was too cold for the frost to melt, and the wind nipped through the holes to ruffle Clare's hair and make her bundle her scarf around the lower half of her face.

She moved silently as she crossed the area. She couldn't risk making noise in case she and Dorran weren't alone in the attic. Instead, she kept her feet light and skirted around furniture and stacks of storage, giving any shadowed areas a wide berth. She approached the closest wall and peered around it.

Dorran was on the other side, facing away from her. She felt a swell of pride while watching him. He'd brought a lantern, which he held high. His movements were steady and assured. An overcoat's collar had been lifted so that it curled around his chin to protect him.

He was scoping around a set of dilapidated wardrobes. One at a time, he bumped the doors open, stepping back in the same motion. He waited just long enough to check that the insides were empty before moving on to the next set.

He's gorgeous. Clare took a step closer, and a board creaked under her foot. Dorran swung at the noise, eyes blazing and teeth bared as he lifted a crowbar.

"Sorry! It's just me. Sorry." Clare raised one hand and risked an apologetic smile.

Dorran's expression morphed into a mix of horror, frustration, and incredulity. He crossed to her in two long paces and grasped her arm. "You can't *be* here."

Clare took advantage of his coat's high collar and tugged on it to pull Dorran closer until their eyes were at the same level. "Remember how you promised to let me win our arguments?"

His shoulders slumped, and even though his eyes stayed tight and worried, a smile creased the corners of his mouth. "Incorrigible."

"I am. You can take me back to my room, but I promise I'll find a way to get out again and again and again. It's going to be safer to keep me with you than to let me wander the house alone." She narrowed her eyes, daring him to argue with her. "I don't even know what half of this place looks like. I could get lost out there and starve in some long-forgotten third parlor."

"It is not *that* big." He chuckled then sighed, resting his forehead against hers. "Very well. I am not too proud to admit I've lost this battle. But please, you *must* be careful."

"I will be."

"Stay behind me when we move into a new area. Don't try to explore alone. And if anything becomes too dangerous, you must promise me you will run. There is no shame in retreating if it means surviving to fight another day. Yes?"

"Yes."

He kissed her tenderly, the touch heartfelt and lingering. "If you care about me at all, put your own safety first."

"It won't come to that." Clare rose onto her toes to meet his lips in return and felt him shiver. "We'll be okay."

Dorran's fingers brushed across her cheek as he smiled down at her. The wind screamed as a harsh gust funneled snow into the attic. Reluctantly, he let Clare go and adjusted his grip on his crowbar. They turned to face the length of the attic. "Let us continue."

CHAPTER 33

FROM HER NEW VANTAGE point, Clare had a taste of how vast the attic really was. It had to run across the entire house, though its temporary walls helped break up the space. She suspected there were several other ladders leading into it.

Like the staff's areas downstairs, comparatively little care had gone into maintaining the attic. Some of the walls had wallpaper, though age had worn away the glue and left strips of it hanging loose. Other walls had been given a thin coating of paint or left as bare wood. None of the furniture, not even the doors, matched.

"Sometimes staff were made to sleep here if there was a shortage of space below." Dorran led her along the attic, his eyes bright as they searched around old furniture and inside cupboards. He spoke in a whisper, but Clare kept close enough to hear him clearly. "Which was far from reasonable. The attic can become cold, even in the warmer months, and there are always unused guest rooms below. But my mother would rather die than allow one of her *servants* to sleep in a guest bedroom."

He used his crowbar to nudge open a cabinet. Inside was empty. They kept moving.

"They put up with it?" Clare asked, keeping her own voice to a murmur.

Dorran lifted his shoulders then let them drop. "She didn't tolerate insubordination. They either bowed to her will or were removed from the house the same day. And many of them, especially the ones who had been here the longest, adored her."

They reached another wall, which stretched halfway across the attic's width. Dorran opened one of the doors, one arm held back to keep Clare behind him. He stayed still a moment as the lantern's light danced over incalculable piles of cast-out goods, then he gave her a brief nod before stepping through.

The new section was messier, with jumbles of furniture on ragged wood floors and old carpets rolled up in the corner. A broken tea set balanced inside a display cabinet. Dorran crouched to check under the furniture then led her onward.

A gust of freezing air snatched Clare's breath away. They turned toward it, and Dorran exhaled heavily, letting the lamp drop. "Ah. I think we may have just found how the creatures got into the house."

They faced one of the larger holes in the roof. Dark, broken tiles littered the floor. The insulation had been torn, and snow was piled below the hole. It was easily large enough for a person to crawl through. Dirty scuff marks spread out from the opening, spiraling in different directions until they became too faint to follow.

Dorran muttered under his breath as he shook his head. "How did they scale the walls? Regardless, there is no purpose in searching the remainder of the house if they can easily come back in again. We will need to seal the hole. And not just this one, but any others that are large enough to allow the creatures through."

Clare looked behind them. The roof was dotted with damage. She could see at least three other breaches that would be large enough for a person to fit through. One of them had its own set of dirty footprints leading away from it. Her heart sank. "I thought the wind and hail were breaking the roof. And I guess they were...but only because it had been weakened. I think the creatures made the holes themselves. I heard something that sounded like scratching on the roof my first night here."

It was a horrible mental image—the distorted humans crawling over Winterbourne like insects, surrounded by the blizzard, frost growing in their hair and over their skin as they clawed at the tiles.

Dorran's lips pulled back in a snarl. "If that is true, then closing the holes will not work. They can simply make more."

"Can we seal off the attic? Barricade the trapdoors?"

"Yes. That may be the best option. Eventually, we will have to eradicate them from the attic as well, but I think this is the only choice we have at present. Please, would you hold this?"

He passed his lamp to Clare then led her out of the makeshift room and toward a stack of building equipment.

Massive planks, old tins of half-used paint, and workmen's tool chests stood propped against the wall. Dorran opened one of the chests and retrieved a pot of nails and a hammer, then he began gathering boards. "From the house's last expansion," he explained.

Looking closer, Clare saw that all of the equipment appeared to be ancient. The wood was old and cracking in some areas, and the tool chests were all rusty. Dorran picked through the wood until he found pieces that seemed solid, then they crossed the room to one of the trapdoors.

For the next twenty minutes, the attic was full of deafening bangs as Dorran nailed shut three of the four trapdoors. They moved carefully. Every time Dorran put his head down to work, Clare stood as sentry, the lamp held high above them as she scanned the space. They didn't try to search for the monsters, and they weren't disturbed. Either the hollow ones had all moved to the lower levels, or the hammering was loud enough to keep them hidden.

As Dorran finished securing the third trapdoor, Clare asked, "Are there any other exits from the attic?"

He brushed sweaty hair out of his face as he stood. Plumes of mist rose with his every breath. "Just the one we came in by. We can carry some planks down with us and nail that shut from the outside. Then we will need to search the remainder of the—"

A low, quiet creak echoed from the back of the attic. They glanced at each other.

Clare spoke in a whisper. "Should we…"

Dorran looked conflicted. "We can leave and avoid confrontation entirely. But there is no guarantee the creature will not try to follow us or stop us from nailing the trapdoor shut. No. I had better deal with it now." He picked up the crowbar, and Clare saw that he was clenching it tightly enough for his knuckles to turn white. "It will need to be done eventually anyway."

Her stomach turned cold. Dorran moved toward the back of the attic, and Clare hurried to keep up with him. The lantern's glow danced over the walls as it swung.

"Careful," Dorran whispered. "Stay well behind me."

Up ahead was the attic's back wall, shielded by a folding screen. Clare could barely make out hints of motion in the gaps between the slats. Dorran circled around, moving silently as he tried not to draw attention.

Clare tightened her grip on the fire poker. This encounter felt different. Before, in the forest, they had been attacked. She had acted in self-defense. Now she was going to strike first. It left her feeling uneasy and dirty. She didn't want to kill something defenseless, something that might just have been trying to hide.

You can't think of them that way. The monsters were beyond reason and beyond saving. They had lost too much of their humanity. She'd seen their eyes in the forest. They were wild, driven by pure animalistic impulses. They barely felt pain. And they certainly hadn't felt remorse when they'd bitten into her.

Even so...hunting them seemed wrong.

She thought Dorran's mind might be running along similar tracks. She could see the tension in his face and across his shoulders. His eyebrows were drawn together, but the expression didn't hold any ferocity. It was full of dread.

Something scuffled across the wooden floor, just out of sight. Dorran took three sharp steps to round the barrier and raised his weapon. Clare followed, the lamp thrust in front of herself, poker aimed outward like a spear.

The woman on the other side snarled. Her teeth jutted out of her jaw, protruding at odd angles, each one nearly three inches long. A bald head and the remains of a dress's collar shone in Clare's lamp. Her back curved into an S shape, bending in then out again in a way that made her spindly legs and overturned pelvis seem like they didn't belong together.

Dorran's crowbar was raised, but he didn't move. The woman coiled, her muscles bunching as she prepared to spring, but then the distorted head rolled to the side. She hissed and scuttled back. The shadows coiled around her as she vanished into the wall.

Dorran's crowbar dropped. He inhaled quickly, his breathing ragged, as his expression turned bitter. "I couldn't do it."

Clare rolled her shoulders, feeling the cold sweat sticking the dress to her back. "I couldn't either."

"She used to be human." He turned his head aside. "She…she wore a dress. Did you see? She still had its collar around her neck. She was a woman not long ago."

Human. Inhuman. Where do we draw the line? How much mercy can we show without bartering our own lives? Clare didn't have an answer for that…or for Dorran's next question.

"What did she do to earn that fate while we survived?"

They stared at each other for a moment, both lost, both conflicted. Then Dorran turned back toward the opening the woman had stepped through. Clare squinted at it. It looked like a door, except it was set into the back of the attic. Logically, the opening should look into the snowy, early-morning sky. Instead, its insides were pitch-black.

Clare took a step forward. Dorran held out a hand to keep her back, but she still craned her neck to see over his arm. "Where did she go?"

He shook his head. "I do not know. This should be the back wall. It makes no sense to have a door here, unless it's a storage closet."

He approached and reached his crowbar toward the wooden door. He nudged it closed, and Clare saw that it only looked like a door on one side. The other was covered by the same blue wallpaper that ran over the wall. The edge was jagged where it had been ripped, but once it was closed, it blended perfectly into the rest of the wall.

A secret door.

Dorran hooked the crowbar into its edge and pulled it open again. Clare leaned closer, lamp extended, to see inside. Behind the door was a passageway. It was wider and taller than she would have expected from the door's size. Thick wooden steps led down. Clare stepped into the opening and stretched her lamp out as far as she could, but she still didn't see the stairway's end.

"Can you guess where it might go?" she asked Dorran.

He looked grim. "I have no idea. We should be standing

above the east wing. But there is no way to reach the attic from that section of the house. And certainly not through a stairwell like this."

"It probably explains how the creatures got into the rest of the house, though. The retractable attic ladders would be too complicated and noisy for them."

He muttered something furious. "I don't like this. If we go down there, I will no longer know the floor plan or how to escape if something goes wrong. We could be trapped."

"We'll have to follow it, though, won't we?" Clare ran her fingers over the ragged wallpaper edge. The idea made her feel sick, but she couldn't see any way around it. "If you don't know where the passageway comes out, it's probably another disguised door somewhere else in the house."

Dorran was silent for a moment. His dark eyes darted across the stairs, then he rested his hand on Clare's shoulder. "I would like you to return to your room."

"We've already had this argument."

"This is different. I don't know how easily I can defend you in this passageway."

"That's okay." She flexed her grip on the fire poker. "It will be safer with two of us. Besides, if we don't know where the passageway lets out, no part of the house is safe. It might even open into our room. I saw one of the creatures in there, after all."

"I sometimes wish you were less deft at logic," he said. "Very well. Stay behind me and be careful."

They took up the same positions—Dorran leading, Clare

holding the lamp and following closely enough to light their way. The boards creaked as they stepped on them, but the noise seemed insulated, as though the walls were too thick to let it carry far. Their breathing echoed. It didn't take long for the attic to feel like a distant world. Twenty steps in, the passageway turned at a right angle. It cut out the last traces of the natural light that had leaked through the attic's roof. Clare started breathing through her mouth. A heavy musky scent seeped out of the passageway. It smelled like rotting flesh and oily hair. The farther she went, the stronger it became, until she almost gagged on it.

"I was hoping we might be in a disused staff passageway from an old edition of the house." Dorran sounded hoarse. "But look at this."

Clare moved closer to where he indicated on the wall. The lamplight revealed the support beams. They ran up the walls and over the ceiling like an archway. The wood was solid and carved into an elegant design. She frowned. "There isn't anything like this in the other staff regions."

"Exactly. And it has been dusted within the last month." Dorran nodded for them to continue.

Now that Clare was thinking along those lines, it seemed equally strange that the hallway was so wide. She bent to see the floor and confirmed what she'd suspected—they were walking on dark wood. It was dusty and scuffed compared to the main parts of the house, but no less decadent.

What is this place?

She had a suspicion, but she didn't want to say it out loud.

Dorran was stressed enough, and if she was reading the tension in his neck and the angle of his eyebrows correctly, he'd already had the same thought.

The stairs leveled out into a straight hallway, and they came to a halt. The passage continued ahead, but a narrower branch led to the left. Dorran looked over his shoulder to get Clare's approval for their direction, and she nodded. They continued straight ahead.

In the distance, Clare thought she could see a trace of light on the right wall. It was fine—razor-thin and near the floor—and barely a meter long.

As they moved toward it, Clare became aware of subtle scratching noises surrounding her. Coupled with the unrelenting stench, it gave her the impression of being surrounded by rats. But the noise was wrong for rodents. She knew it from the week she'd spent trying to ignore it. *Fingernails on stone. Fingernails on wood.* She swallowed and tasted fear.

Dorran stayed alert, but his attention had turned to the sliver of light. When he reached it, he crouched to feel around it. Lamplight painted deep shadows over his face. He pressed his fingertips against the wall and pushed. A muted crunching noise echoed, then the section pushed out, swinging silently on well-oiled hinges.

They stepped through the opening, and Clare lowered her lamp as natural light replaced it. Dorran rubbed his palm against his forehead. Although his expression was stony, his lips twitched.

As Clare looked around them, she thought the scene was

familiar. She recognized the tall walls, dark, intricate wallpaper, and elaborate architraves. A support pillar jutted out of the wall every ten feet. To her left, at the end of the hall, was a window that had once had a curtain hung over it.

They had arrived back in the third-floor hallway.

CHAPTER 34

"THERE ARE SECRET PASSAGES in my home." Dorran's smile was bitter, and his lips continued to tremble. Whether it was from repressed anger or shock, Clare wasn't sure. "I've lived here my whole life, and I never knew. Apparently, trust is considered a luxury in this family."

Clare wished she could say something to help, but her tongue was dry. The first time she'd seen one of the strangers, she'd been standing at the window at the end of the hallway. She could have sworn she'd seen a figure lurking in the darkness. But a second later, it had vanished. They were now standing where *it* had stood, at one of the support pillars. The door had been molded to blend in with the pillar's edges. Clare could have walked past it a thousand times and never noticed the hairline cracks.

When she looked back through the opening, she could see the secret passageway continuing, dipping into stairs shortly ahead. That answered the question of how the hollow ones had been moving through the house without being seen. But it raised another question: how far did the pathways go? She dreaded finding out the answer to that, but she could guess some of their destinations.

The cellar.

Dorran twisted to the right, toward their bedroom door. Clare followed his gaze and felt her heart skip a beat. The tall creature hovered near the stairs. Its arms hung limp at its sides. Its slack jaw twitched into an expression that might have been a smile or a grimace. It took a staggering step closer, its bowed head scraping across the plaster as it moved.

"Careful," Dorran said. "Get behind me."

The creature's arms swung like pendulums as it rocked nearer, saliva dripping from its open maw. Dorran took a step forward, feet braced and crowbar raised.

Something moved beside him. Pale limbs glistened in the concealed doorway. Fingers, mottled and eight inches long each, reached out, aiming for Dorran's head.

"No!" Clare lunged, bringing her poker down on the grasping hands as they snagged Dorran's collar. Bones crackled. The lamp swung precariously as Clare desperately shoved Dorran out of reach of the hands.

Dorran reacted quickly, twisting toward her, but the hands were faster. Clare swung at them but missed. Fingers tangled in her hair and yanked her so sharply that she could barely gasp. They dragged her through the doorway and into the darkness inside the walls. More bony hands wrapped around her arm and tightened on her ankle. They wrenched her in opposite directions, and Clare fell, flinching as she hit the floor hard. The lamp shattered. Its flame exploded upward as the oil spilled, but almost immediately, something large flopped over it, extinguishing the light.

Dorran was halfway through the opening, weapon raised and teeth bared. That was a mistake. The tall woman was on him in that split-second of inattention, dragging him back and forcing him onto the hallway's carpet. Clare tried to yell, but cold fingers pressed over her face, stifling her.

Then the door slid closed, and Clare's world was enveloped in blackness. The smoke from the broken lamp blended into the rancid stench and what smelled like burning flesh. Clare fought blindly, swinging her poker at the creatures holding her. One blow hit its mark, thudding into flesh and bone, but the creature didn't loosen its hold. Clare kicked. Her foot passed through empty air. Something heavy pressed into her back, forcing her over so that she was facedown on the floor. All around her, she heard scrabbling, scratching noises. Then Dorran yelled. It was faint, insulated by the thick walls. He sounded like he was in pain. Clare reached to where the door had been, but something sharp crushed her outstretched hand into the floor. She tried to scream, but with the hand over her mouth and her lungs starved of oxygen, all she could manage was a whine.

The creatures were chattering. The soft, animalistic noise grew in volume. She could feel a presence approaching her, but she was blind in the darkness. She writhed, trying to throw them off, and managed to get one arm free. Two more hands grasped it and yanked it down at her side.

The chattering swelled, turning into something that sounded like a chaotic chant, and Clare squeezed her eyes closed. Something hard and heavy smacked into the back of her head, and her vision exploded into a swirl of darkness and dancing red dots.

The pain was intense, like molten lava being poured over the back of her skull and into her eyes. She no longer felt certain of which way was up, and her limbs refused to move properly. The clammy fingers pinched as they dragged her along the hallway then down the stairs, each step jarring the pain in her head and making her twitch. Consciousness faded in and out, and with it came nausea. She wanted to scream, to make them stop, but innately, she knew that noise would bring another blow. Instead, she gritted her teeth and tried, as much as she could, to be aware of where she was being taken.

They dropped down a sharp step, and Clare's head smacked into the floor. The pain intensified until it was unbearable. More sparks danced across her eyes then faded out.

When she opened her lids again, she was lying on her side on something hard and freezing cold. She knew she must have passed out, but she didn't know for how long. She was blind. A horrible fear rose that the monsters might have clawed out her eyes, and it took effort to suppress the panic. Her eyes hurt, but not enough to be missing.

She wasn't alone. Noises coursed around her. Quiet enough to be whispers, the clacking of dozens of nails across stone and phlegmy, rasping breaths bled together into a terrible symphony.

Fear choked her. She fought to push it down, to keep it under control, to keep her mind working. She lay perfectly still in an effort to avoid attracting attention. With her eyes useless, she had to rely on her other senses. The stench from the hallway was stronger than it had been before. It wasn't helping her nausea. Only the panic clenching her stomach kept it at bay.

By the scope of the sounds, she knew she must be surrounded by the creatures. She didn't understand why she was still alive. She'd assumed they were mindless, that all they cared about was eating, that they would have consumed her the first chance they had.

Moving very carefully, trying not to make any noise, Clare extended a hand to feel the surface she was lying on. From what she could tell, it was a rough slab of rock. Uneven edges jabbed into her, and the section below her cheek was cold enough to make her face ache. It was helping the headache, though, which was a small mercy.

She no longer had her fire poker. Both her jacket and boots were gone, leaving her arms and feet cold. Clare tried to mentally run through her body, assessing for damage. She didn't think any bones were broken. Everything hurt, from her head to the bruises across her side and back. Something solid pinched the skin around her ankle. When Clare tried to move her foot, a chain link clinked.

Her fear crept up to a new level. She had a shackle around her foot. If this was the creatures' doing, she had vastly underestimated them, their motives, and their intelligence.

Dorran...

Among the rough breathing of the bodies moving around her, Clare tried to pick up on any sign that she had human company. If Dorran was there, he was staying perfectly silent. Clare closed her eyes against the repressive dark and tried not to hyperventilate.

She'd distracted him. He'd turned his attention away when Clare yelled, and it had allowed the tall creature to rush him and force him to the ground.

Dorran was strong, fierce, and resourceful. But he was also exhausted.

Her heart ached. She'd wanted to be with Dorran to keep him safe, and she'd done exactly the opposite. If he'd been hurt, she wasn't sure she could forgive herself. A dark part of her mind took it a step further and asked what would happen if he was already dead. The pains across her body suddenly felt insignificant to the way she ached inside.

Clare moved as silently as she could. She breathed through her mouth to minimize the noise and try to reduce the overpowering smell as she curled her body. She kept her leg still so as not to disturb the chain and felt around the restraint. It had been manufactured out of thick metal. The shackle had been intended for someone larger and didn't fit around Clare's leg properly. She thought, if she could turn her foot at the right angle, she might be able to squirm through.

The chattering noise around her rose in volume, and Clare froze. A slow, steady clicking—louder than the sounds around it—was coming closer. Clare tried to pinpoint its direction, but the darkness was too disorienting.

Quick. Before whatever's coming arrives. This might be your only chance.

She gave up trying to be silent. Clare got her fingers under the shackle, testing its size, and began to pull it over her foot.

The fit was close. But even with her heel pulled in and toes pointed, Clare didn't think she could get her foot through. Not without something to help it slide over the skin.

"She is blind. Let us have some light."

Clare froze. The voice belonged to a woman, but not like any woman she'd ever heard before. The words were spoken slowly and enunciated crisply, with a faint accent that Clare couldn't pinpoint. The voice rang with authority. She could easily imagine it belonging to some kind of aristocracy. At the same time, it had been distorted. The words sounded too dry, almost cracked.

She shrank back from the voice. A moment later, a soft hiss was accompanied by the glow of a freshly lit candle. The light was weak, but Clare had spent so long in the dark that she still squinted.

The hissing and chattering grew louder. Shapes scurried back from the light, their distorted faces watching it warily. Then Clare saw the woman holding the candle and had to bite her tongue to stop a scream.

The woman stood tall, well over seven feet. Her papery-white skin was creased, partially from age and partially from the distortion her body had undergone. Lines around her lips told Clare that they had been pursed often in life. She suspected she would have seen frown lines around the eyes as well, except the lower lids had drooped. They created dark crescent-moon shapes below the eyes, where once-pink skin had turned black. It made the stark-white eyeballs seem poised to slip and tumble out. Steel-gray hair had been wrapped into a bun on top of the creature's head, though wisps sagged out of the formation.

The woman wore a dress that would have been magnificent before it had been torn. Its high collar brushed her chin, and its dark-red bodice was entwined with black lace trim. She clasped the candle in a bony hand, unconcerned with trying to protect her fingers from the dripping wax. She had eight fingers on each hand. Then Clare's eyes moved down, and the malformed hand became the least of her concerns.

The dress's skirt had been shredded. Dark silk strips rustled with the woman's every step, and behind them, Clare could see legs. The woman had *insect* legs.

Clare pressed her hand over her mouth as she tried to shuffle farther back. Her thigh slipped over the edge of what she realized was a dais, and she froze.

The woman's legs moved rhythmically, almost as though she'd had them her whole life. It was clear she hadn't, though. Gore still stuck to the exposed bone segments. They ended in sharp protrusions, like a crab's legs, and had too many joints. Clare counted six full-grown legs, but others were still developing. Two more had burst from the woman's waist. They wiggled uselessly in the air with every step she took.

"Well?" The woman's upper lids descended in what would have been a slow blink if the lower lids had met them, then they fluttered back up. "Show your respects to the mistress of the house."

CHAPTER 35

"MADELINE MORTHORNE," CLARE WHISPERED.

The woman's chin lifted a fraction of an inch. She swept toward Clare, the horrible clicking from her spindly feet echoing through the space. The candlelight flickered around them, and Clare tore her eyes away from the woman. The area she was in seemed to be a cavern. Rough stone walls surrounded her, and she couldn't see the ceiling. She tried to count the creatures in the space. There seemed to be more than a dozen, but it was hard to be sure when they were moving incessantly, scurrying across the ground or climbing the stone walls.

She hazarded a question. "Where am I?"

Madeline's nostrils flared, but her voice was steady and measured as she answered. "Below the cellar. In my private rooms."

That meant the secret passages had to spread through the whole house. They were well built but not well used...until recently. She guessed previous generations had installed them as shelters for a worst-case scenario. A paranoid woman who built her family's home in the middle of the forest seemed like just the sort of person who would turn them into a maze of secrets.

Her head throbbed, and her arm ached. The cold metal was an unpleasant weight on her ankle. As Madeline circled her, Clare chanced a look at the chain. It was short and bolted into the edge of the stone slab, trapping her on the dais. The shackle wasn't quite large enough to pull over her foot, not without scraping the skin.

And once she got out, she had no idea which direction to go. No matter where she looked, all she saw were unyielding stone walls and the relentlessly chattering hollow ones.

"You're not like the others." Clare spoke carefully, afraid of flaring anger, but trying to feel out the exact extent of the situation.

Madeline's eyebrow quirked up. "Of course not. They are only servants."

Clare swallowed. Now that she was looking, she realized the pitiable creatures were still wearing scraps of maid uniforms. She recognized the woman from the basement, with the many-jointed arms. She crawled upside down, her breastbone pointed at the ceiling and saliva trailing down her cheek and into her hair. The spines growing from her back scraped across the stones. The dress clinging to her jutting hips had the neat black-and-whites that Clare guessed the staff must have worn before the world fell apart.

She looked aside and saw the maid she and Dorran had encountered in the attic. He'd commented that she wore the collar of a dress. It was discolored and had been splattered with blood from some gory feast. If it hadn't been so stained, Dorran might have recognized it as the collar of one of the staff's uniforms.

"These are your entourage," Clare muttered.

"My *servants*." The voice took on a biting threat. "My personal maids who care for my needs. They have gone witless, but they still know their mistress well enough to mind my commands. Most of the time."

As she passed one of the creatures, Madeline extended a hand. Her multitude of fingers curled under the maid's chin as it cowered, eyes wide and adoring. Madeline's fingers twitched, and pricks of blood appeared at the creature's throat. Then Madeline stepped away, and the maid crumpled to the ground, shaking and head bowed in reverence.

Disgust curled through Clare. Madeline was treating them as something even less than pets. And they seemed to adore her for it.

"Why am I here?"

Clare dreaded the answer, but none came. Madeline's thin, bloodless lips curved into a smile. She continued to pace, a hint of satisfaction shining in her eyes, content to let the silence stretch. Clare had the distinct impression that they were waiting for something. She tried a different question.

"You must have been outside the forest when you changed." She knew she was reaching, but Clare needed to know if Madeline remembered what had happened to twist her so viciously. "You were traveling to Gould, right? You and the rest of your family."

Madeline's face tightened, and for a moment, her drooping lower lids twitched. "You are right. The car stopped. They had instructions to travel without break, so I opened my door to understand why I had been disobeyed, and I heard them screaming."

"Who?"

"The others." Her hand flicked out in a dismissive wave. "My family. And the servants in the bus. They were going wild. Clawing at their own faces as though they were animals. Biting at each other. It was all I could do to gather my maids and lead them home."

Another of the creatures quivered as Madeline passed. She was circling the dais. What for, Clare couldn't tell.

"Did you see or feel anything?" Clare cleared her throat at Madeline's sharp glare. "When *you* changed, what happened?"

"The air." Her expression grew distant. "It was sour. Oh, it burned when it was swallowed. How my darlings screamed. But it made us strong. It made us able to endure…"

Wax was dripping over the edge of the candle. It trickled over the woman's many fingers, but she didn't so much as flinch. *Whatever it was, it dulled their nerves.*

Madeline saw her staring. A hint of a smile ghosted over her pale lips. She reached out and overturned the candle.

Clare was too slow to react. She screamed as burning wax splattered over her neck. Her headache flamed up, scorching like an inferno, as she hit her head on the dais, fingers clawing in an effort to scrape off the wax.

Madeline laughed. It was a gentle, fluttering noise, like something Clare might have heard at a dinner party. "Oh, you are delightful. You look so sad and helpless when you are in pain. It is no wonder my son took a liking to you."

Tears blurred Clare's eyes. She hunched over, gasping, fingers shaking as the fresh wax hardened over them.

Madeline leaned down to stare into Clare's face. Her spine didn't move naturally. The upper back remained straight as she twisted at the waist, creating the impression of an insect bending its thorax. "Oh yes, I know. I saw him carry you back into the house. I listened to him talk to you while you were asleep. You have done a pretty job of seducing him."

Clare squinted her eyes to see through the pain. "Leave him alone."

"So opinionated, so small-minded." Madeline sighed delicately as she returned to pacing. "He is the last of his family now that the others have been lost. My only child. My love, my pride."

Clare had plenty of words she wanted to spit at the creature, but the burns on her throat still throbbed, and the candle flickered threateningly. She bit her tongue.

"He was so sweet when he was little. I would hold him close and shush his tears as I picked the scabs open. In the evenings, he would sit quietly and let me poke sewing needles into his back as long as I kissed him and told him I loved him."

Clare closed her eyes as nausea choked her. *Oh, Dorran. What hell did she put you through?*

"It is my fault he has gone astray. In my love, I allowed him to grow willful and proud." Madeline lifted her chin to stare at the ceiling. "As he grew older, he became hardened. He no longer seeks his mother's love or listens to her guidance. Spoiled, proud, willful. I gave him everything, and in return, he shows nothing but disdain."

Liar. Proud and spoiled were two concepts so far removed from Dorran that Clare's mind struggled to connect them. He was kind, gentle, and patient. But apparently those weren't traits Madeline valued.

"You have never had children, I suppose." Madeline's exhale rasped over a dry tongue. "You cannot understand. A mother's love is infinite. You would do anything to save your child. Even when he scorns you. Even when the future you sweated and bled and sacrificed to build is hurled back into your face."

"Are you talking about this?" Clare, unable to stay silent any longer, raised her burned hand to gesture around them. "A life spent trapped in this house? The last scraps of a wasted fortune? The honor of a family name no one remembers anymore?"

Madeline's glance was cold. "A history. A legacy. Being born to the Morthorne bloodline is an honor I cannot expect you to understand."

The words left Clare before she could stop them. "At least I understand basic human decency."

Madeline's eyebrows rose. Then she exhaled a fluttering laugh.

"You are impertinent. I should have your tongue cut out. But I suppose that would compromise your purpose."

Dread rose in Clare's stomach, cold and sticky. "My purpose?"

Madeline's long fingers flicked, as though waving the question aside. She turned to face the wall opposite them.

Clare's fingers still stung under the hardened wax. She shot a glance at her ankle. The wax wasn't a perfect grease, but it was oily enough to help. She pulled her legs up to her chest, hoping it would look like she was simply curled from cold or fear, and squirmed one of her burned fingers under the metal.

"I wanted to let you go, you know." Madeline's hand twitched around her throat, adjusting the collar. "It was not your fault you were brought into our house. You would have been permitted to leave my estate unharmed. But you relinquished that privilege the day you set your sights on my son. Evidently, he does not have much resistance against a pair of pretty eyes. You have been leading him astray, reinforcing his arrogance, encouraging his selfishness. And now I will require you to be a part of his education."

Clare paused her work to glance up. "Education?"

"I was forced to teach him a lesson many years ago." She faced away, her chin lifted high as the claw-like protrusions at her stomach twitched. "It was a difficult lesson, one about priorities and loyalty. It took many of my family to make the point, but it was worth it. He began to value his mother's guidance again."

The cyanide in the wine. Clare swallowed the words that wanted to crawl out of her and continued fighting with her shackle. One of the chain links clinked, but Madeline didn't seem to notice.

"It appears he has forgotten those learned morals in spite of the care put into them and the price that was paid. Now he will have to learn again." Madeline looked over her shoulder and smiled delicately at Clare. "He loves you. He is coming to look for you. I will allow him to see you one final time. And then he will watch you die."

Clare kept her body curled around the shackle. She had finished smearing the wax across the metal and quietly, subtly tried to squirm it over her foot. It was still too tight. The chattering was growing louder as the hollow ones scurried through the room. They were becoming excited. Clare prayed it wasn't a sign that Dorran was near. She needed more time. "Dorran won't be the heir you want, no matter what you do to me."

"Oh, you are wrong there, child. He is not quite broken yet, but he will be after today." She sighed and pressed a hand over her breast. "This body…it is strong. It is a gift. But I know my son will not see it that way. He will use it as an excuse to be repulsed, to reject me, if he can. That is why we hid, biding our time, waiting until he would be ready, until grief broke him enough to be malleable again."

"The cyanide tablet I ate was your fault, wasn't it?" Clare winced as she squirmed her foot in the shackle. The skin was scraping raw, but she was getting closer. "Dorran thought he'd made a mistake, but you swapped the bottles."

"You would have suffered less if you had let the tablets take you. It was a mistake to fight it."

"So you're going to kill me now instead. To get Dorran back.

That makes no sense. Do you really think this will make him love you?"

"I think that he will need comfort. He will long for someone who will care for him. *If* he believes he is responsible." She held up a finger. "He does not know I am here. He saw you dragged away. By the time he finds you, he will be too late to save you. My darlings will have started their feast."

The chattering was growing louder. The creatures were becoming bolder, their incessant laps around the space bringing them closer to Clare. She had a horrible suspicion she knew what Madeline meant. "Feast?"

"My poor darlings are starving." She smiled down at them as they groveled. "I allow them to eat one of their sisters on occasion, but it never ends the hunger. I would know. I feel it too. A pit in my stomach, ravenous, unfillable, no matter how much flesh I consume."

Clare's mouth was dry. She hadn't seen the maid with the hole in her side. The girl had probably been one of the unfortunate meals.

"My son will find us soon," Madeline murmured. "I left bread crumbs for him to follow. When he is near enough, I will give my pretties the permission they crave, and they will begin to eat. By the time he reaches you, you will be too far gone to save. You will be sure to scream for us, won't you?"

"They'll kill him," Clare said.

"Oh no, they shall not. My darlings hunger, but they know better than to cross me. They understand that he is off-limits."

She adjusted a strand of loose hair, tucking it back into the bun, her smile lifting a fraction. "I will allow him some time. To bury what is left of you. For his grief to break that maddening spirit. And then, once he is ready, I will emerge from the forest. His mother. The only one who cared for him above all others. The one who was willing to sacrifice her brothers and her sisters to correct his rebellious streak. Yes, he will return to me. He will have no choice."

"Why?" Clare spat anger into her words to hide the pain and fear. Blood trickled over her heel as the sharp edges of the shackle cut into her. "The world is gone. What do you think will happen? You'll live holed up in this house with Dorran, surrounded by ruin and mindless servants while you wait to die?"

"There is honor in remaining steadfast in the face of the changing world." The friendliness vanished from her voice. "Our family has ruled here for hundreds of years. And so we will continue. I will not shame my grandmother. I will not be the one to fail the empire that she has built."

Clare drew ragged breaths. Her foot smarted, sticky blood glistening around the heel, but the shackle was off. She reached her red-tipped fingers into her pocket and found the small knife she'd hidden there. Madeline was turning toward her, the protrusions around her waist twitching with agitation and excitement.

They were both out of time. Clare lunged.

CHAPTER 36

SHE HIT MADELINE IN the chest, right above the twitching claw-like protrusions. The blade embedded itself, but Clare knew that wouldn't be enough to hobble her. The pain would be a distraction at best. Instead, she relied on the momentum to throw them both to the floor. It worked. Madeline's spindly legs fell out from under her, and her malformed eyes widened with shock.

They met the stone floor and rolled. Clare pulled the blade free as she sprang away. She couldn't win in a fight against the matriarch and her underlings. Her best weapon was the element of surprise and the seconds it would buy her to escape.

While she'd been struggling to get the shackle off, Madeline had been staring at one of the walls. Clare thought she could see the hint of an archway there. She guessed it would lead to the main parts of the house, and it was the path Dorran would be coming from. She ran for it.

The candle had survived the fall, but it didn't survive Madeline. The wick hissed as she squashed it, and the room fell into pitch-blackness. Clare moved recklessly, one hand reached ahead of herself, the other clasped around the bloody knife. She couldn't afford to feel her way. She just had to run and pray for the best.

Madeline didn't make a sound. There were no screamed instructions or commands. But Clare knew the underlings were obeying her somehow. The scraping of nails on stone swelled through the cavern as they gave chase.

Clare hit a stone wall. She gasped as the air was forced out of her. The throbbing headache robbed her of her balance, and she held on to the wall as she stumbled along it, desperately searching for a way out.

A hint of light appeared to her right. It was barely anything, but it was enough to highlight the edge of an archway. Clare reached toward it. Something sharp cut into her thigh, and she screamed.

"Clare!"

Dorran's voice was distant, but she could hear the terror in it. She had no breath left to answer. She stabbed the knife down and felt it cut into skin. The pressure was released. She lurched forward, out of the fingers' reach and through the archway. Hot blood ran down her leg. Pain radiated from the cuts with every step, but she closed her mind to it and spent everything moving forward.

Flickering light glistened on the rough walls of the natural tunnel. The passage curved to the right and sloped upward. Clare set her sights on the warm glow ahead.

Then fingers snagged her dress and dragged her down. She

gasped as she fell, and her vision exploded white then black as her head jarred on the floor. She rolled over, gagging as she tried not to throw up. Teeth bit into her leg, then her arm, then her shoulder. She opened her mouth to scream, but the noise caught in her throat.

No. Please. Not like this.

She twisted, threw her elbow back, and felt it hit bone. Pain overwhelmed her, blinded her. Hands pawed at her limbs, squeezing. Then, in an instant, the teeth released their hold.

Bright light arced overhead. Clare squinted her eyes open. Flames hissed and spluttered, a trail of sparks spiraling around her. The hollow ones howled, their eyes bulging as they flinched away. Dorran appeared in the light, his face twisted into a vicious snarl as he planted himself above Clare. He wielded the flames, a burning cloth tied around the end of a wooden pole.

One of the hollow lunged toward him, but Dorran reacted quickly, jabbing the torch forward to meet it. Guttural shrieks rose, and the stench of burning skin swelled around them. The hollow one lurched away, clawing mindlessly at its face, shredding the scorched flesh. Its companions backed out of Dorran's reach, swaying. Waves of anxious chattering rolled through them.

Dorran crouched at Clare's side, not moving his eyes from the monsters. "Can you put your arms around my neck?"

Everything ached, but Clare reached up, hugging him, and his spare arm slipped under her legs. He kept the flame moving, threatening anything that drew too close, as he lifted her and began backing up the passageway.

"It's your mother." Clare struggled to speak and breathe at the same time. She needed him to know in case they were separated again, in case the worst happened. "She's been here the whole time. I don't know how, but she's controlling the other monsters."

He muttered something she couldn't quite make out. The creatures continued to dance around the edges of the light. Dorran was breathing heavily, trying to share his strength between carrying Clare and wielding the torch. "Hold on. We're almost there."

"I can walk." She wasn't sure if that was the actual truth, but she hoped she could carry through on the promise. "You can put me down."

"Not yet." Dorran sidestepped. Clare noticed a small metal door set into the side of the stone tunnel and braced herself. Using his shoulder, Dorran shoved the door open. Its hinges had springs, and as they stepped through, the door bounced closed with a bang. Dorran shoved his foot into it, and Clare heard a latch click as it caught.

He staggered back a handful of steps, dropped the torch, and very gently lowered Clare to the floor. As he pulled back, she tried to read his expression through the spluttering light. He was ashen gray, and his lips were white. Blood beaded in a scratch across one cheek. Stress clung around his eyes in shadows and harsh lines. "Clare—"

"It's okay. I'm okay."

He pressed into her, kissing her lips then her cheek before pulling back just far enough to look into her eyes. "I thought I'd lost you."

"I'm not that easy to get rid of." She laughed even though it hurt.

"Stay still a moment." He pulled back to reach a bench near them. It held a lamp, which he opened and lit half-blind. The space was warmer than the tunnels they had come from. The homemade torch on the ground was burning itself out, but it wasn't the only source of light. Clare looked behind herself and saw a glow coming from one of the five massive furnaces. Dorran had brought her to the basement.

The lamp came to life. Dorran knelt at Clare's side. His smile faded as he saw the blood dripping off her shoulder. The tension returned to his movements as his hands roved across Clare's body, assessing the damage, finding all of the bites and scratches. "Oh, Clare. No. No. I am so sorry. I am so sorry—"

"Not your fault." She ran one hand over the side of Dorran's face to pull his attention away from the cuts. Sweat dripped into her eyes, and her fingers shook, but she put conviction into her voice. "Listen to me. You don't apologize, because none of this is your fault. You didn't *do* this."

His eyes met hers then flicked away as he tugged his jacket off. "I promised to keep you safe. I should have been more careful. I should have gotten to you faster."

"It was my stupid ass that got grabbed. And you not only found me, but you got me out of there, which is more than a lot of people would have." She winced as she adjusted her position. "I'm still alive. I'm calling that a win."

He used a knife to cut his jacket into strips then began

319

wrapping them around the cuts on Clare's arms and legs. They bled freely and hurt like crazy, but as far as she could tell, there were no missing chunks, just tooth marks. Dorran tied off one of the bandages then applied pressure to another wound. "Try not to move. As long as we can get these to clot—"

"We can't stay here for long. The monsters—the hollow ones—they're mindless, and they probably won't figure out the door. But Madeline will."

He glanced at her sharply. "Are you certain it's her?"

"Yeah. Gray hair. Fancy dress. Surrounded by maids. They used to be maids, at least."

He squeezed his eyes closed and muttered under his breath.

"She…" Clare didn't know how to say the next part. No matter how much bad blood existed between Dorran and his mother, Madeline was still his closest relative. It was hard to know how much loyalty might live under the surface or how painful the news might be. "She was caught in the quiet zone. It changed her."

He didn't look up from his work. "How?"

Clare flinched as he tied off another bandage. "She…she has a surplus of legs."

"All right." He was quiet as he examined the bite mark on her shoulder, and Clare tried to read his expression. He kept it carefully guarded. She thought it might be possible he didn't know how to feel. It was a lot to try to process when there were so many other things to be worried about.

Dorran caught her watching him and glanced aside. "You said she is controlling the others?"

"She is. She said she brought them back here after they changed. They must have been hiding under her orders. They had instructions to stay away from you, which is probably why you never saw them."

"And she knows the secret passageways, which means she has an advantage." Dorran looked at the door behind them. A rock façade had been fastened over it. Now that it was closed, it was almost invisible as it blended into the rest of the wall. He sighed. "Oh, Clare. There are tunnels everywhere here. I don't know how far they go, but I must have traveled through half of the house trying to reach you."

"So no matter where we go, she'll have access to us."

"We can lock ourselves into a room. Perhaps if we can find somewhere secure, we can wait it out and let them starve. They must have been without food for a long time."

Clare closed her eyes as she struggled to think through the headache and the pain. "They're cannibalistic. The maids. That's what they've been surviving on—each other."

He groaned and tied off the final bandage. "Then we cannot wait them out."

She didn't know what to say. Fighting an uncoordinated band of creatures in the forest had been one thing. They could be outsmarted. But with someone like Madeline at their helm—clever, ruthless, and motivated—it was hard to believe anywhere was safe.

She ran her hand over Dorran's cheek, just below the scratch. He leaned into the touch. "Clare." He kissed her palm. "You are alive." He pressed another kiss to her hand, this one feather light. "And you are with me. For that, I am grateful."

She tried to smile. "No matter how this ends, I don't regret anything. I don't regret being with you. I want you to know that."

His shoulders shook as he pulled her close. He was careful to only hold her in places she wasn't hurt, but once he had his arms around her, he held her so desperately that she felt like he might never let go. "Dearest Clare, stay with me a little longer. I will figure this out. Somehow, some way, I will make it right."

"We'll make it right together," she whispered.

Scratching noises echoed from the wall behind them. One of the creatures picked at the door, scrabbling around the edges and clawing at the handle. Clare's heart dropped, and the hairs rose on the backs of her arms.

"Stay with me," Dorran murmured, tightening his arms around her. "We will get out of here."

CHAPTER 37

WITH DORRAN'S HELP, CLARE stood and swayed. Her muscles were stiff, and every motion jarred the cuts on her legs. Dorran moved to lift her, but she shook her head. She couldn't let him carry her again. It would put him at too much of a disadvantage if he had to fight.

Dorran scooped the torch off the ground. It had burned out while they talked. He ripped away the old material and wrapped the remainder of his jacket around it. Then he picked up a jug from the shelf and poured fuel over the cloth.

"We'll aim for our room," he said as he used the lamp to light the torch. Flames bloomed, sending stark golden light across the space before reducing to a manageable size. "It is a long walk, so we may need to shelter somewhere closer. But if we can reach there, we have supplies to get us through the rest of the day and allow us to regroup."

His arm went around Clare's back, and he helped her across the cavernous space. She had to limp, but Dorran took a lot of her weight as they passed the furnaces and moved toward the stairs in the opposite wall.

The running furnace—the one funneling heat into the gardens—was down to coals, but the heat coming out of it was still immense. The metal stairs glittered in its glow, like strips of orange running up the wall. As they drew closer to the stairway, Clare pulled Dorran back. "Wait."

"What's wrong?"

She squinted into the shadows surrounding the staircase. The space was too dark—she couldn't even see the walls. When she turned her head, she could still make out the scrabbling noises at the secret door they'd come through. Her mouth turned dry. "It's a trap."

Dorran's eyebrows pulled together. "You think so?"

"Yes. It's too easy. If we were just dealing with mindless hollow ones, there would be nothing strange about them picking at a locked door. But Madeline is in control. She wouldn't send them to waste their efforts at that door—"

"Unless she wanted to herd us away from it," Dorran finished, realization crossing his features. "Which means she must be waiting for us ahead."

"Somewhere." Clare continued to scan the dark stairwell and the walls surrounding it. She couldn't see anything. But almost as though the creature behind them felt their hesitation, the scrabbling intensified.

Dorran held the torch ahead of them, trying to light the space as much as possible. Clare felt torn. They couldn't stay in the furnace room. Her energy was quickly dripping away, and the hollow had seemingly limitless endurance. But if she and Dorran tried to climb the stairs, they would be doing so essentially blind.

"Put more wood in the furnace," she murmured. "They're trying to lure us into their element—the cold and the dark. If we're going to confront them, it should be on our terms—right here, where it's warm, and where we can see what's happening."

Dorran nodded and fixed the torch into a holder in the wall. He unfastened something from his belt and offered it to her. Clare realized he'd been carrying the fire poker she'd dropped. She wrapped both hands around it like a bat as she alternated between watching the stairwell and watching the furnace.

Clare tried to listen for the telltale scraping noise heralding the hollows' approach, but it was hard to be sure what she was hearing through the furnace's crackles and the unseen creature attacking the far door. Dorran moved swiftly, gathering wood from the stack in the nearest wall and tossing it into the furnace. The logs were big, but the heat was intense enough that they caught quickly. He built the fire up until it was roaring, and all traces of cold left Clare. When he returned to her side, sweat dripped from his jaw. "That's as much as I can manage without cooking myself."

"It's perfect." Clare squinted at a shadow near the stairs that might have been a rock or might have been something more. The furnace's light spread out in a semicircle, beating its way through the shadows and dousing the environment in a red tint. "Let's throw the torch up there and see what we can shake out."

Dorran took the torch from the wall and crept toward the stairs. Clare followed closely, her poker held at the ready. They stopped twenty feet from the base of the stairs, and Dorran wound his arm back then hurled the flaming torch up.

They watched it spiral. Its light caught on the walls and on parts of the stairs then, horrifyingly, illuminated three pairs of glinting eyes.

"There they are." Clare took a step back as the torch clattered onto the stairs. The creatures, hissing and spitting, scuttled away from the light. The metal clanged as they charged down the stairs. Dorran picked up the shovel and stepped in front of Clare. As the first of the hollow neared, he swung. A meaty *thwack* rang out as his weapon connected with a skull.

The creature skidded across the stone floor, but the other two quickly took its place. Like the hollow ones in the forest, they were moving recklessly, unafraid of the weapons. Clare brought her poker down on one of the monster's protruding shoulder blades, dislocating it, and Dorran followed up with a swing that connected with the creature's side. The blow sent it tumbling away in a mess of limbs and teeth. It came to a halt in front of the furnace. Dorran followed it, darting in just long enough to jab the shovel's edge into its chest and force it into the inferno. The monster let out a deafening screech as the flames swallowed it.

The second monster charged Dorran. Clare moved to deliver a jab, throwing it off balance and allowing Dorran to get behind it. A solid blow sent it skidding after its companion. It convulsed as it fell into the furnace. Already, the other hollow one seemed to have disintegrated in the flames.

Something's not right. Panting and shaking, Clare inched close to Dorran as she watched the third and final hollow one regain its feet. The fight seemed...not *easy*, but too convenient. There had been more than a dozen maids in the cavern. One was still occupied with the door, but the rest were unaccounted for. *So why are we only being made to fight three? Madeline acted as though she had control over them, as though they obeyed her orders. So why aren't we being swarmed? Unless...*

A sprinkle of sand caught in the light as it fell. She looked up. High above her, two eyes flashed in the light. Something large moved across the ceiling. Clare took a sharp breath as the shapes resolved themselves.

Madeline led the remainder of her fleet. Her claw-like feet dug into the stony ceiling. Strips of her torn dress fluttered around her like flags. Behind her were the remaining hollow. Their pale bodies contorted horribly as they squirmed across the ragged ceiling like insects.

Clare gasped and yanked Dorran back, closer to the furnace. "Above!"

He bludgeoned the hissing maid away then looked up just in time to see the monsters release their hold on the ceiling. They plunged down, twisting in the air, extending their arms and legs toward the floor. Dorran and Clare had only a second to move, and they both leaped back to avoid the outstretched limbs.

Madeline hit the ground in an explosion of dust and cracking stone. She rose out of the plume, standing tall, back straight and neck high as her insectile legs lifted her to tower over them.

A choking noise escaped Dorran. Shock froze his expression.

Madeline's unblinking eyes fixed on him as she stretched one long hand toward her son. "Dorran. Come."

The words were said with such unyielding authority that Clare flinched. She looked at Dorran, afraid of how he might react. For a second, his eyes reflected pure, blind terror. Then they cleared. He braced his feet, his face hard, and raised the shovel.

Madeline's nostrils flared. "I said *come*."

He matched the harshness in her voice. "No."

His mother's expression twisted. She threw her hand outward, and five maids swarmed Dorran. Clare tried to block them, but they scuttled past her, pushing Dorran back, separating him from Clare.

Madeline turned toward Clare. The matriarch's eyes seethed with loathing, and her lips twitched, barely containing her fury.

Before, it wasn't personal. She wanted me gone because Dorran liked me, but that's all I was to her: an inconvenience. Now she really, genuinely hates me because I ruined everything for her. Dorran knows she's here now. He knows what she's done. And she's a woman who isn't used to being crossed.

Clare backed up, matching Madeline's pace as she stalked forward. Each step the older woman took made a soft clicking noise on the stone. Then, faster than Clare had thought she was capable of, Madeline darted forward. One bone-tipped leg shot out. Clare sidestepped and swung her poker, trying to break the appendage. She only managed to swipe it aside so that it missed her. Clare moved back, putting herself out of reach, but stumbled on her injured leg. Pain bloomed out from the cuts, and Clare swallowed a gasp. The makeshift bandage was saturated.

She risked a glance to the side. Dorran was trying to reach her, but every movement was foiled by the monsters surrounding him. Their bony arms wrapped around his, slack jaws chattered into his face, and talon-like claws dug into him. He lifted the shovel repeatedly, slamming into them, knocking them back, but there were too many. The creatures never stayed down for more than a second before rising again and rejoining the fray.

He was running out of energy. Clare tried not to think about what would happen when he was exhausted. Madeline claimed she had control over her maids and had instructed them not to kill her son. But as their bulging eyes fixed on Dorran's exposed skin, Clare had the sense that their hunger was at risk of overcoming their loyalty.

Madeline circled Clare, her eyes unblinking. Her arms stayed at her side, but she repeatedly clenched her fingers into fists then relaxed them. That and the coldness in her eyes were the only visible signs of emotion.

"You're out of choices." Clare held the poker ahead of herself, wishing it shook less than it did. "Dorran won't be coming back to you. But there's still time to save yourself. Take your maids and leave us alone. You can start a new life without him."

"Insolent. Ignorant." The words hissed through clenched

teeth. Madeline's expression flashed dark. She darted forward, two of the legs stretched out to impale Clare.

Clare had anticipated the attack, but she didn't try to escape it. Every step sapped her energy and caused fresh blood to trickle down her leg. She had to end the fight quickly. It was their only chance. She took a risk. Instead of trying to dart back, she stepped forward.

Madeline had been expecting a retreat. Her legs went wide of Clare's new position and stabbed thin air. Moving forward pushed Clare right into the woman's personal space. Her eyes were level with the twitching claws extended from the matriarch's stomach. They wiggled, agitated. Clare could hear Madeline's exhale. See the sweat glistening on her neck. Smell the stench of breath tainted by rotten meat. She angled the fire poker toward the ceiling and stabbed up in the same instant Madeline lunged down.

CHAPTER 38

HOT LIQUID DRENCHED CLARE'S arms. She squeezed her eyes closed, knowing she would either pass out or be sick if she had to look at what she'd just done. The fire poker twitched in her hands as Madeline convulsed. Then it was wrenched out of her grasp entirely as the woman lurched back.

Clare's nose was full of the harsh metallic tang of blood. It coated her, sticking to her hair and face and dripping from her arms. Clare finally opened her eyes. Madeline stood a pace away. The metal pole impaled her head, running through the underside of her jaw and with the sharp tip poking out from her steel-gray hair.

The woman's upper eyelids fluttered, and the sagging lower ones twitched. Clare let her arms slump. Madeline's lips parted as though to speak, and Clare caught a glimpse of the black metal inside her mouth. Then the matriarch crumpled backward.

A plume of dust billowed up around her when she fell. Her spindly insectile legs tangled over themselves. One gave a feeble twitch then fell still as the dust began to settle.

"Oh." Clare couldn't hold herself upright any longer. She dropped to her knees and retched. She was dizzy, and she couldn't tell if it was caused by blood loss or shock.

Through the buzzing in her head, she was faintly aware of noises in the room. Scratching. Clattering. Her consciousness made a final bid for coherence.

Dorran is here. He needs help. You've got to get up. Don't leave him to fight them alone.

She struggled a few inches off the ground then slumped back down. Everything was turning numb. She couldn't see properly, but suddenly, she wasn't alone. Hands caught her, and she heard Dorran speaking her name.

"Did she hurt you? Clare, my darling, I need you to talk to me. Where are you hurt?"

She blinked, and Dorran filled her vision. Tracks of sweat and blood ran through the gray dust coating his face. He held her, one hand on each of her shoulders, keeping her upright.

"I'm fine," she mumbled. She squeezed her eyes closed as she waited for the nausea to fade. "You...you killed them?"

"Two of them. The others ran off when..." He glanced over his shoulder, toward his mother's corpse, and when he returned his attention to Clare, his expression softened with mingled relief and sadness. "You were very brave, my darling. They ran when she fell. I think we are safe now."

Clare nodded. Her eyes burned. Tears began to escape, and she was too tired to stop them. Dorran moved closer and circled one arm around her back so that she could rest against his shoulder. She knew she must smell awful, like blood, sweat, and the oily musk that permeated the basement. But he didn't try to recoil. As he ran his hand over her hair and murmured soft words of comfort, Clare felt safe for the first time in a long while.

"I can take you somewhere more comfortable where we can clean up and rest. We can worry about this mess later."

Clare looked from the fallen matriarch to the crushed bodies of the two dead creatures. She nodded sluggishly. Dorran kept one arm around her back and reached the other under her legs to lift her.

"I can walk," she mumbled.

"I know. But this is easier."

Clare's eyes were already drooping. "You're tired."

She could hear the smile in his voice. "I'm never too tired to hold you. Rest now. I will take care of everything."

Clare drifted into sleep. Her subconscious was vaguely aware of the bumps of ascending stairs, but whenever she stirred, Dorran rocked her and lulled her back under.

It was night when she woke properly. The familiar bed and crackling flames told her she was back in the bedroom. Blankets were draped over her. She rolled over, moving gingerly as aches flared.

A warm body lay at her side. Dorran watched her, his eyes half lidded.

"Sorry," she whispered. "I didn't mean to wake you."

"You didn't." He smiled, and feather-light fingertips brushed stray hair away from her forehead. He ran his fingers across her cheek in a caress then relaxed again, leaving the hand resting on the crisp sheets between them. Clare squirmed her own hand out from under the blankets and took Dorran's. Their fingers wrapped together. It was a small touch, but it felt intimate and good.

She was clean, and she realized he must have undressed and washed her while she was asleep. Fresh bandages were wrapped across the bite marks and scrapes.

It was a sudden reminder of the first day she'd met Dorran. She'd woken in his bed, wearing nothing except her underwear and bandages. Back then, she'd been terrified of him. Now she couldn't think of anyone she trusted more.

Outside, the storm raged, hurling sleet against the walls and rattling the windows, but Clare had never felt so comfortable.

"We'll have to face the real world again soon," she murmured.

He smiled, his thumb grazing over her fingers. "Unfortunately, my darling. But not just yet."

"Do you think any of the hollow are left in the house?"

"It is possible. But I suspect most of them have fled. There are tracks in the snow outside leading toward the forest. With Madeline gone, perhaps Winterbourne is no longer a hospitable place for them. They may have realized food will be more easily found in the forest, where there are rabbits and rodents to hunt. They don't seem interested in the greens in the garden."

"Oh no—poor garden. We must have cooked it."

He chuckled. "It will be a little warm. But the vent will make sure the lake bears the worst of the fire."

Imagining the sunken hollow floating through the heated lake like some kind of unnatural stew, she scrunched her nose. Then another thought crept into her mind. "Dorran, are you okay?"

"Of course. Nothing worse than a few scratches and bruises."

"I mean…" She squirmed an inch closer. "Last night. Your mother. It…was a lot to have to see."

Dorran was quiet for a moment then said, "I am at peace with it."

His eyes looked sad, and Clare's heart ached for him. She tightened her hand around his as she struggled to find words that might help. "I know you don't like to show when you're hurting. Or afraid. Or sad. You were never allowed to *be* those things, I guess. But sometimes it helps to talk. If you don't want to, I won't push, but I'm here when you're ready, and…" It felt strange to say something that seemed so obvious to her, but she thought Dorran needed to hear it. "I…I won't hurt you."

His shell cracked. The sadness spread from his eyes to flow across all of his features, and he clenched his teeth. He took her hand in both of his, holding it and kissing it as though it were a lifeline. The moment passed, and his face cleared, though his breathing was rough.

"You are good to me." He kissed her hand again. "I…I would rather not talk about *her*. She hurt you. But she is gone now.

I want to spend my life walking forward, not looking over my shoulder."

She smiled. "I can understand that."

"We have a future ahead of us. And…and I would like to spend it with you." He was struggling to meet her eyes, battling caution, fighting to lower the walls for her.

Clare moved a little nearer to him, closing the gap between them. "I like the sound of that. Our life might not be very normal, after what happened to the world. But we'll be together."

"We will," he promised as a smile grew. "And that is more than enough."

CHAPTER 39

Two days later

CLARE STOOD BY THE kitchen's sink as she washed and dried their plates from breakfast. The sky was clear that morning. She knew she couldn't count on it staying that way—the weather could change in a heartbeat—but she was enjoying it while she had it. Outside, light glowed off a fresh field of snow, and the fire in the kitchen's oven made the day feel warmer than it actually was.

It was her first time out of her room since escaping the basement. She limped, but it was growing less pronounced. Dorran had cared for her, feeding her pain tablets when he thought she was uncomfortable and washing and redressing her cuts. He'd wanted her to stay in bed longer, but Clare was eager to feel like she had control over her life again.

Dorran had left her to collect more firewood. Clare found

herself glancing toward the door every few seconds, watching for his return. There was no sign that any hollow ones remained inside Winterbourne. Even so, she didn't like being separated from Dorran.

As they recouped from their fight, they had begun to talk through plans for the future. They would need the food from Clare's car. The garden was recovering, but not enough would be ready before their supplies ran out. How they would reach the car, though, was a question neither of them had an answer for yet. They occasionally saw emaciated bodies creeping through the tree line on clear afternoons.

Clare had picked up a handful of broadcasts on her radio, but most were brief and lacked concrete information. One had been nothing but gibberish—clips of songs and discordant voices mixed in with static. It had unnerved Clare, and she tried to avoid it, even though it was the only channel that played reliably.

Some of the other broadcasts had been useful, though. The cause of the apocalypse was still unknown, though survivors shared rumors like they were currency. So far, the only people Clare had heard about surviving the event had been driving along rarely used roads or had been living off the grid. That led people to believe that populated areas had been targeted deliberately.

The hollow had unnatural strength and didn't die easily. According to the transmissions Clare had managed to catch, humanity's best hope was that the creatures would starve. It had been nearly three weeks since the stillness. Some people reported seeing hollow ones acting more sluggish than normal. Others said they couldn't tell any difference.

Clare was acutely aware of her own luck in being brought to Winterbourne Hall. The people she'd listened to on the radio were all nomads, moving from town to town, trying to connect with other survivors and hoping that the next place they chose to camp wouldn't have a nest of hollow near it.

She'd heard one report of a monster like Madeline: sentient, retaining its memories and personality. They didn't know what made that hollow different than its mindless counterparts. Clare had a theory, though. Madeline had been intensely willful. Clare wondered if strong, rigid personalities had a better chance of surviving the change.

Clare left the radio on Beth's frequency most of the time and always kept it close. Dorran didn't complain. He seemed to understand that Clare needed to hold on to hope stubbornly, even irrationally, despite each day of static repeating the same message of futility. Hope was a rare commodity in the new world, but it was almost as valuable as food or shelter. Eventually, the radio's batteries would fail, and Clare would be forced to give it up, but she wasn't ready. Not yet.

The door creaked, and Dorran entered, wearing a green knit top and scarf. Clare tried not to look as relieved as she felt. "Hey! Did it go okay? Nothing bothered you?"

Dorran returned her smile, but it had lost the sincerity she'd begun to enjoy. "I went to the furnace room."

They hadn't been to the basement since the fight, and Clare

realized the bodies would still be there. She put down the dishcloth and crossed to him. "Dorran, I'm so sorry. I should have come with you."

He shook his head. "It was something I wanted to do alone. The furnace needed reheating before the garden grew too cold. And I also thought if the bodies stayed there for too long…"

They would start to rot. Clare imagined the hollows' already-nightmarish bodies writhing with maggots, and she swallowed. "Can I help…clean them up?"

"No. I took care of two of them. The furnace is consuming the bodies." He leaned his back against the table and folded his arms, his eyes tight. "But there is a problem. I only *found* two of them."

"You mean—"

"My mother's body was gone." He lifted a hand then let it drop. "All that is left is a patch of dried blood."

Clare pressed her fingers to her mouth. She'd felt the bones fracture as she'd impaled the woman's head. She'd seen the life leave her eyes. "Maybe the surviving maids came back for her and carried her body away."

"Perhaps."

As they stared at each other, Clare knew that neither of them truly believed that idea.

"I will seal off the secret passageways," Dorran said. "But I do not know all of them yet. Until we can be certain we're safe, I would like you to carry a weapon. And I will try to never be far from you. Just in case."

Clare couldn't speak. She stepped forward and fell into

Dorran's hug. He pulled her close and kissed the top of her head. "Shh. We will be all right. I will keep you safe, my darling."

It seemed unfair that he even had to. Clare closed her eyes as she and Dorran rocked together. Broad hands massaged her back until the tension left her shoulders. Clare swallowed the anxiety and instead tried to focus on the good in their lives. They didn't know Madeline was alive—not for certain. And even if she was, she couldn't be as much of a threat with a metal bar through her head.

"I will take care of it," Dorran murmured.

Clare tilted her head back to meet his eyes. "*We* will take care of it."

"Ha. All right. Together."

Clare gave Dorran a quick squeeze. "Are you okay?"

"I…will be fine."

"Are you sure?"

"Yes. I have you. And that is everything I need right now." He kissed her forehead. "Just stay close to me."

"I will." She slid out of his arms and turned back to the dried utensils. "I'm just about done here. Did you want to start on the passageways straightaway or visit the garden first?"

"The garden, I think. It will need water. And some of the new plants will have started to sprout."

Clare had been looking forward to visiting their sanctuary again. It was the best part of Winterbourne. Tending to the tiny, fragile plants while chatting with Dorran always made the world seem brighter and warmer. It would be good to return to their routine, as much of a routine as Winterbourne allowed them, at least.

As she stacked the plates, Dorran came up beside her, using the damp dish towel to wipe down the counter. They were close enough that their arms grazed, and Clare smiled as she leaned into the touch.

The radio on the shelf crackled. It had been running for so long that the static had become a part of the background noise, and the sudden change made Clare's breath catch. She and Dorran turned to face the small black box.

A woman's voice floated out, distorted and tinny but unmistakable. "Clare? If you're there, please answer. It's me. Beth."

ABOUT THE AUTHOR

Darcy Coates is the *USA Today* bestselling author of *Hunted*, *The Haunting of Ashburn House*, *Craven Manor*, and more than a dozen horror and suspense titles.

She lives on the Central Coast of Australia with her family, cats, and a garden full of herbs and vegetables.

Darcy loves forests, especially old-growth forests where the trees dwarf anyone who steps between them. Wherever she lives, she tries to have a mountain range close by.

THE HAUNTING OF ASHBURN HOUSE

THERE'S SOMETHING WRONG WITH ASHBURN HOUSE...

Everyone knows about Ashburn House. They whisper its old owner went mad, and restless ghosts still walk the halls. But when Adrienne inherits the crumbling old mansion, she only sees it as a lifeline...until darkness falls.

As the nights grow ever more restless, it becomes clear something twisted lives in Adrienne's house. Chasing the threads of a decades-old mystery, it isn't long before she realizes she's become prey to something deeply unnatural and intensely resentful. She has no idea how to escape. She has no idea how to survive. Only one thing is certain: Ashburn's dead are not at rest.

THE HAUNTING OF
BLACKWOOD HOUSE

HOW LONG COULD YOU SURVIVE?

As the daughter of spiritualists, Mara's childhood was filled with séances and scam mediums. Now she's ready to start over with her fiancé, Neil, far away from the superstitions she's learned to loathe...but her past isn't willing to let her go so easily. And neither is Blackwood House.

When Mara and Neil purchased the derelict property, they were warned that ever since the murder of its original owner, things have changed. Strange shadows stalk the halls. Doors creak open by themselves. Voices whisper in the night. And watchful eyes follow her every move. But Mara's convinced she can't possibly be in danger. Because ghosts aren't real...are they?

CRAVEN MANOR

SOME SECRETS ARE BETTER LEFT FORGOTTEN.

Daniel is desperate for a fresh start. So when a mysterious figure offers the position of groundskeeper at an ancient estate, he leaps at the chance. Alarm bells start ringing when he arrives at Craven Manor. The abandoned mansion's front door hangs open, and leaves and cobwebs coat the marble foyer. It's clear no one has lived here in a long time… but he has nowhere else to go.

Against his better judgment, he moves into the groundskeeper's cottage tucked away behind the old family crypt. But when a candle flickers to life in the abandoned tower window, Daniel realizes he isn't alone after all. Craven Manor is hiding a terrible secret… One that threatens to bury him with it.

For more info about Sourcebooks's books and authors, visit:

sourcebooks.com

THE HOUSE NEXT DOOR

NO ONE STAYS HERE FOR LONG.

Josephine began to suspect something was wrong with the house next door when its family fled in the middle of the night, the children screaming, the mother crying. They never came back. No family stays at Marwick House for long. No life lingers beyond its blackened windows. No voices drift from its ancient halls. Once, Josephine swore she saw a woman's silhouette pacing through the upstairs room…but that's impossible. No one had been there in a long, long time.

But now someone new has moved next door, and Marwick House is slowly waking up. Torn between staying away and warning the new tenant, Josephine only knows that if she isn't careful, she may be its next victim…